FOREVER RED

A FALLEN THORNS STORY

HARVEY OLIVER BAXTER

FOREVER RED

To every goth who thinks they're not part of the community because they don't dress a certain way. It's all in the music.

"But to die as lovers may — to die together, so that they may live together."

— JOSEPH SHERIDAN LE FANU, *CARMILLA*

Content Warnings

This book contains content I believe should be addressed before you begin:
- Depression, anxiety, and suicide (referenced and attempted)
- Reference to self harm
- Religious guilt and self blame
- Parental neglect
- Transphobia, deadnaming, homophobia
- Extreme violence, mutilation and references to bodies and wounds
- Manipulation
- Consensual, moderately explicit sex with blood-play
- Grief and death of a loved one — survivors guilt
- Torture
- Murder
- Emesis
- Extreme drug use and consumption of alcohol — overdosing

INTRODUCTION

Fallen Thorns takes place from October 2018 – January 2019 in Durham, England. Forever Red takes place from Summer 2009 – June 2019.

Forever Red can be read as a standalone or can be read as a prequel to Fallen Thorns. If you're entering this world for the first time with this book, be warned part 5 and part 6 will spoil the story and ending of Fallen Thorns. I have tried my best to make it as accessible as possible for first time readers, but if you are reading this book *after* Fallen Thorns, here is Ben and Casper's story. May I present to you the first ten years of the post-punk, dark-wave vampire band: Forever Red.
Enjoy.

Is this working? Have we got the mics working?
Right. Okay, let's roll.

"Ben Audley and Casper Murphey! Welcome back! It's lovely to see you two again. How are you both doing? A lot has happened since we last spoke!"

PART ONE
'JUST BOYS'

2009

<u>**Interview Excerpt: February 2013**</u>

INTERVIEWER (PAUL NORRIS, 'AND THAT'S GOTH' - Spring 2013): I'm joined here by the founding members of the band Forever Red, the rising stars of the ever-growing eighties revival scene, with their heavy synth and dramatic bass lines. Ben Audley and Casper Murphey! Welcome!

Ben Audley (Vocalist/Bassist/Keyboardist, Forever Red): Thank you for having us.

Casper Murphey (Drummer, Forever Red): It's a pleasure.

[3 minutes of interview redacted]

Paul: So, Casper, why don't we start with you? Tell us where it all started.

[Murphey adjusts himself on the chair, and after a quick glance at Audley, he smiles back at the interviewer and starts to reminisce]

Casper: I grew up in Alexandria, Louisiana, with my four siblings and a mom and dad who worked their asses off to give us all the best lives possible. I was the youngest by quite a few years, which is probably why I felt like we never had any problems as a kid, since I essentially had six parents looking after me. My siblings will probably tell the story differently, especially my oldest sister, Kathy, who grew up when my parents still lived in a rented apartment in a rough part of New Orleans. Kathy's got a soul of steel. She made sure we ate before school, packed our bags, and checked our beds for monsters. I love her endlessly. I'll never be able to repay her for all she did for us.

The twins, Sam and Rhonda, were the troublemakers—the rebels, my uncle called them. They weren't bad, just passionate about making sure everyone had a good time. [*laughs*] We had a fun childhood, you know. Our parents kept us in our place, but we never had any big troubles. Again, that was always my perspective anyway. Mom and Dad would never share if they were struggling; they would never want us to worry.

Then there's Jesse. He's seven years older than me, but he always felt the most like a brother than a carer. He was the quiet one who minded his own business a lot of the time. Jesse actually got me into music—good music, that is. Hell, this was the nineties; a lot of trash was floating around! I think my earliest memory was Purple Rain by Prince, a true masterpiece. Jesse worships Prince.

[*Ben nods*]

Casper: When all my other siblings grew up and moved away, Jesse stayed home. He got a job at a local record store; he's one of the lucky few who found his best friends at a young age and always kept them close. When he got that job, I used to tag along with his friends every Friday after school. He'd let us stay until the store closed, and we got to pick albums to blast on the speakers. It was the best.

[*redacted*]

Out of all my siblings, we keep the most in contact. He's flown over a bunch of times, and I'm trying to get him to record more stuff with us. He claims to be our number one fan.

Casper

Summer 2009

"I GOT IN! Jesse! I'm going to England!"

Jesse wrenched me in for a hug, nearly cutting off my circulation. He's a big guy, strong, but his hugs always came from the deepest parts of his soul, like he never wanted to let go.

The elation lingered until the realisation kicked in. I was moving—not just to the next state, but a nine-hour flight across the Atlantic to a country I'd never been to, to stay for *three* years. Of course, I'd thought about it. I'd planned and prepared; I always like to push myself, and I don't tend to dwell too much. But it finally sunk in then that I would be leaving this place. Leaving Louisiana. My family, aunts, uncles, my grandparents. My friends. Jesse. Home.

It was going to take a lot of getting used to. I'd been on many online forums of people comparing the two countries. What to do, what not to do. What to say, and what not to say. The more I researched things, the more it stressed me out, and I nearly pulled my application multiple times. There was also a bunch of legal stuff I had to sort, which had me questioning; would it really be worth it? But I decided, ultimately, yes. Yes, it would be. I gotta live my life, right?

"Hey, Casper. You listen to me. You're gonna do this, and you're gonna have the time of your life. You're living the dream." Jesse pulled my head to his, then slapped my back with proud force. "I'll support you no matter what."

I leaned into him, laughing. "I know. I know. It's gonna be good. It's gonna be good." I reassured myself, shaking out my arms.

"And hey, it's not like I'm never gonna see you. We'll video call, I'll call you—I'll even write you letters."

"Letters?" I laughed. "What is this, the nineteenth century? You gonna seal it with the family crest?"

"Family crest? Wow, you're becoming a Brit already. Don't go all royal on me now."

"Never." I winked.

"Hey, I heard there's a castle near your college." My brother tapped my knee, shifting the subject.

"Even better; they got a whole ass *cathedral.*"

Interview Excerpt: February 2013

Paul: Does Jesse play drums like you?

Casper: Nah, he loves his guitar and saxophone. He uses my dad's hand me down acoustic, re-stringed and polished like new. My uncle used to be in a blues band; I think my dad used to try and be like him, but he never properly played, not really. But Jesse —Jesse makes *music.* He did the sax on some of the tracks in our latest album, you know.

Paul: That's what I was getting to; I noticed he was credited.

Casper: We flew him out for a few sessions in the studio. Honorary member.

Paul: A future permanent member perhaps?

Casper: [*winks then smiles*] Who knows. Maybe.

[*redacted*]

Paul: Okay, but what about you though? Why drums?

Casper: Someone's gotta be the drummer. [*laughs*] No, in all seriousness, I wanted to do something different. I never really enjoyed sports or anything like that. I liked going to the gym and sticking to my own routine, but my siblings encouraged me to join track or try football and basketball because of my height, and those never stuck. I even tried ice hockey at one point. I'm not really cut out for physical team stuff like that, though. It's too competitive.

We had a set of drums at my high school that some local guy donated after clearing out his garage, so I thought I'd give them a shot. I got to playing, and my teacher—shout out to Mr Rogers—encouraged me massively. He taught me the basics, got me to feel the rhythm and understand its importance as an instrument. I fell in love with it. We couldn't really afford or fit a drum kit in the house, but Mr Rogers let me play whenever I wanted. It got to the point where the Principal had to authorise opening the building out of hours so I could practise. I was *obsessed*. Just feeling the beat all around me and knowing *I* created it. Oh, it's *powerful*.

Paul: I don't doubt that. I would have loved to have had a go at drums.

Casper: I'm sure I can arrange that.

Paul: You didn't study music at university though, did you? You studied Law, correct?

Casper: Yeah, Law. Believe it or not, it was the only other thing I had any enthusiasm for. Justice, rights, ya know. I only did things I was passionate about, and by some miracle, I got accepted into *Durham* of all places. I honestly don't know what I was thinking. I think I'd painted such a rose-coloured image of the place in my mind—I'd grown up seeing all these old English villages in movies and TV shows and was in awe at their beauty. I developed such a serious interest in architecture and history, and I wanted to become part of *this* story. Durham is nice and all, but it's not a place I'd choose to go to if I had the choice again, not when it comes to the environment and community, if you know what I mean. I probably would have stayed in the states where I *knew* things, you know. I could know what to expect. British people are very good at disguising their bigotry as something... *'justifiable'*. But anyway, sorry, that's probably not what you wanted to hear. [*smiles*] I believe everything happens for a reason, and I know I was meant to go there at that time, to start the band and meet Ben.

He's my best friend, and I wouldn't change it for the world. [*looks at his bandmate and grins*]

Paul: No, no. This is good, thank you for expanding on that. You're right. [*clears throat*]

[*2 minutes of interview redacted*]

Paul: So, Ben, what about your childhood?

[*Ben's smile fades*]

Ben: Oh, *my* childhood? Far less exciting. Just me, my mum and dad. Pretty average childhood.

Ben

August 2009

"OH. I ACTUALLY DID IT," I said to an empty room. It's a bit embarrassing talking to myself. My gran always caught me, and I'd suddenly realise I must've done it all my life without noticing.

She was downstairs watching the television—there wasn't much signal in the front room, so I laid on my bedroom floor with the WI-FI box beside me, refreshing the admissions page. My gran was going to drive me to collect my A-Level results later, but I didn't really care about them, just as long as I got into Durham.

I refused to settle for my second choice. I was young, naïve, and very stubborn. If I didn't get my first-choice uni, I planned to take a gap year and try again. I was very particular about my path.

But yeah, I got in. I said it aloud in utter disbelief, ran to the landing, and shouted down to my Gran, who, bless her soul, jumped to the doorway and let off a party popper. It was as if she'd known.

I ran down the stairs to hug her.

"Oh Benjamín, I knew you'd do it! I'm so proud of you."

"I'm going to Durham! I'm going to Durham!" I was practically jumping.

"Go and ring your mother, she'll be dying to know."

<u>Unpublished interview excerpt: March 2014. (Unpublished through the request of Benjamín Marco Audley and his manager Mars Rosario)</u>

BEN: I was born in London but moved to Nottingham with my mum and dad when I was two. We couldn't really afford to go away much, but when we did, they made it special for us, planning the entire trip so not a single moment was wasted. You know, I've got so many happy memories from that time, like when you're a child and problems don't exist. You have no worries or fears because you have your mummy and daddy to make everything all right.

We were pretty devout Catholics; I was an altar boy for a brief time when I was about nine or ten. My mum claims she re-found her faith with my dad and constantly shuns her younger years before him, but that's normal, though, isn't it? When you're young, you like challenging things that came before you. Her dad —my grandad, Marco—managed to leave Franco's Spain in the late fifties, came to the UK with his sister, and met my gran not long after. They were both raised Roman Catholic, and they bonded over their faith. He taught her Spanish, and it was all so movie-script romantic, but my mum and uncle found it hard I think—sometimes being forced into something as a kid probably makes you resent it? I dunno. I don't know what I really believe in now, but I've got my own found faith. [*touches his crucifix necklace*]

I was eleven when I found out that my dad wasn't actually my dad—not biologically, anyway. He was my dad in every way that counted, but discovering the truth was confusing, regardless. It's weird because when you look at the three of us, you'd think I was their biological son. My parents were married not long after I was born, and we all had the same dark, curly hair, with my parents having come from Spanish and Italian backgrounds. I share the same green eyes as my mum, and people told me I had my dad's features. But there was one difference that made me stand out the most, and that was my freckles. I mean, just look at me. [*stretches out his arms*] I'm covered in them. I didn't get those from either of my parents. When you're a kid, you don't question it, it doesn't matter. But when I got a bit older, I did. Innocently.

[*inhales deeply from his cigarette and taps it on the ashtray*]

Ben: I'm honestly surprised they managed to go so long without me ever suspecting.

"Mum, are we related?" I asked one night.

She laughed at first, but then briefly glanced at my dad, her expression sobering. "Why would you ask that?"

I told her my list of reasons, and she looked at my dad again before ushering me to the sofa. There, she explained everything, my dad inputting where necessary.

When my mum was twenty-three, she went on a trip to New York with her friends. They were all fresh out of university and had saved to go travelling.

[*redacted*]

Sorry, I went off track a bit there. Anyway, so yeah; she went to New York with her friends and they, in her words, 'had a bit too much fun.'

Interviewer: As we all do at that age.

Ben: Yeah, I suppose.

She met this guy and briefly described him as 'a charming lone traveller' which made me laugh, but I think she just meant he was mysterious, a man with a backstory, you know?

[*both laugh*]

[*Ben reaches for his glass of water and lights another cigarette*]

Interviewer: Aren't you worried about your health?

Ben: [*shrugs and laughs*] Maybe I'm already dead.

[*redacted*]

Ben: She always says she could never place his accent, but that he sounded sort of English—maybe Scottish or Irish—but he was clearly very well-travelled or was perhaps born in a different country, his accent evolving over time. She kept his description vague, but the gist is: he had an interesting enough voice to let him buy her a drink.

My mum was never spontaneous or easily charmed by guys; she made that clear to me, but I think she was just living in the moment. She was leaving for London again in two days and didn't want the trip to end, so she got with this guy, gave him her contact address, flew back to London, then bam, nine months later, I arrived. He never contacted her once.

That was such a horrible way to tell the story, sorry mum. Can we do that again please?

[*redacted*]

Ben: My mum hates herself for what she did, but she didn't really do anything wrong. The number of times I had to follow her to the confession booth at church was ridiculous. It's all that American guy's fault, if he even was American. To be honest, I reckon I've got siblings across the globe.

But yeah, my dad might not be related to me by blood, but I have no desire to find my biological dad, not after what he did... Why am I telling you this?

[*redacted*]

Interviewer: You mentioned you moved in with your grandmother when you were fourteen? Any particular reason?

Ben: When did I mention that?

Interviewer: [*looking flustered*] Oh, erm, I must have read it somewhere.

Ben: My parents split up. I was starting my GCSEs. I didn't need things to get complicated, so we all decided it would be best for me if I moved out. I'm still in contact with them both, though. They're my mum and dad, and nothing will change that. They might not love each other anymore, but that does nothing to my love for them. I see my mum more than I do my dad; he lives back down south now. I wish he... never mind.

[*redacted*]

Ben: Don't release this interview.

Interviewer: Of course.

Ben

26th September 2009

"Jake, I swear to God, if you don't turn that down, I'm going to throw it out of the window."

Me and my best friend Jake had just moved into our accommodation. We'd known each other since I moved to Leeds in 2005 and were lumped together as 'the new boys.' He'd recently moved schools due to a bullying issue, and I'd moved because it was the nearest school to Gran's. We got on, bonded over our shared music taste, and recreated Bauhaus riffs in his dad's garage on weekends until our fingers were red raw and our throats dried out from imitating that deep, gothic charm.

Jake wasn't studying music, instead, he chose philosophy. He'd never struck me as someone who would choose that path, but looking back, I think he just wanted to stay close to me. We basically went everywhere together, so I should have predicted it. We booked our accommodation the second we got our offers.

"I'm setting the tone for the surrounding occupants," Jake remarked sarcastically as he turned down his CD player on the windowsill, the window wide open.

I sucked in my lips, holding back my temper. "I'd rather not be branded a nuisance before the term has even begun."

Jake pulled the CD player away from the ledge and balanced it on his knees. "You can go back to your room then. My room, my rules." He stuck out his tongue in jest, and I playfully kicked him in the leg before heading to the front door for a cigarette.

IT WASN'T long after I became friends with Jake that I tried my first hit of nicotine. In Spring 2006, we went on a school trip to some residential site in the middle of nowhere. It was stupid of me, I know, but I wanted to fit in, wanted to be cool—*accepted*. I'd never really managed that before, and at that age, I thought I was mature enough to start making my own decisions—going against what people told me to do.

One afternoon, I followed two boys in the year above me behind the main building during our free time and asked for a tab. They laughed at first, but didn't object, offering me a tab and lighter. I'd been with them earlier when something funny had happened, and we all laughed together, making that brief interaction enough for my naïve brain to think they would be friendly with me. That I was *like* them.

My first drag made me cough, but I'd already taken two more drags before they had a chance to judge. They watched me wide-eyed, and I grinned. I was so smug, like I'd somehow shown them how cool I was.

Jake smelled it on me the second I went back to our bunk and scolded me, like a friend should. "You're already cool," he said. But I didn't listen.

I continued to get cigarettes from those boys right up until they left in June, but by then, I'd developed enough of an addiction to pluck up the courage to go into my local off-licence store and ask for a packet of Marlboro Red. The only brand I knew. I wasn't even fifteen yet, but the law was different then, so no one cared. After a brief hesitation, the guy produced a packet and smiled, taking my money and throwing in a lighter for free.

I wonder where he is now. I liked that store. Nice selection of pop.

I hid it from my gran. It wasn't hard, though; she had a bit of an issue with her sense of smell anyway, so she never questioned why I always smelled so overpoweringly of aftershave despite not having a single hair on my face at the time.

My dad smoked, but my mum never allowed him to do it in the house or anywhere around me in general. *Sorry mum.*

But yeah, it stuck.

3rd October 2009

I THINK it was the first week of term, or maybe freshers; they all sort of blend into one. I'd only been in the city for about two weeks and was out for a stroll to see if any clubs or societies looked fun enough to join. But nothing caught my interest, until I stumbled across this small poster. 'Band members wanted,' it said, typed in a Victorian, gothic font. 'Must like whiny guitars that transport you to a pit of despair.'

I remember laughing and thinking that whoever had created that abomination of an advertisement was definitely worth meeting.

Casper
3rd October 2009

"YOU THINKING ABOUT IT?" I'd been hovering behind this guy for a good minute, studying his side profile as he examined the poster. He looked like the perfect candidate: long leather trench, curly black hair, and hands pushing casually into his low pockets. A piercing dangled from his left ear, too—a dagger, if I remember rightly.

The guy turned to me, whipping his headphones off in shock, and smiled in a rushed panic. I'm not going to be one of those people, but, well, I suppose I am: he was beautiful. His green eyes glistened in the light, completely entrancing, and the cute freckles splattered all over his face made him a work of art. I smiled back, perhaps a little too intensely.

Up until this point, I assumed I was straight, or more, I'd convinced myself I was. I never let myself consider otherwise. It was easier that way; I didn't like standing out.

"Yeah... I think. You made this?" He gestured to the poster. Not my finest graphic design work, but it did the job.

"You play?" I asked him, trying to stay cool, calm, and collected. I couldn't let this guy in on the fact I was already thinking about the softness of his lips. Like, simmer down, dude.

The guy shrugged, smiling, which made his response look effortlessly cool. "I'm actually a pianist, but I can play bass too. I'm not the best; I've only been playing a few years, but I can just stick to keyboards or synth, if that's easier, whatever you need the most."

I heard what he said, but all I could think about was how I could see this guy again, regardless of whether he fit the bill. His voice was so much deeper than I expected, which didn't make things easier... he was *perfect*.

"Bass and keyboard sound good. You up to practise a bit? Share tastes and stuff?" So smooth, Casper; *so* smooth.

"I mean, yeah. Sure. My mate plays guitar, too; he likes the same sort of stuff as me. Alt eighties kinda stuff. Can he tag along?"

"Gosh, yeah. The more, the better. You're literally the only person who has expressed interest. I thought I'd picked the wrong place to move to." I tried to sound funny, but I don't think he picked up on it. His laugh was considerably delayed and likely one of pure politeness.

"You're American," he observed, brow quirking.

"Yeah, long way to come for a course that would make more sense if I did it in the States, yada yada." I'd heard it all before.

I think I offended him slightly because his face faltered. "Oh no, I was just confirming. You see, my mate and I have had this bet for years that we can tell the difference between American accents and Canadian accents. He said I couldn't do it; I'm always proving him wrong." He laughed then. "And I'm completely boring you and embarrassing myself at the same time. Wow, I'll stop while I'm ahead."

I didn't care, of course. I'd already decided there and then that I could listen to him for eternity. I knew he was the one in every aspect of the word. We were meant to meet each other.

"You free tomorrow night?" I asked.

"Yeah, yeah, I think I am." A cute dimple appeared when he smiled. I really had to control myself, jeez.

"Nice. Cool. Meet here tomorrow at six?"

"Sure, we'll be there."

"Cool."

He nodded and then began to walk away, but I was too stunned to move, my brain turning to mush. He'd already put his headphones back on from around his neck and held a packet of cigarettes in his hand when I called out to him again. *Fuck. Just when I thought he couldn't get any hotter.*

"Hey, wait. I didn't catch your name!"

"Oh, yeah, sorry. It's Ben. Ben Audley." He walked back over and extended his free hand, clad in bulky rings and nails chipped with black polish.

"Casper. Murphey. Casper Murphey. Nice to meet you, Ben." I shook his hand. It was so soft...

"Nice to meet you too, Casper. See you tomorrow!"

I had no idea my life would change the way it did from there on out...

Band
Members
Wanted
MUST LIKE WHINY
GUITARS THAT
TRANSPORT YOU
TO A PIT OF
DESPAIR

PART TWO
'THE BURDEN OF LOVE'

2009-2011

<u>**Interview Excerpt: July 2014**</u>

INTERVIEWER (BRIGIT LEIGH, 'SIXTEEN SECONDS' - Summer 2014): So, you guys met by chance, really, didn't you?

[*Ben and Casper smile*]

Ben: It was the graphic design that caught my eye.

Casper: [*tips his head back, laughing*] What can I say? I should have gone into advertisement.

Francesca Young (Vocalist/Lead Guitarist, Forever Red): [*covers her mouth and snorts*] Dolly the Dancing Elephant.

[*they all laugh at this inside joke*]

Ben: It worked, though.

Casper: It did. And the rest is history, I suppose.

Lawrence Marigold (Bassist/Acoustic Guitarist, Forever Red): Until I joined, of course.

[*they all laugh again*]

[*Fran playfully taps Lawrence's back*]

Brigit: Of course! You wouldn't be the band you are today without Fran and Lawrence, [*looks to the founding members*] but you guys started it all.

Casper: Yeah, we did.

Ben: Just boys playing around with instruments; we didn't need an audience.

Casper: Yeah, those first sessions were something else.

Brigit: Oh, I'm sure your fans would love to hear those recordings.

Ben: [*laughing*] I assure you, they do not.

Brigit: Am I right in saying there were three of you originally, though?

[*they all quieten*]

[*Casper clears his throat and glances briefly at Ben, who is no longer smiling*]

[*Fran and Lawrence remain silent*]

Ben: [*clears throat*] Yeah. Jake.

Brigit: Yes, Jake Walters.

Casper: [*interrupting the interview*] We don't need to talk about that, though.

Casper
October 2009

"No way, you know Clan of Xymox too?" Ben looked at me with joyous wide eyes.

This was our second meeting; in the first, Ben shared his cool bass riffs, and Jake Walters, Ben's long-time best friend, showed off on his guitar, proving that the two of them were far more experienced than they claimed to be.

"Their first album is literally a masterpiece." I'd been playing one of my many mp3 playlists on the docking station for inspiration.

"They're one of my favourite bands! I've never met anyone who has heard of them before!" Ben was still beaming.

"You do have a pretty cool music taste, Ben," Jake piped up from the corner where he'd been tuning his Telecaster.

"He got you into them?" I guessed.

Jake nodded. "Xymox, The Chameleons, Sisters of Mercy. The list goes on."

"I just find songs I like, then blast them," Ben explained, blushing slightly from the attention.

"Well, maybe we could start with some covers then? Something we all know." I sat behind the drum kit and readied my position.

I'll admit, I always believed that Jesse and I had a superior music taste to my siblings. We had the best albums and cassette collections, which turned into shelves and shelves of CDs as time went on. None of my high school friends liked the stuff I did, nor did the rest of our family. Only me and Jesse felt that sort of music in our souls, and now I'd met two English guys who just *got it*.

Everything felt *right*.

November 2009

"Casper, what you did just there was brilliant! It worked so well with Jake's guitar. It's like we're one."

It was a few weeks later, and we'd more or less settled into university and our respective courses, while continuing to find the time to practise what we loved. We played mostly simple covers but occasionally put our own twist on things, until eventually, we delved into the territory of creating wholly new material, which was surprisingly a lot less daunting than I'd originally thought. Ben and Jake were easy to work with, and I quickly picked up on what they were putting down. We gelled perfectly.

Ben's comment there, though, led me to believe this could work and that we could actually take off. *We might make it.*

I also found myself becoming more and more infatuated with Ben. He was smart, charismatic, sweet, and oh lord, was he stylish. Ben had to have known how *attractive* he looked when he walked around in those outfits, looking like some goth rock star who didn't even *have* to try.

I told myself I had to stop, though. It had been a while since I'd been in a relationship and getting with bandmates was strictly off limits, right? That's the unspoken rule. They always end in disasters. *Right?*

"Yeah, if I just slow down my tempo before we hit the chorus, and then Ben holds off on that bass note for just a second longer, we can come together in unison there; that would sound amazing. Well, it does in my head, anyway. Let's give it a go." Jake adjusted the tone on his guitar, and Ben and I exchanged a brief glance and nod.

"Great, let's try that."

Interview Excerpt: Leeds Festival 2011

Interviewer (Aniyah Fay, 'It's So Dark In Here'): You started in local clubs, I believe? Around bars?

Casper: [*brushes his braids behind his shoulder and grins*] Yeah, turns out the alternative music scene is a little bigger than we anticipated in Durham. We gained quite an eclectic group of teenage followers—some fellow uni students must have spread the word to their friends or family members with similar interests. We were by no means '*big,*' but we definitely got more popular, especially around campus, which I don't think the university approved of at first. We were hardly an academic image.

Ben: Yeah, it sort of happened quite fast, too. One minute, we're messing about and recording; the next, people are coming up to us and going, 'hey, we like your stuff,' and I'm always lost for words. We're not used to this attention, are we? [*looks to band-mates, Murphey and Young, who nod in agreement*]

Casper: It was a shock because we only really did covers then; occasionally, we had the confidence to play a few early, unpolished versions of our original songs, but people *liked* us regardless. They wanted to hear our whiny guitars and heavy drumbeats. I think the biggest audience we got was like thirty people in this one pub, and people were buying us pints afterwards, and I remember... [*laughs*] I felt sick because I was only like nineteen at the time, and obviously, in the states, you can't legally drink until you're twenty-one, and I was worried I'd somehow get into trouble.

Ben: [*whispers*] Naughty, naughty. [*playfully taps his band-mate's shoulder*]

[*redacted*]

Aniyah: So, Francesca, when did you come into all of this?

Fran: Oh, not quite yet. I didn't join until October 2010; I'm a year behind these guys, you see. And a lot happened before I came.

Ben

December 2009

THE FIRST TERM went pretty well. I was anxious to move away at first. Having only just settled in with my gran, I felt guilty for leaving her all alone, but she was having none of it. I was 'chasing my dreams,' after all.

Me and Jake got on so well with Casper, and every time the three of us came together, it was like we were the only people in the world. We *were* the music. Casper was probably the busiest out of all of us with regards to our courses. He was doing Law and bit off more than he could chew with our band stuff, but he was one of those people I always envied; he always managed to find time for everything. He studied, he practised, he went out, joined a gym, and he actually *slept*, too. Such a rarity for university students.

I unintentionally joined the orchestra, where we met up twice a week. It didn't take long for me to realise how boring the music was and how I'd much rather be playing with Jake and Casper. Apart from being semi-decent at an instrument, I had nothing in common with the people on my course. I didn't want to admit it then, but I will now: the music course wasn't at all what I expected, and in hindsight, I probably wouldn't have wasted my time with it. All my life, I tried to do what I thought would look the most impressive instead of what I wanted. I was good at piano, but did I want to spend my life being a pianist in an orchestra? Playing solos in churches or opera houses? No, not at all. So, why did I... never mind. I did the course. All three years. But I don't know how I managed; I really don't.

The first week of December that year, I went on a date with this guy from our halls. He'd spoken to me in the kitchen a few times, caught me out the front with a cigarette and lit up beside me, you know, casual stuff. He wasn't really my type, but he was nice enough, so I agreed to get food with him one night. Less than an hour later, I was sat on Jake's bed with a greasy, cheesy garlic pizza bread burning my lap while I complained my heart out.

It turns out the guy was only after one thing. He lied about getting us a table at this nice restaurant, instead informing me he'd booked us a hotel for the night to 'do stuff.' Imagine being that forward on a first date? Naturally, I left him.

"You know what uni gays are like—hit by that long-delayed epiphany and assuming you all think the same. Let him bother someone else; you saved yourself there." Jake sat at the head of his bed with a notebook open on his lap. I'd clearly interrupted one of his rare study moments, but he seemed relieved he had an excuse to stop.

I took a bite of my pizza and burned the roof of my mouth off in the process. I offered the box to Jake, who just laughed at my slobbery mouth noises.

"He wasn't really someone I could see myself being with anyway," I admitted.

Jake paused. "Hmm. What sort of guy do you see yourself with then?"

I shrugged; I didn't have a definitive answer. "Dunno, really. Someone with similar interests, a personality I can meld with... good record collection." I chuckled at the last part.

Jake smiled, his eyebrow quirking, pre-empting some sarcasm. "You've definitely got someone in mind."

"Maybe."

I can't recall if that sparked my wandering thoughts or whether I'd already planted that seed in my brain before then, but from that point onwards, I became increasingly aware of how much I thought about Casper.

The guy had made a pretty solid first impression. He was outgoing, confident, yet honest and humble. Tragically uncommon traits to have all at once.

Casper was a marvel to me. Everything he said or did intrigued me. He had so many things on his mind, and a lot of the time when he spoke to others, I could see the cogs whirring in their heads. He was so passionate that people couldn't wrap their heads around what he was saying half of the time. But I understood every word. I felt like we were connected on some deeper plane of understanding.

I know how dramatic and childish that sounds, but that was how I felt. Like we were destined to meet and become friends.

So, the next day, after my disaster of a date, and after Jake and I devoured a whole tub of ice cream between us, binged rented videos, and quietly strummed on our guitars until the early hours of the morning, I began to observe Casper. Stringing together the puzzle in my head. I honed into every detail: the tone of his voice, the smile in his eyes, how his t-shirt caught around his waist when he moved his arms, how tall he was, how well-fitted his trousers were, his battered docs with odd laces; his feet were very...

"We're going from the top, yeah?" Casper crossed his drumsticks, and I was suddenly aware of how my thoughts had drifted... My eyes widened. I don't know if either of them noticed the shift in my energy—I hoped to goodness they hadn't.

"Let's go again, Ben. Little lighter on the E string, yeah?" Jake shot two finger guns at me, then popped his pencil back into his mouth, preparing to play again.

Jake was definitely starting to take control of our practise. I don't think he realised it; he was just so engrossed in what we were producing. We all had our ideas, but Jake was getting more and more confident at voicing his thoughts. He was nearly always spot-on with his suggestions, though, so neither me nor Casper had an issue with him taking charge. It was inevitable that someone would have to fill that role. Otherwise, we'd get nowhere.

<u>Interview excerpt: September 2016</u>

[*INTRO REDACTED*]

Casper: Oh, I definitely shot my shot the week later. By then, I'd wanted to ask him out for a couple of weeks but wouldn't let myself. He'd never openly discussed his sexuality, and I was still trying to convince myself I was straight. But then Ben said he was going on a date with a *guy,* and it was like my heart sank and leaped at the same time. I had a chance, or at least I was closer to having a potential chance. Man, I was so dramatic.

Interviewer (Graham Hobbs, 'Goth Gays' – Winter 2016): You swooped in like a knight in shining armour after that failed date, then?

Casper: [*shrugs*] You could say that. I gave him space, of course. I didn't want to scare him off too soon or make him think badly of me, but I was growing impatient. I really, *really* liked him.

Ben
December 2009

"Hey, Ben. Wait up."

A week before the Christmas break, Casper decided to stay in the country to save money and settle into Durham more; Jake had already booked his train home, and I was weighing out my pros and cons of how long *I* should stay home. I wanted to see my gran, but I also wanted to have some free time to explore what was by far one of the prettiest cities I'd ever lived in.

Casper caught me after one of my lectures, and his voice alone sent my mind whirling with a million things at once.

I stopped walking and turned. "Yeah?" *Had he been waiting for me?*

I paused while he caught his breath. He looked gorgeous in that outfit: a beige turtleneck, short braids tied half-up, half-down, reading glasses on, and a grey chequered scarf loosely draped around his neck. I smiled at him.

"I was wondering if you wanted to get together later to talk about stuff?"

I presumed he was talking about our band. "Yeah, I'll text Jake."

Casper closed his eyes and flinched as though I'd slapped him. "No, I kinda meant just... just *us?*" He opened one eye in an unsure, questioning manner.

My heart sped up. *Oh.*

I took a deep breath and sweat formed on my palms, my ears burning. "Erm... yeah. Yeah sure, of course."

Casper let out a long breath, then beamed. *Pretty.* "Ok. Nice. Great."

"Where did you have in mind?"

By this point, I panicked, fearing I'd misinterpreted his proposal. My mind went static as I waited for him to clarify.

"The Italian up near the cathedral. Seven o'clock."

So, I hadn't misinterpreted. My smile grew wider, and my breathing went all funny. He'd planned this. He knew I wanted to try that restaurant, too... he'd listened to me. He *knew* me.

"Oh, so..."

"Yeah?" Casper was shaking, too; his hands were restless by his side, and I was hit with a wave of his scent. Had he always smelled that good?

"When you say talk about stuff..."

"Just stuff. Anything. Us. Talk about us. Music aside." He was so nervous.

"So, this is a..."

"A date. Yes. Ben, I'm asking you out, and I'm seconds away from passing out here because I—god, sorry, ahh." He covered his face in his hands and swung around so we were no longer facing.

I didn't even hesitate.

"Yes. Yes, Casper. I would love to go on a date with you. Yes. Yes. Yes." I noted the shift in my voice as I stepped around him, coming close to his face until he dropped his hands.

"Yeah?" He was breathing heavily.

"Yeah. I like you. I want to get to know more about you. Music aside."

"Okay. Wow. I really didn't think you'd agree to it. Wow." Casper reached out and squeezed my shoulders in a giddy burst of adrenaline, then strode away with a noticeable bounce in his step before turning back to me, eyes wide. "Seven o'clock. Don't be late."

I beamed back at him, a breathy laugh leaving my mouth. "I'll be there."

I SPENT TOO much time planning what to wear, which felt absurd because it was *Casper*. We'd seen each other every day since the start of term. He knew all my clothes and jewellery; I didn't *have* a special outfit to put together.

Casper

I KNEW EXACTLY what to wear.

Jesse and my parents got me a bunch of new clothes to take with me. Crisp, white shirts and a pair of black, straight-legged trousers. They told me they were 'only for special occasions'.

I'd not had a 'special occasion' yet.

Until that night.

Ben

I COULDN'T DECIDE whether to tell Jake or not. After all, he was my best friend; we told each other everything. But I didn't want him to know we were going out because then he'd just tag along, and then I'd have to explain it was a *date,* and then what if it didn't work out? It would have made things too awkward for us all. I decided it would be best not to say anything until the next day and see how the night unfolded first. Jake had briefly mentioned having something to do that night anyway. I knew it would be fine and I shouldn't worry too much; I just needed to enjoy my night.

Casper

I'd never been on a date with a guy before. I'd figured for a while I probably liked more than one gender. It boiled down to personality over anything else, but I'd never run with it. Would I have to act any differently? What was the protocol for guys dating guys? Who pays? Who carries the bags? *Kathy and Rhonda would roll their eyes at these thoughts.*

Ben

Before that point, I'd been on a grand total of two dates, both of which never amounted to anything. My longest relationship was exactly one month and three days long, and ended mere moments after the words: "Oh, we should get a girl involved." We were sixteen.

Despite my wardrobe dilemma, I was ready by six, having settled on a simple black shirt with a pinstriped waistcoat and the slimmest-fitting jeans I owned. I don't know what image I was going for, but it would have to do. I spent the following forty-five minutes replaying every possible scenario in my head.

This was really happening.

I was going on a date with Casper Murphey.

I was early, of course, but couldn't sit in my room any longer.

Casper clearly had the same thought process, too, because at quarter to seven, he was already standing outside the restaurant.

He looked so hot.

God, Ben.

The night went perfectly, as I'd so desperately hoped.

We spent hours talking about our lives, interests, and hobbies. I learned so much about his family, hearing story after story about his childhood and all the fun and not-so-fun events that shaped him into who he was today. I also learned how he wound up flying over half the world to study in Durham, of all places. He wanted to push himself. To try something new and out of his comfort zone. Carpe diem. I thought I was making a bold move taking an hour and a half train up north. I had no idea, did I?

He spoke so fondly of his brother Jesse, and if Jesse was anything like Casper said, I wanted to meet him. He sounded sweet, just like his brother who sat opposite me, drinking gin from a crystal glass and staring at me with eyes like, well... like I was the only thing that mattered in the world.

I had no idea he felt *that way*.

"Tell me more about you; you're always so secretive."

We were a few drinks deep at this point, and my edges were well and truly softened. I told him the general stuff about my mum and dad, how I came to find out my real dad was actually a sleazy, American dude.

"Maybe I know him; I could easily conjure up a list of overbearing white dudes in my hometown alone," joked Casper.

I laughed at everything he'd said throughout the night, but I suppose he could have said anything, and I would have laughed and laughed until my lungs gave out.

I *really* liked him.

Casper

By then, I knew I loved him. A minor issue, really, since I couldn't admit it yet without creeping him out. I'd liked him since the moment I met him, but as far as Ben was aware, this was the first time I'd ever expressed any sort of feelings towards him. I needed to take things slowly to avoid messing things up, a skill I'd become increasingly good at: rushing into things without thinking and speaking before my thoughts had even caught up, you know... the downfalls of an overactive mind.

This had to work out. I'd hate to think what I would have done if it hadn't. Life was going so well in every sense of the word, but it was the questionable amount of alcohol I'd consumed that gave me the confidence to ask what I did once we got up to leave.

"Hey, do you maybe want to come back to mine? Continue the conversation? I've got cans."

Ben's eyes widened, but he was clearly trying to hide his reaction. In hindsight, I shouldn't have worded the question in a way that implied things I hadn't intended to imply. I really did just want to continue talking to him. I hadn't even thought about anything else. Well, that was a slight lie. Of course, I'd thought about *the stuff that comes after*. I'd thought about kissing him and learning what he likes and dislikes, waking up with his arm around me, his soft curls on the pillow, the smell of smoke and apples filling the air...

"I think I should probably just head back to my room... I've got a couple things I want to finish off."

"Oh, no, yeah. Sure, of course. No problem. I'll walk you back?"

"Oh, you don't have to. I live a lot closer than you do; it wouldn't be worth the hassle. Don't worry about me!" Ben played with the necklace beneath his shirt's collar; he'd pulled it out at some point in the evening, but only then did I realise it was a crucifix. He never mentioned he was religious...

"See you tomorrow?" My chest was constricting. Had I done something wrong? Had it not gone as well as I'd thought?

"Yeah, of course. See you tomorrow!" Ben was smiling, but his expression was unreadable.

We parted ways not long after that. We split the bill; I was going to offer to pay, but I didn't want to embarrass him if he took it the wrong way. I wasn't very good at this. I should have paid...

after all, I was the one that arranged. I'd asked Ben out; he didn't have to say yes...

All the way back to my room, I replayed his words in my mind. *He was just being polite, wasn't he?* Was that his way of kindly letting me down? *What went wrong?*

I slammed my door behind me and threw myself onto my bed in the pitch blackness. I landed on a deodorant bottle, flinched at the sharpness of it, and threw it across the room in a fit of rage, where it hit the mirror and made an awful noise before rolling across the floor.

I felt like such an idiot.

This is why you should never date bandmates.

Ben

I SAT in my room for about five minutes before I called myself stupid, stomped my feet a few times, then got up and went back out.

I panicked. I hadn't wanted Casper to know how much I really wanted this; I didn't want him to think I was that eager, but instead I'd scared him off. I was ready to do stuff to him that I'd only ever done to people in my dreams. I *wanted* him so badly. I needed to get away before I ruined everything; before it even had a chance to manifest as *something*. I was so afraid of commitment. It was easy to drunkenly sleep with someone at a house party, but this was nothing like that. This was *real.*

I eventually came to my senses.

Casper definitely thought I didn't like him back. I'd went too far...

'Stay awake. I'm an idiot.' I texted him.

I didn't wait for a response.

Casper

'*STAY AWAKE. I'M AN IDIOT.*' His message read.

He'd sent that fifteen minutes ago. A few minutes later, after I vomited up my heart and flushed it down the drain, there was a knock at my door.

I forgot to breathe.

Ben

I LIKED HIM. A lot. A *lot,* a lot. I know that doesn't make sense. I don't care.

Casper

WHEN I FLICKED on the light and pulled the door open, there he stood. It had started to rain, and I smelled the fresh dampness on his jacket, the scent of his aftershave... *him.*

"You said you had cans?" Ben said, short of breath.

Oh, fuck it. I pulled him inside and crashed my mouth to his, letting the door slam shut behind him. Ben didn't pull back, even as I held him closer, moving one hand to his hair.

Yup, of course; I breathed in his smell of smoke and apple shampoo, twirling my fingers into the thicker curls at the back of his head. I noticed he'd been letting his hair grow. He pulled at my belt loops and then wrapped one arm under mine, bringing us flush together. His hand splayed over my back, and I felt his warmth through all the layers I wore.

He pulled me in even tighter, and I nearly toppled forward, pushing him backward and breaking the kiss.

"We're on the same page then, yeah?" Ben looked me dead in the eyes, panting for breath.

"Definitely."

"Perfect." He pushed me towards the bed, surprising me with his strength, but I was most definitely *not* about to protest anything he was going to do next.

Ben pressed me into the sheets with his weight, his black trench coat hanging around him as his head shielded the light, forming a halo on his head. *He's like an angel,* I thought. The way the light shone behind his hair made him look too good to be true; I was undeserving of this—of him and his beautiful green eyes. Ben glanced down at my lips, and *he bit his lip. He bit his lip.* God, so help me.

"I really like you," he said, pressing his arms firmly either side of me. His crucifix necklace dangled below my face, so I instinctively reached out to hold it. Ben pulled back on his knees and straddled my waist, taking the jewellery in his own hands and considering it.

"You never mentioned you were religious," I said, internally yearning to break the distance.

"I'm not, not really. I just..." He glanced down at the chain between his fingers. "Anyway, let's not discuss this now. What we're doing is hardly..."

I didn't let him finish; I reached out with both arms and pulled him against my chest, holding his weight in my hands.

"Kiss me again," I muttered close to his face.

"My pleasure." He leaned down and peppered kisses along my lips, cheeks, nose, and brow.

"You really are a wonder, Casper Murphey," he said, nibbling my ear.

I love him.

"I do try," I think I said. It might not have been the time for sarcasm, but it did the job as he sped up his kisses.

I helped him out of his jacket, uncaring about where it landed. He pushed back at my shirt collar, and I sat up, finally taking off my own coat.

"Damn the weather."

Ben stayed the night.

He was my boyfriend by the end of the week.

Ben

I decided to stay in Durham.

I told Jake about us the very next day, though I had no choice really, seeing as he knocked at Casper's door at noon. I hadn't answered my door, and Jake rightly concluded that this was the only other place I could have been.

Like he already knew.

Jake said he was happy for us and took us out for coffee that morning.

Everything was perfect. Just perfect. I wanted to lock myself in time and relive the joy from that day over and over and over for eternity.

We spent the whole week together on the run up to Christmas; we explored the cathedral and the riverside, and we even booked a train to York to see the Christmas markets before heading to my gran's house for Christmas Eve.

I'd rang ahead to let her know my 'American friend' was joining us because he had no one to spend Christmas with. It was the perfect excuse because even in the short two weeks we'd been together, I had already grown too used to sharing a bed with him.

Jake had slept at mine on many occasions when we were at school, so my gran didn't even have to query who Casper was to me. It was all very normal.

I wasn't ashamed or embarrassed to be in a relationship with him; I just didn't like making a big deal about it or having the whole 'this is my boyfriend' talk, and answering all the follow-up questions from my family, even if they knew I wasn't straight anyway... This was the first time I actually felt serious about a partner, so, for the time being, we collectively kept it between us, Jake, and, of course, Casper had told Jesse, who was apparently dying to meet me.

My parents knew I was gay. I'd come out to them when I was fourteen, which probably wasn't the best time for them, since they were dealing with their own relationship stuff. My dad said he was confused because I'd apparently once said Beyoncé was pretty—though I don't remember saying that—and even if I had done, I would have been a child. Children think everything is pretty. My mum was also a little shocked, saying she never would have guessed. She hugged me, regardless, promising as long as I was happy, she was happy. For so many years, I blamed myself for their divorce, thinking that it was my coming out that drove them apart, even though they had been struggling to work things out with each other for years without me even knowing.

My mum came up for Christmas and met Casper. She pulled me aside later that day after a few glasses of Asti and said, "He's not just your friend, is he?"

When I shook my head, she held me tight and said he was a 'nice boy', and she could see how happy I was. Mums always have a way of knowing us like that.

I walked back into the living room afterwards and caught Casper in the middle of his round of charades. My gran was perched on the edge of her seat, shouting the word 'THE' way too enthusiastically. My mum's brother, Uncle Robert, was on his feet already, hunched over as if his body language won him points. Casper glanced up at me and grinned. He was glowing. I took in a deep breath, then beamed back.

This was everything.

· · ·

I CALLED my dad that night. He asked me how I was and said I should have a little present waiting for me when I arrived back in Durham. I told him I loved him, and that he would have to come and visit me some time. He paused, then released a slow breath. "Of course, son. I'll see you soon. Love you too."

JAKE TEXTED me on boxing day to tell me he'd dreamed about vampires and thought we should name our band Forever Red. He provided no context, but I showed the message to Casper, who agreed. It had a gothic ring to it, which was how we'd always intended to market our band. Neither of us had any other ideas, so it felt right.

And thus, we became Forever Red.

Oh, the irony of what was to come.

Casper

ME AND BEN had essentially moved in with each other. Half my stuff was at his; half of his was at mine. We were a shared soul. On New Year's Day 2010, I kissed him and told him I loved him, and he didn't even hesitate to say it back. He was my soulmate.

Jake was overwhelmingly supportive of us and promised to keep things quiet until we were ready to announce things. We waited a long time before telling everyone else. Durham was surprisingly queer-friendly—given its snobbish reputation—but it was 2010, and we already stood out like sore thumbs, regardless of whether we were together or not, so we agreed there was no rush in coming out. At the end of the day, we had each other and were extremely happy. Our families knew now, and that was all that mattered. Being 'alternative' in a sea of tweed and satchels was alienating enough, we just wanted to take our time.

We released our first original work on YouTube in March that year. 'Angelic' we called it. Very dark and grungy—too many pedals for my liking, and none of us had the guts to sing on it, so we left it as a seven-and-a-half-minute instrumental track, which weirdly hit 1k views within a few days. When 1k soon turned to 5k, we couldn't believe our luck. Me being me, I went to every media site to scrounge for any mention of us besides the seven comments on the video. I found a link on Reddit; two people commented they'd check it out. I think it was under a thread r/quietgoths or something super random. I have no idea how I managed to find it.

About a month later, someone reposted our audio to YouTube with a pixelated slide show of graveyard stock images. The description claimed we were an American band, which made me smile at first, but the one singular comment it had at the time said, 'I think they're British, actually."

I rolled my eyes.

I THINK it was around April time when Ben and I got our first tattoos together. I got a moon on my bicep, and he got a cluster of stars on the side of his hip—a spontaneous decision for us both, I admit, but we had no regrets. Ben pierced his nose and shaved the sides of his hair; he was a star in the making. People would always comment on his stylish appearance when we played in bars. His long leather trench, steel capped boots, mesh tops, and skull rings. He seriously looked the part, and I wanted him to be the face of our band, but he always refused. He had no idea how perfect he was.

"I'm not cut out for that," he'd said to me one night.

"You don't even have to try—everyone thinks you're the

coolest guy in the year." I wasn't even exaggerating. People spoke openly about him around campus. That was one of the perks of our relationship being secret at the time—people had no real idea who I was. Of course, our other friends knew me, and a few people vaguely recognised us three together as 'the boys from that student band,' but everyone always forgets about the drummers at the back of the stage. And that's how I liked it. I felt like I was infiltrating secret territories without being spotted.

I should have enjoyed that privacy while it lasted.

"Let go, I'm going to go bald!" Ben snatched for the brush in my hand as I pasted the bleach over his roots. We sat in his tiny student bathroom beneath the buzzing light bulb and whirring fan. I remember noting how our height difference was more dramatic than normal, until I glanced down at my New Rocks and saw Ben was barefoot. I liked being able to see over his head, though. I was always very protective of him. Despite his gloomy attire, he had such a young and innocent-looking face, and I liked to remind people how strong and mature he really was.

"I'm not going to let you go bald," I promised.

He turned to face me, wide-eyed. "So, you've done this before?"

I clenched my jaw. "Well... not exactly."

At that, he successfully managed to grab the brush from my hand and threw it into the sink, yanking on his own set of plastic gloves before working his hands through the top of his head.

He was so stubborn. I held in my laugh.

"You need to ensure it's spread evenly," I added.

"I know, I know," he snapped, though not unkindly. He was in full concentration mode.

"This was a mistake; my mum is actually gonna kill me," he joked after a beat.

"You can't stop now, you'll just have a giant ginger patch on your crown."

"Maybe I can make it work. Start a trend!" Ben snorted at his own realisation.

"I would love you, regardless, but I would definitely question your decision." I bit down my laughter.

"Urgh, why did I do this? Why did I do this?" He began muttering under his breath as he sectioned off the layers and added more bleach.

When he came to me with his proposal, I'll admit that I hated the idea at first, knowing his beautiful raven black hair would be no longer.

"Why?" I'd asked him.

"I think it will give me more confidence. You know, take me out of my comfort zone."

"Is this because of what I said?"

"What did you say?" His tone answered my question with a resounding yes. He was our front man—the face of the band—and now he wanted to try and fit his own image of what that meant.

Ben believed in Forever Red so much that he wanted to do everything in his power to make us the best we could possibly be. No matter the cost.

He would never admit that, of course.

We washed it off, and Ben cringed at the coppery aftermath. He ran straight for the purple shampoo he'd bought in preparation when Jake walked in and gasped.

"Jesus Christ, what have you done?" he said, throwing his hands to his mouth and taking in the scene.

Ben hung his head over the bath and brushed a towel through his hair. "Making bad decisions for the greater good," he joked, face damp as he turned to our friend.

Instead of having a go at Ben, which I'd expected him to do, he stepped into the bathroom and picked up the bowl of peroxide. "Any left?" he asked.

Jake's hair was practically blonde anyway, so it proved a much easier task to get his desired results, one round turning his hair snow white. He'd recently started wearing long jackets similar to Ben's, and thus had now virtually become a Billy Idol doppelgänger.

I kept forgetting we were still essentially just kids. Ben was still only eighteen, and none of us really had any serious life experience —we were just having fun.

We created our image then, though. Cemented ourselves as the post-punk goths of the year. Of course, we would never have been let off lightly with what we were becoming. No one parades around the streets of an old English city looking like nineteenth-century grave robbers without the stares and under breath remarks, but we were high on life and felt unstoppable.

At the end of our first year, we played a local charity gig for nearly two hundred people. Granted, most of the guests were fellow students who wanted to add 'donated to a charity' to their CVs, but the atmosphere was insane regardless. Two hundred people? It was incomprehensible to us at the time. We were three boys with far-fetched dreams, living in our bubble of denial.

Ben had bought himself a few new pedals and a looper to upload some pre-recorded keyboard parts to some of our songs. We were starting to feel *professional*.

Sure, it was still a fairly small venue, and we were relatively unknown outside of the university—and a very niche corner of the internet—but we didn't expect much to come from it, aside from our enjoyment and experience.

But then a group of people stayed at the end and asked for photographs with us.

And *autographs*.

I remember Jake laughed and said, "I can't write," before whipping out a pen and signing a clearly practiced signature onto a black and white photo of the cathedral. The girl who asked grinned giddily, then asked her friend to take a photo with the three of us. I agreed, as did Jake, but Ben stepped back slightly, a look of panic washing over his features. His hair had started to grow out, showing his darker roots, and he'd begun to wear Victorian button-up shirts. I remember looking at him and thinking how lucky I was to call him mine. Then, I remembered how he'd once told me how much he hates posing for photographs, and my excitement at our current situation faded.

"Oh, I'll sit this one out," he said politely, jokingly, shaking his hands in protest, but I heard the twinge of embarrassment in his voice and caught the look of confused disappointment on the girl's face.

"Casper?" Jake looked at me, desperate to get the photo out of the way to avoid prolonging the awkwardness for Ben.

With one last look back at my boyfriend, I posed for the photo as the girl positioned herself between us and draped an arm around each of our backs.

It was a bittersweet moment.

"WHY DIDN'T you just do it, Ben?" Jake asked once we were back in my room; Ben sat on the edge of the bed, gripping the mattress with a distant expression.

"I just, I dunno." He didn't look at either of us.

Jake joined his side and wrapped a friendly arm around him. I admittedly felt a slight twinge of *jealousy* as I watched this intimate moment, but cursed myself for even letting my mind go there. Jake was Ben's oldest and closest friend; it was perfectly normal. I joined his other side, resting my hand on Ben's thigh. I rubbed it for reassurance. "It doesn't matter really, does it?" I said to Jake over Ben.

Jake shrugged, then withdrew his arm. "We're gonna have to get used to this, though. This is what we wanted, wasn't it? You're our frontman." He had a point, but his tone was too harsh.

Ben finally spoke. "I just felt *off*."

"That's fine, Ben. No one is forcing you to do anything you don't want to," I quickly responded before Jake could add anything else.

"Look, I'm just saying…" Jake stood and started pacing. "That was a pretty insane experience. A photo? With us? I would have liked my best mate to have been involved in our first fan interaction." He playfully kicked and nudged Ben's foot with his, garnering Ben's attention.

"I just didn't feel like it, okay, Jake? Can we leave it, please? It's not that big of a deal," he snapped.

Jake clearly didn't expect Ben's reaction.

"God. Sorry. I didn't think…" Jake raised his hands apologetically and threw himself back down on the bed beside us, lying flat with his hands stretched out. "It's all so surreal. I never planned for this. I mean, we have *actual* fans. It's all just happening so fast! I mean, it's cool. It's so cool, but wow… do you reckon we should start making merch?" He tried to change the subject, propping himself up on his elbows.

I scoffed. "Merch? We've only got, like, two original songs out in the open. We have no marketing experience whatsoever, and I may have a bit of knowledge in design, but…"

Ben silently laughed, and then I laughed, too, thinking back to my terrible poster. The weight of the room lifted.

"There's no way we'd be able to come up with a good enough font or logo on our own," Jake said.

"We could look up some freelance artists in the area and check out their rates?" Ben contributed, seeming to cheer up.

"We could. I don't really want to spend the entirety of my student loan on a font, though." Jake still stared at the ceiling, lost in thought.

"I could try and see what I can do. Even if I draw something by hand and then scan it in?" I suggested.

"My mum has a bit of graphic design experience. She used to take a night course when I was a kid. I mean, their technology won't have been as good as modern tech, but I could still ask her," Ben suggested.

"Good idea, as long as she wouldn't mind." I nodded at the proposal.

Ben looked at me, his dimples showing. "Oh, she won't mind; she'd probably quite enjoy it."

"There's a freelancer here who does font design at a decent price."

We both looked at Jake, who had since pulled out his new phone and quickly searched the internet.

"Mars Creations. Says they're based in Durham. Could be a shout." He continued reading.

"Let's have a look." Ben leaned down beside Jake, staring at the tiny phone screen. Jake started scrolling while Ben pulled a face of pleasant surprise.

"That *is* decent," he said. Ben looked at me, gesturing me over with his hand. Jake passed the phone over, and I had a look for myself.

WE EMAILED THE ARTIST, who got back to us a few hours later saying they would love to design a logo for us. They asked to hear some of our music, so I sent over a link to our YouTube video. They said we sounded super unique, and within two days, we had a perfect logo; they also offered to throw in a bunch of printed t-shirts for us to sell, completely free of charge.

Back then, Ben and I never met Mars in person, but Jake went over to collect the t-shirts one afternoon. It turned out they were a third-year student in the neighbouring city with their apartment here in Durham. It seemed odd but we didn't question it.

"They were so fit." I believe were Jake's exact words. Ben rolled his eyes.

I FLEW BACK to the states the following month for a few weeks. Jesse never left my side as he bombarded me with questions about England, the band, and Ben. I didn't mind, though; I was proud of everything I'd been blessed with that year. It still hadn't even fully sunk in. I'd successfully completed year one of a Law degree, while also (sort of) becoming a music artist. I really don't know how I managed to juggle it all and not let either thing suffer. I was good at hiding my stress, but regardless, I did it. I succeeded.

Ben hated his course. I'd figured it out a while ago, but he managed the year and said he would take year two with a different approach. I'd told him it would be fine if he dropped out, switched courses, or even wanted to put the band on hold, but he wasn't having any of it. He didn't want to admit to his family that the course he'd been so unbelievably set on doing wasn't for him. You see, he gets embarrassed very easily.

Ben flew out for a week in August, and I introduced him to my family. My dad nicknamed him 'The Cure' boy, but Ben seemed to take it as a compliment, joking about his own fashion sense. He got on brilliantly with them all, with my mom even calling him her son by the end of his trip. She's always so motherly and dotes over everyone who sets foot in our home. I love my mom.

By September, we were back in Durham. We'd decided months ago to get an apartment to share, renting a house on the opposite side of the city. It only made sense. Jake's course friend, Henry, occupied the fourth room for the first few weeks until he spontaneously decided to move out and live with his girlfriend because they 'could not bear to be apart.' Good riddance. I didn't like Henry.

In October 2010, we did our second 'not in a pub' concert for freshers. It felt weird getting back to it all, but I remember feeling so relieved that I was finally back home. *Home.* Because that's what it was to me now: Ben and the band. Home. Forever Red.

At the end of the concert, I noticed a short, white-haired girl lingering around the door. She looked like a buzz cut Debbie Harry, if she'd booked out a tattoo parlour for her eighteenth birthday.

"Hey, you okay?" I asked her, my drumsticks still in hand. The other two were packing away their guitars and gear.

"Hi, yeah. Well... I know this might be a weird and possibly insane request, but do you think I could maybe... join the band?"

I definitely wasn't expecting that, but I didn't dismiss it.

"You like us that much?" I asked.

She grinned back, a little shyer this time when she spoke: "I mean, obviously, we'd have to try stuff out, so you can decide if you like me or not, but I absolutely adore your music. It's right up my alley. I saw you three with my friends last year, and you made such a big impression on me. And I thought, hey, shy bairns get nowt."

Her accent took me a moment to absorb, a really strong version of the one I heard a lot around the city. But I definitely didn't struggle over her statement. *We made a big impression?*

"You play?" I asked.

"Guitar, vocals, whatever you need me to do. And I'm not at uni or anything so I'm basically free whenever. I'm in between jobs, you see." She sounded like she'd rehearsed her response.

I paused, trying to figure out the logistics. We needed an extra member to alleviate Ben's many roles. He'd talked about not wanting to be our permanent singer; still a little stage-shy in that respect.

"Hang on, I'll be right back," I said. She nodded with an innocent smile and shrugged with smooth confidence.

I walked back to the stage and told the guys the situation. Jake looked hesitant, but Ben didn't even pause before saying: "Sure, bring her over!" He looked genuinely excited.

. . .

Interview excerpt: Leeds Festival 2011

[*INTRO REDACTED*]

Aniyah: So, you joined them right then?

Fran: More or less. They were super chill about it; got me to play some stuff on Jake's guitar and sing a bit for them. By the next week, we were recording together in their flat, and then I decided to move in because I was travelling in from home nearly every day. We essentially became the 'Forever Red' house.

[*redacted*]

Fran: You see, my dad used to be in a band in the eighties, they had like one hit song, but they never split up and continued touring small venues. He had stored up all this equipment over the years and would let me experiment around with stuff when I was a kid. Music is one of those things you keep in the family. Once one of you takes it seriously, there's no stopping generations and generations from feeling it, too.

[*all nod in agreement*]

Casper: Fran's dad helped us out massively, even helped us record our first EP. In fact, we have him to thank for our current location.

Ben: Oh, without a shadow of a doubt. He's like our unofficial manager.

Fran: [*laughing and looking at the camera*] Shout out to Beck Young.

Aniyah: The man, the myth, the legend.

Ben

December 2010

WINTER IN 2010 WAS AWFUL, and definitely the worst snow I'd seen in a November. We were essentially stuck in the flat for days and days, so we used our time wisely, the four of us practising every day until we were the strongest we'd ever been as a four piece. I think Jake got a little jealous that Fran was slowly yet unintentionally becoming our front woman. I know he always wanted the role after I more or less stepped back from it, but Fran was made for the part. I believed she was meant to lead us—the guidance and grounding we'd always needed. She kept us focused, and we always produced the best stuff when she took charge of the lyrics and we created the melodies around it, as opposed to the other way around. It was as though she'd been with us since the start.

But despite our occasional disagreements, the band was thriving.

I will never understand how a band like ours found success in the area we lived, but we did. It was overwhelming.

One random day, someone asked me, "You're Ben Audley, right?" I was standing in the queue at a coffee shop. I turned around, expecting it to be someone from university, but it wasn't. It was a middle-aged, balding man with expanders in each ear lobe, and more hair on his chin than his head. He was sporting a Talking Heads t-shirt and had a worn-out, badge-covered canvas bag over his shoulder.

My eyes widened.

"Yes... I am," was all I could say.

He laughed and shook his head. "Sorry kid, you probably weren't expecting that, were you?"

"Yeah. No. Yeah." I had no idea what to say.

"I'll leave you be, but I just wanted to say, I'm a big fan. My friend Richard is one of your tutors. You're going far kid. So very far."

Then he turned to shout at his wife who was sat down a few tables back, double checking her order.

You're going far, kid.

I felt like I'd just been visited by punk Gandalf or something.

But yeah, some older guy liked our stuff. In fact, older generations started coming to our gigs more and more until our audiences were a balance of young and old. It was surreal. These were people who grew up in the original goth scene, and they wanted to see *us*?

WE DECIDED to create a social media page; it was the thing a lot of people were starting to do then. We sold all our merch and hired Mars with the money from our previous gigs to produce more; they even designed some aesthetic background art pieces for us to use to advertise upcoming shows. RIP blurry ravens from Tumblr.

Casper had tried—God bless him—to design some things for us, but it just... didn't fit the look we were going for, shall I say.

"I DID SOME DOODLING, what do you think?" Casper turned his laptop screen to face us. The three of us on the sofa stood in unison for a better view. It was... interesting to say the least.

"It looks like a pig; is that a pig's shadow?" Jake went straight for brutal honesty.

"I was going to say an elephant—a dancing elephant to be exact." Fran gestured to the design, trying and failing to hold in a laugh.

Casper shook his head in comical self-disappointment then looked at me for my input. I really didn't want to crush his spirit, but once I realised he was inviting criticism, I joined in.

"We should give it to the travelling circus; they might have a horror routine to advertise."

Casper paused before bursting with laughter. God, I loved his laugh.

"Dolly the Dancing Elephant!" He wiggled his fingers as if introducing his next act, failing to hold the act for more than a few seconds before falling into hysterics again.

"I'm glad we're all in agreement then," Jake said, though slightly more seriously. Our laughter faded.

"Yeah. I think we should call that Mars person again; I can input some cash where necessary." Fran held composure.

I THINK the weirdest part of gaining more attention was how quickly people became interested in our personal lives. Me and Casper hid our relationship extremely well from the outside world —we didn't want our relationship to have anything to do with the band. We didn't want to be the main focus; we just wanted to play our music. Most people worked out I was gay back in school, house parties were never private affairs, and everyone loved to gossip, but since moving to Durham, I'd not told a soul.

But somehow, despite all that, we garnered the attention of a small group of serious followers, who liked and commented on our every post; it was flattering at first, but then it started to get... weird.

We still weren't big by any standard, but these guys *adored* us.

It all got a little too much when a photo was shared of me and Fran on a cig break, just chatting between recording sessions, like friends do. Obviously, we were oblivious to the fact someone had essentially invaded our privacy, but what got me the most was the caption.

'*You can't tell me these two aren't seeing each other,*' it read.

"You know this sort of shit is gonna start happening. Fans crave for their dreams to come true. They get obsessive and start theorising. It's pretty harmless for now, so there's nothing we can really do," Fran said. All four of us sat around our living room table, critiquing the image.

"It's so blurry, like they were hiding in the bushes or something." Casper winced, and my feelings plummeted.

"Weirdos. Get a life," Jake said to the photo. "I don't see how they think that even... I mean, no offence, Fran, but you two have little in common with each other. You two are probably the least close out of all of us. I don't see how fans can even see it working." He seemed pretty defensive for someone who wasn't even in the photo, and my brow furrowed at his tone. Fran shrugged silently; after all, we'd only known each other a few months.

I enjoyed spending time with her, she was a very easy person to get along with. Fit herself into any conversation naturally, making small talk actually quite enjoyable. I knew she'd fit in well with us from the start, but I never expected fans to read *that* deeply into the moments we shared. Did I give off flirting vibes? I never even thought about it...

"I could ask them nicely to take it down, or debunk it," I suggested, my voice coming out a little higher pitched.

Jake chewed his bottom lip. "We could, but then when will we stop? This is bound to continue and inevitably get worse. We need to think about the sort of image we're creating for ourselves."

I was puzzled by his wording. "So, you're suggesting I just leave it? Let these people think Fran and I are dating?"

"It could be quite fun to toy with them." Fran smirked.

Casper said nothing, seeming deep in thought.

"You think?" I wasn't sure about that, at all. What if they started seriously pairing us together? What if people made up stories about us? Sure, Fran was lovely, and we would undoubtedly get closer as friends, but I loved Casper more than words could say, and I couldn't fathom the idea of being with anyone else, even for a joke.

"I just think maybe if we start interacting with this sort of media, it could come back to bite us in the ass, which is essentially what I was trying to say. Things stay on the internet *forever*. We should probably keep it professional. You don't want anyone to know about you and Casper yet, so maybe keeping this going will act as cover. Just a suggestion." Jake rubbed his chin.

"We could maybe start looking for a proper manager? Get a little advice on pr and stuff?" Casper suggested, breaking his silence.

"Maybe you're right," I mumbled, relaxing my shoulders.

Casper leaned over to kiss my head. Jake looked away.

Interview excerpt: June 2015

Interviewer (Max Fletcher, 'It's So Dark In Here' – Paparazzi interview for immediate release): So, let's address the elephant in the room. You've worked together on a bunch of solo projects, and now this single. You both are seen together a lot of the time, alone, too. Fans have speculated for years that you're maybe more than friends?

[*Ben and Fran remain silent*]

Max: Any comments? Want to settle the rumours?

[*Ben looks visibly uncomfortable*]

Fran: Look, look. Whenever you get even a smidge of fame, there's always people who want to know more about you, people who think they know you and can figure stuff out. Me and Ben are friends; we have been a for a long time now. We work together on lyrics, on guitar and bass lines. We like to push our boundaries and experiment with our ideas. We work brilliantly together on stage, and I love him. In fact, he's my best mate now, but we are *not* together. Happy?

Max: [*clears throat*] You heard it here then, guys. Rumours put to rest after many years.

Ben: [*interrupting, staring directly at camera as if to address fans*] Please stop trying to figure us out. Please.

Casper
February 2011

THIS 'FAME' stuff hung heavy over us during our second year. Not necessarily in a bad way, but it made me more aware of its effect on Ben.

I was lying on my front, face turned towards him in bed. Ben had just sat up and lit a cigarette, leaning over to lift the window up a crack. (We were *not* getting the deposit back on the house, but I'd given up trying.) I think he thought I'd drifted off, but my heart was still racing, and my eyes were slightly open, watching his every move.

"When did you start smoking?" I asked.

He looked down at me with a clueless expression. "Just a few seconds ago. You want me to put it out?"

I didn't have to open my mouth; I rolled my eyes and waited for it to click.

"Oh, you mean... erm." He tapped the cigarette on the ash tray on his nightstand. "Fourteen, I think. Nearly fifteen." He took another drag, tilting his head away to blow the smoke out of the window.

I recalled having had this conversation before, yet the answer still shocked me. So young.

"Do your parents smoke?"

Ben shrugged, pouting his lips and tilting his head. "Dad did. A *lot*. Mum hated it. They used to fight about it, and she made her points very clear." Another drag. "He never smoked in the house, though; he always went in the back yard to do it or when he walked to work."

"So, why did you start?"

"Dunno, really. I got bored at school. Someone handed me one. It stuck." He shrugged distantly again. "What's with the questions anyway? I can put it out."

I moved to sit up beside him, a draft of icy air hitting me. "No, no. I'm just curious. I'm in a quizzy mood. Sorry."

Ben smiled, and there was that god-damned dimple. "It's okay, I like quizzes." After his final drag, he added, "I hope I will have the sense to stop in the future; I'm well aware of the effects, but for now, at least, it's only this and not the drugs."

The way he so casually brought it up shocked me. I would never have pinned Ben as someone who actually *did drugs.*

"Drugs?" I said, trying to not sound as controlling as I feared I might. I was just concerned; he'd never mentioned taking them before.

Ben waved me off. "Don't look so worried. It was just a blip in sixth-form. I tried some stuff a few times at house parties, it was unfortunately very normalised, but I had enough sense to stop after..." His eyes widened upon realising he'd never shared this story with me before.

My eyes widened. "After *what*?"

Ben looked at me and bit his lip in guilt. "After I stopped breathing, and Jake had to force me to be sick."

I lay motionless, my eyes fixed on Ben's face.

"How old were you?"

"Seventeen."

I stayed silent, absorbing it all.

"Sorry, I forgot I hadn't told you," he added.

Then I dove up and threw my arms around him, pulling him close to my chest. I held on tight, nestling my head in the crook of his shoulder while Ben slowly wrapped his arms around my back. The contrast of his cold hands against my warm body made me shiver, but I didn't move or speak a word—I didn't need to.

The more I learned about Ben, the more I realised he was hiding things from me—from us all. He was a quiet man who isolated himself too much. He blamed himself for a lot of things in his past, things that were completely out of his control, and though I wasn't entirely sure how to fix that, I sure as hell would try my best.

"I'm always here, you know that, right?" I said into his ear. I felt his heart thumping against my chest, fast and strong.

"I know. I'm sorry, Casper."

"It's okay."

I held him all night.

March 2011

I suppose you could say this was the real beginning of our career. The moment we all sat down and went: 'Wow... so, we really are taking this seriously then.' The moment we dropped our first, self-titled EP onto streaming platforms and sat back and let the world decide our fate. We rerecorded 'Angelic' with Fran doing some ethereal backing vocals, and then worked together to perfect all our performances.

Beck helped us a great deal with marketing and production, helping us even get it out on CD. He offered to manage us until we found someone suitable to work with—which was a lot harder than it seemed—but we were no longer just 'that band from university.' We'd transcended that.

We travelled to Manchester for the release and enjoyed a night out. Jake and Fran had already drunk their weight in alcohol before we even made it to the second bar. Although we spent most of the night as a group, when we strolled through the gay village, Ben and I wandered off a little. No one knew us there; it was the first place we could just be ourselves and blend in.

We found Fran and Jake a little while later. Jake had a girl on his lap—dyed jet-black curls and fishnets from head to toe. They were deep in some sort of winking conversation while Fran casually lounged against a white concrete pillar, drink in hand, chatting up a much taller woman with a twinkle in her eyes. We took one quick assessment of the scene and thought it best to simply leave them both be; they'd find us when they were ready.

We moved on to another bar and bought a couple more drinks. I wouldn't call myself overprotective, but I refused to let Ben out of my sight. He liked to float around a bit, and after consuming the amount of alcohol he had, he grew a lot more confident and would jump into random conversations. I followed him outside a few times so he could have his cigarettes, but kept enough distance to let him enjoy himself—it was a rare thing to watch Ben open up, smiling and laughing in public. It calmed me to see him like that.

At one point, we were outside, chatting with a couple of other guys, when I somehow lost him. After wandering through crowds, I rang him and waited beside the alleyway so he could spot me.

I stood there awkwardly on my own, drinking just for something to do, but then I heard a scratching noise beside me and some sort of splutter. I had to shove my heart back into my chest for a moment, nearly dropping my drink. I turned to my side, but I could barely see anything. It was so dark. Slowly, I edged back towards the light, then turned the corner away from the sound and back into the crowd.

I heard it again, but this time it was higher pitched, like someone was in pain.

I turned back, unable to zone out.

"You okay?" I shouted into the alleyway. I was still backed-up enough to run to safety if anything leaped out at me. It felt stupid to shout into the darkness, but I couldn't live with myself if I left someone injured, or worse.

No one responded, but I heard more movement. Someone was down there, and after another shuffling sound, I could make out a silhouette of a person crouched against the wall, head down.

"Hello?" I called out, less sure of myself this time.

The figure let out a gasp for breath.

"Hello?" I said again, stepping closer. "Is everything alright? Do you need me to call someone?"

I stepped further into the abyss and crouched down to the figure, whose heavy breathing echoed along the alley. I lowered my voice as I softly asked: "Are you hurt? Shall I call an ambulance?"

Heavy, ragged breathing followed, then, "No. No. No ambulance. Nothing. Please, leave me... ahh... alone." They cried out in raspy pain, their voice young and tortured.

I don't know what encouraged me to reach out, but I did, and I eventually found the cold arms of the injured body. I felt what I could only think of as a long, tattered skirt. The figure flinched.

"Please, let me help. I can help; I'm not going to hurt you." Which was exactly what someone who would hurt you would say.

"I just need to have a look, where are you hurt?" I reached for the torch on my phone while this person struggled to breathe.

"No. No. No." Their voice grew more panicked and afraid; they inched back slightly before crying out, the movement clearly worsening the injury.

"I'm going to have to have a look; otherwise, I can't help you. Please, let me..." I reached out again with one hand on my phone, ready to shine the light on where I suspected the wound was.

I turned on the torch.

It was not a leg wound.

I jumped back in a flash of terror, dropping my phone face down beside me on the concrete, torch still beaming.

I will never forget the sight before me for as long as I breathe.

It couldn't have been human, or at least, it couldn't have been alive. Its eyes were entirely red, with dark, curly hair matted to its forehead from crusty, dried blood, the same dried blood coating its entire face. Thicker, blacker trails of crimson stemmed from the mouth and dried onto the chin. Its horrified eyes regarded me while it held its entire chest wall in the palm of its hands, blood still seeping from the edges as it tried to hold the skin over its exposed flesh and bone. It cried out in pain as if to say, 'I warned you not to look at me.' I should have listened... I...

"Casper? What are you doing down there?" Ben's voice brought me back to reality; I startled, spinning to face him and running back down the alleyway to join his side. The look of confusion on his face was prevalent.

"You okay?" He searched my eyes for answers and glanced back into the alleyway. "Who were you talking to?"

I turned back to the darkness, blaming my drunkenness for my lack of memory. "I... I don't know..." I didn't know—my brain felt *empty.*

"We should probably head off soon and catch up with those two."

I nodded profusely. "Yeah, yeah. Good idea."

Ben glanced back to the alleyway once more and peered down at my hands, red smeared along my palms. "Was someone hurt? Are *you* hurt?" he asked, a manic edge to his voice.

"What? Oh, no, no." I brushed my hands onto my black trousers. "That's just paint."

Just paint.

SALES for the EP were steady at first, which we expected, until nearly a month after the release, somehow, we got noticed. We appeared on an indie chart, and a small local radio station played our song 'Ink Black.' They called us for an interview a week later.

Radio interview excerpt: April 2011

RADIO HOST (HANA DANES, 'Eighties Revival Hour'): What was your reaction when you heard your song on the radio for the first time?

Ben: Oh, I couldn't believe it! I genuinely thought I was dreaming.

Casper: Yeah, it was crazy.

Fran: Thanks for playing our silly little song.

Hana: Well, how could we not? You guys are like a breath of fresh air.

[*all look shocked*]

Casper: We're just doing what we love.

[*redacted*]

Hana: So, I believe you guys have three big tour dates coming up?

Casper: Yeah! Newcastle, Manchester, and then Ben's hometown, Leeds. [*smiles at his bandmates*]

Hana: What does it feel like performing in your hometown, Ben?

Ben: Oh... it will be weird, definitely. But exciting. I'm excited. I'm hoping I don't see my old school mates, though. That would be awkward.

Fran: Nah, it'll be great.

[*redacted*]

Hana: Aren't there four of you in this band?

Ben
May 2011

JAKE DIDN'T ATTEND the interview. At the time, he said he had uni work to complete, which was perfectly valid—it was nearing the end of our second year, and we all had final assessments looming. We had a lot on our plates, balancing uni with the band, but this was such a big thing, and I thought Jake out of all people would have cancelled *anything* to be there... it just didn't make sense.

At first, I wasn't good with the publicity side of things; it took me a long time to get used to being recognised and not curling inwards at every acknowledgement. Jake and Casper were the opposite; they were outgoing and positive right from the start, but then as our fame grew, they both settled down a little, but in Jake's case, he almost seemed to stop caring at all.

"You're coming out of your shell, I can tell," Jake said to me the day after the interview. I, of course, questioned him further on his absence, but he brushed me off and changed the topic, which somehow turned to me instead.

"Yeah, you think?" I took a drag of my cigarette before stubbing it against the side of the ashtray. We were sat outside our house on the back steps, my usual morning haunt. Jake had brought me a coffee like he did some mornings.

"You're changing," he said, yet I couldn't read his tone.

"What do you mean?" I turned to face him, but his face was averted, staring off into the distance.

"I dunno... It's just you seem different to what you used to be. It isn't a bad thing; in fact, it's great. You're so much more confident and surer of yourself. The Ben I went to school with would be amazed at the Ben you are now."

A smile twinged on my lips. "Hmm, do you reckon?"

"You promise me you're okay, though?"

I looked at him, puzzled. "Of course; what do you mean?"

"I just want to make sure my best friend is happy."

I flashed him a boyish smile, teeth showing. "Why wouldn't I be?"

"You'd tell me if something was up, right? Just like in sixth-form."

I heard 'sixth-form' in the form of a sting to the centre of my chest, but I nodded. I promised I would always share if I felt off. I didn't really know what caused him to question in that moment, but I was just glad we were talking like we used to. Ever since we started taking the band seriously, I'd felt Jake drift from me slightly. I knew our dynamic would inevitably change as we grew up and established ourselves as fully grown adults, but every now and again, in moments of clarity, I found myself clinging on to the way things used to be.

I think I was aware of it on some level—that I was no longer overthinking everything. I was increasingly becoming more spontaneous and throwing myself into things more. My fears and consciousness never left me, but I think I was starting to manage things better. I always thanked Casper for that, but looking back, maybe I should have thanked Jake for it, too. Hindsight is a wonderful thing.

But then, just as I was starting to feel like I'd reached the happiest point in my life, everything changed. Like the flick of a switch, I plummeted to my lowest point and lost sight of how I ever managed to cope. Reality hit, and I was exhausted. Just one damn text was all it took. *Why do our minds do this?*

Casper

BEN CANCELLED on me for the first time in our relationship. It was the end of the busiest month of our lives; we'd just completed our end-of-year assessments on top of playing three gigs in the north, so had a trip to London planned for just the two of us. I'd never been to London before, other than for connecting flights, and Ben promised to show me around. So, we made a proper plan for seven days, travelling around to different cities in the south. We both deserved this; we'd worked so incredibly hard this year—hell, Law was kicking my ass, and my original plans of becoming an actual lawyer seemed further and further away, but I loved this band so much; I loved our lives, and I was beginning to forget why I even cared so much about getting a degree in the first place. I know we'd both gone from being obsessed with the fact we got into such a prestigious university, to not even caring in the slightest, so much so that we didn't even bother applying for our placement years. We didn't want the distraction. Our courses came second, the music first. Always music first. We were on cloud nine.

We obviously had to rearrange plans to suit us both, but this? I really didn't see it coming.

"Wait, so you're just not coming anymore?" I asked Ben, his voice groggy on the receiver.

"I'm sorry; I just can't go." He didn't elaborate, which annoyed me, but then I remembered the Ben I met back in 2009. The quiet and shy boy who always kept himself to himself. What happened? Was it my fault? Had I done something to make him feel this way?

Instead of cancelling, I let Francesca go on the trip with her then girlfriend, Maddie. I stayed at home and didn't see Ben for nearly five days. He asked for some time alone and went to see his gran. Once he got back, I was at his door, waiting impatiently for him to open up. There was no answer, even though I'd heard him enter the building. I tried the handle, and thankfully, he'd left it unlocked.

"Ben?" I called out into the empty room. There was no sign he was there, except from his discarded duffle bag and flannel thrown onto the bed. Then, I heard a sharp cry come from the bathroom, and all thoughts left my head except one.

I dove towards the door in an instant and swung it open with a bang. Everything blurred as I moved to grab him and pull him close. He stood shirtless with his head hung low over the bathroom sink, his hands trembling. I wrapped my arms tightly around his bony waist, catching his arms, too, and dragging him away from the sink, metal clattering in the faucet. I pulled him into the bedroom and lost my balance, falling onto the mattress with Ben on top of me. He didn't fight my grip; he came willingly, as though all fight left in him ceased to exist.

I pushed us up to a sit and kissed his crown, rocking him and whispering assurances into his hair. I had him.

"I'm sorry, Casper. I'm sorry," he repeated over and over, his heart racing out of his chest and straining against my arms. His body was warm and clammy.

"You've got nothing to apologise for. Don't, please. I love you. I love you. I love you."

"You still do? I love you, too. I love you, too." He bent to kiss my arm, his lips barely touching my skin.

I blanched yet held him tighter. "What do you mean 'still do'? Ben, what would make you think... Ben, what's happened? Please tell me. I can help. I promise I can help." I nearly started crying as a dull pain rose in my throat.

"I've not..." His breathing faltered. "I've just not been there for you. I've been selfish."

How dare he think that.

"Oh no. Ben, no. Please don't *ever* think that. Are you talking about London? You realise I don't care in the slightest, right? We're allowed to have time apart, you know; we're allowed to *be* apart." I was trying so hard to reassure him, and he fell silent, his heart rate less frantic, his breathing shallow.

"I'm sorry," he whispered. "It all just gets a bit..." A deep, strained breath followed, and he coughed from deep in his lungs. "It gets a bit much sometimes, but I'm managing it. I promise I'll manage it better. I wasn't actually going to..."

All I did was hold him tighter. We sat there on the floor, talking for what felt like hours. Then, later, we curled up into his bed, and I let my arm go numb beneath his body, refusing to let go of him.

I rang Jesse the next day, asking for advice. He had very little experience in looking after people this way, too, but I needed to hear my big brother's voice. He told me not to push subjects Ben was not ready to talk about but to always listen whenever he had something to say. Of course, I knew that already, but Jesse's advice was a calming confirmation.

A few days later, I found out that Ben's dad had cancelled on him. He'd made up a half-ass excuse as to why he couldn't come and see his son, then hadn't replied for two whole weeks. I don't know if that was the sole cause of Ben's sadness, but it definitely played a part. Ben was always sensitive when it came to his parents and the impression he had on them. He still blamed himself for their divorce, despite knowing it had nothing to do with him.

Honestly, I think the fame stuff was getting to him a little, too. Ben refused to admit that, but it was clear. It was a big deal for all of us, and Ben seemed to always believe we'd never make it, as if someone like him could never achieve such a thing. He used those words on multiple occasions—'someone like me.' I never fully understood what he meant, and maybe he didn't either. He just wasn't used to happiness.

I made Ben sleep beside me for the entire week that followed. He kept promising me he was okay, and I wanted to believe him— I knew Ben enough to trust him like that—but sometimes, you just don't know.

Jake's strangeness wasn't helping, either. He stopped joining us in rehearsals—stopped everything, in fact. For whatever reason, I never got to know Jake as well as I knew Ben and even Fran by that point. He was a boisterous sort, but private too. I could never read what was going on in his mind, nor could I predict his next moves. Outside of the band, I probably would have never been friends with him. That was nothing against him, of course. He was a charming guy with a great sense of humour, and an ear for good composition, but that was where our similarities ended. He went from being the guy who wanted us to rule the music world, to the stoner who left the house for days at a time and didn't even bring his guitar to rehearsals anymore. It just didn't make sense, and I know Fran noticed too.

"Stop me if I'm out of place here, but have you noticed a shift in... I dunno, vibes? Does that make sense?"

I'd met with Fran for coffee one afternoon after some lectures. She called me and asked if we could talk, and I feared the worst. People only say 'we need to talk' for super serious things. I'd not known her well enough then to figure out what constituted as a serious matter for her, so I was in the dark, and a little afraid to meet.

She immediately started talking about Jake.

"Jake's not really trying anymore?" I inferred this form her words, mixed with my own thoughts.

"Well, yeah. And you know, I'm still the new kid here so I don't want to sound like I'm taking over, or imply that I know any of you better than you know yourselves, but I chat to Ben a lot when we go out for a tab, and lately he just seems off. And then Jake missed that interview, he turned his phone off for days, then Ben didn't want to go to London, so I put two and two together and wondered if the pair of them had maybe fallen out?"

It wasn't my place to offload Ben's personal experience, one I was only just managing to scratch the surface of myself, but her concern was not misplaced. I'd thought many times that part of his feelings were linked to his childhood friend.

"University is a trying time for everyone, we're sometimes not ourselves," I said with a bitter smile, knowing fine well it made me sound oblivious. I just wanted to piece more of the puzzle together myself before I started discussing things with other people. Not that I didn't trust Fran, she just wasn't the first person I wanted to talk to about things concerning Ben. Not yet, anyway.

Fran sighed, flopping her hands heavily onto the table. "Nothing? You've noticed nothing?"

"Oh, I have. I know exactly what you mean. I just don't have the answers yet." I tread carefully.

"Look, I like Jake and all, and I really don't want to be that person, but he's hiding something—holding something back, and I think it will affect us all eventually." Those were Fran's final words on the matter, before she bought another coffee and changed the subject. It sat with me for the rest of the day though. What could I do to prevent this?

ON THE ONE occasion Jake bothered to turn up to a rehearsal that month, he snapped at Ben. We all watched in open-mouthed disbelief as it happened. I could have punched him. The look on Ben's face crushed me. Ben only suggested something in his usual calm manner, and Jake *went for him*, calling him selfish and slamming his hand on the stereo.

He apologised profusely after calming down, but Ben's face didn't recover for the rest of the session. Ben doesn't let things go easily; he takes them on, adding them to an internal bank of other troubles until breaking down completely.

Now, I know I shouldn't have judged Jake so harshly. After all, I had no idea what he was going through. I would always be on Ben's side until my dying days, but I needed to be the bigger person, so, that same evening, after speaking to Ben, I asked to go on a walk with Jake. He paused, seeming confused at my offer, but finally nodded. I met him outside his room an hour later.

We walked down by the riverside, and I approached the topic carefully.

"We don't talk as much as I think we should," I began.

Jake nodded, peering up into the trees. "I think you're right," he said without looking at me.

"I just don't feel like I know you very well, you know? Despite us having spent nearly every day together for the past two years."

Another nod. Jake sucked in his cheeks slightly. "You got to know Ben, though," was all he said.

I paused, trying to figure out his implications. Then, I went for it. A streak of annoyance hitting me.

"You know, has Ben done something? Has he hurt you or something? What was that today?"

Jake shrugged and laughed distantly, nodding as though I continued to talk to him. He took in the information slowly. "No. No, it's not that." He wagged his finger at me with a pained smile and heavy eyelids. "You know, Ben doesn't have a single bad bone in his body. He couldn't harm anyone even if he tried. I shouldn't have snapped at him, I was just having a bad day. I've had a few bad days lately, well, for a while actually."

I was confused where this conversation was leading, but Jake decided to continue, shoving his hands into the pockets of his low-cut jeans. "You know, Ben saved my life once. He straight up *kept me alive* when I thought it was the end. And then, I saved him. We did *everything* together; he was *always* by my side. But he's changed, and I can't see the old him anymore."

I pondered my next response. "Oh," was all I managed.

"Ben's great; he's the best person I'll ever know, but he's changed, and I don't like it. I'm admitting it now."

"Changed how?" A defensive streak washed over me, my brow tensing.

"You know. I know you know."

"He's more confident now, but that's healthy. He's always

being himself." I didn't know what else Jake meant. Was he implying he didn't *want* Ben to find himself?

"Do you want me to spell it out? He doesn't *think* about us anymore, doesn't plan things with us, doesn't even put the band first. It's just *you*..."

"What about me?" I tried to stay calm. "Are you jealous or something?" The last part came out way too harshly, and I probably—in fact, definitely—should *not* have said it.

"Woah, mate. Get off your high horse."

So, he is jealous. I'd pieced it all together by that point. I just needed his confirmation.

"When you said 'us,' you meant just *you*, didn't you?"

"Obviously." Jake's fire simmered.

"But he's your best friend; you said it yourself. Ben adores you; he always talks highly of you. He's told me so much about the things you did together. He loves you to pieces. I never had a friend like that."

Jake threw me a side glance and took a deep inhale. "Ben adores *you*. I'm just his mate." He spat the last words; it was impossible not to read the bitterness in his tone.

"I just don't know how you can see Ben changing as a bad thing. He's growing out of his shell; he's learning more about himself; he's happy," I said.

"Is he?" Jake quirked an eyebrow, disgust in his features.

I gulped. We both knew Ben was hiding things. My mind flashed back to that night. How long was I going to stay in denial?

"So, you know too, then?" I sighed. Immediately reminding myself these two had most likely seen each other at their worst. I dreaded to think what that point was.

"I've known long before any of you. Ben is my longest friend. I know him inside out. He's forcing himself to change and be someone else, and he's not happy. He's not. But he refuses to see that. He only sees you."

I felt a pain in my chest that left me speechless. What was I going to do?

"It's always been about Ben, hasn't it?" I said.

"When was it not?"

We walked the rest of the way in silence.

THAT NIGHT, I went to Ben's room and said I couldn't sleep.

"You want to hug me? Had a bad dream?" Ben laughed from his bed. He still had his bedside lamp on, a notebook open on his lap, his legs under the covers. His face changed as he noticed mine.

"What?"

I looked down and Ben shuffled over, making room beside him in bed. I reached out and held his hand. He gripped it tightly. I looked into his eyes and watched his throat bob.

"What did Jake say?" he asked.

I shook my head and took a deep breath, trying not to worry him. "I..."

"Casper, talk to me. Please. I'm worried."

"Ben, I need to ask you something."

He flinched, as though I was about to hit him. "What is it? What?"

"I'm sorry I don't think this is the best way for me to go about this, but I need to ask—I need to know."

"Casper, please."

"Have you ever hurt yourself before?"

"What do you mean?"

"Ben, please just answer the question."

"No."

I half sighed. "No, as in..."

"No; I've never hurt myself before. And I was never going to.

You know, *that* day... I wasn't going to... I don't..." Ben choked up and looked away.

The silence was deafening.

"Ben, have you ever thought about—"

"Don't." His head snapped back to me, and I saw the glisten of a tear in his eye beneath the lamplight.

"You have."

"No, Casper. I..." He shook his head frantically. "Can we not talk about this, please? What's caused this?"

My heart was in my throat as I pictured all the worst possible scenarios.

I leaned closer, prompting Ben to close his book and place it on the nightstand. He wore a white shirt unbuttoned to his navel; soft black hairs graced his pale chest. I thought of his heart and how it beat so powerfully under his skin—keeping him alive, keeping him here.

Without speaking, I glanced down at his hands and took one in mine, guiding it to his chest. I pressed it firmly there while Ben watched in confusion.

I lifted my eyes to meet his. "Listen. Can you feel it?"

He nodded slowly.

"It's beautiful," I whispered.

"I don't..." He began to protest.

"Shhh," I closed my eyes and shook my head. "Just listen."

We stayed in that position for a minute or so while the steady thud of his heartbeat pressed against our palms. His life source.

"I love you, Ben. You are the greatest creation this Earth has ever seen. You are a beautiful soul; your heart is kind; your mind is exquisite. It is an honour to share these breaths with you. Out of the millions and millions of endless years you could have existed, you exist here now with me. No matter what anyone tells you or what you believe, you deserve the world, you just have to let yourself have it."

He didn't speak for a moment, and I thought perhaps I'd gone too far or sounded too dramatic to be believed.

"You really think that?" he asked quietly.

"I know that."

Ben kissed me, moving his hand to cup my face. I held onto his wrists as his green eyes pierced mine.

"You make everything okay," he said. "It is my honour to share this time with *you.*" His smile lit up the room.

Everything was going to be okay; I'd make sure of it.

I just needed to check up on Jake.

Ben

June 2011

I THINK on some level I saw it coming. But I pushed it down because I didn't want things to be different. I wanted to cling to all the happiness I found, and to maintain that, I selfishly didn't want anything to change. But that was completely ignorant of me. I was so blinded by my own thoughts I hadn't even considered how anyone else felt until it was too late.

Jake was my oldest and closest friend until one day, he just... wasn't.

WE'D HAD a petty argument at a bar the night before— something so pathetic I can't even recall it, but it was dramatic enough for Jake to storm out and prompt three separate people to check if I was alright. *I* was alright, but Jake wasn't. I needed to do something. I didn't go after him, even though I should have. I should have tried to resolve things between us, but instead, I took in a deep breath, turned back to the bar, and ordered a much stronger drink before chain-smoking myself into oblivion on the balcony overlooking the river. Alone.

I'D CRAWLED BACK to Casper's room in the early hours of the morning and was out cold until nearly two in the afternoon. I don't even remember speaking to Casper or if he even stayed in the room with me. I just remember waking up, face down, with my jacket still hung over me, a half-used cigarette in the ashtray on the bedside table, and a head seconds away from exploding.

I had three missed calls, all from Jake. I rolled onto my back and rubbed my eyes, letting out a dramatic sigh of frustration.

I heard the front door open, and in came Casper, a look of pity on his face.

"You should have let me come last night. You didn't even call."

"I'm sorry. I didn't..." I groaned.

"Come on. Get changed. I think you've got someone to speak to." He wandered over to open the curtains, and I hissed at the brightness. Casper's tone was calm and sympathetic.

Casper sat on the edge of the bed; his braids were nearly down to his waist at this point (one of my favourite looks of his), and he rubbed at my feet, still booted.

"Jake," I said, sitting up slightly, head pounding.

Casper nodded then glanced out of the window, away with his thoughts before looking back at me. "I think you two need to have a talk alone—not in a public space, and definitely not while you're drinking. You are best friends; you know each other the best. Talk to each other properly. Get stuff off your chest. We need you; we need you both to be okay. We can't continue with things the way they are, Ben. We *need* you."

Jake was barely at rehearsals anymore, and whenever he did show, I'd say something that would somehow rub him the wrong way, and then the session would go nowhere. I was never intentionally mean or cruel, but it was like everything I said held different meanings to him than it did to anyone else. I would look at Fran and Casper as if to say, 'help me out here,' but they would both stare back, confused. Then the next minute, Jake would crack a joke with me, acting like the moment before had never happened.

I wished I could read minds. Well, not really. It wouldn't go well with my anaemia or constant headaches. Really, I would have just loved to understand what was going on in Jake's head, and to know what I could do to fix things.

It turns out, I didn't need that ability after all, because he told me that very same day.

I agreed to meet him outside the house, and we walked to the riverside. We were silent the entire time, except from the odd generic observation on the weather.

We stopped outside one of the many boathouses and sat on the steps inches away from the river.

"Are you okay?" was the first thing Jake asked.

I nodded despite my lingering headache.

"I'm sorry about last night," he said.

"I'm sorry, too..."

"No, Ben. Please, just accept my one-sided apology. I had no right to snap at you like that; I never have."

I looked at him in silence, processing.

Jake sighed, then peered out across the water, stretching his legs.

"Look, Ben. I'm just gonna come out and say it. There's no point in me denying it any longer, and after last night, it was all I could think about. I know it's selfish of me and perhaps inconsiderate, but I can't let it eat away at me anymore." Jake sat back with his palms on the concrete, his eyes very far from mine as he spoke. "I love you. I've loved you for years. Since the day we met, you were never just my best mate."

Out of all of Jake's possible confessions, this had never made the cut. I knew he was bi; he knew I was gay, but we really were just good mates. We did things mates do, but we never crossed *that* line. At least, I was never aware that we did. Maybe we had. But if we had, I'd never noticed.

"Don't look at me like that." He sucked in his lips.

"Like what?" I said defensively. I wasn't aware of how I looked at him, too preoccupied with absorbing his admission.

"Like you had no idea."

"I didn't..."

Jake stopped me with his open hand, jabbing the air. He let out a laugh of disguised agony, and my heart sank. I really had been so blind. Flashes of every moment we'd spent together over the last six years came crashing back in seconds. My heart was on the floor.

He continued. "I thought about asking you out a while ago, and I nearly did, but then I saw the way Casper looked at you, and then I started to notice the way you looked back at him, and then the next thing I know, you're seeing each other, and you're sleeping in his room nearly every night, and I feel you drifting away from me. I just can't deal with it."

Panic set in. I was about to lose my best friend, and it was all my own stupid, *stupid* fault. "Jake, please. I'm so sorry..."

"Have I taken this too far? God. I can't stop now. I'm sorry. I really am. I'm so very sorry, but how do you think I feel? Day in day out, I watch the guy I love being swept off his feet by some other dude." Jake was shaking, worryingly so.

"Casper isn't just some *other dude*, God! Jake, do you hear yourself? Casper's our bandmate. He's your friend, too. I can't help that I..." It all spilled out as my defensive streak reared its ugly head.

"That you what?" Jake wasn't going to let me stop.

"That I..." I paused, trying to compose myself. A couple walked past us with their dog, and we threw them a fake smile, waiting until they were out of earshot. I leaned closer and lowered my tone. "That I don't love you. At least not in the way you want.

I do *love* you, but I'm not *in* love with you... I—You have always been my best mate, but I never saw it any other way. I'm sorry. I really am."

Jake didn't speak for what felt like an eternity until he voiced the inevitable. "I can't do this anymore."

"What do you mean?" I knew exactly what he meant; I just needed to hear him say it. To make it real.

"I mean, I'm leaving, Ben. I'm quitting the band. I can't cope."

"You don't mean that."

"Oh, I do. I've been thinking about telling you for months, but instead, I just chickened out and took it out on you and the rest of the band. I'm aware I've been a complete dick, and I'm sorry about that, but I'm leaving. That's my final decision." Jake was already on his feet.

"But Jake, let's at least talk this out! We can make it work. What about the future of the band? Me and Casper don't have to..."

"But you don't get it, do you? No matter what you promise, what you hide, or whatever, that still doesn't change the fact that I *can't* be with you. I cannot just stand around like some third wheel. I've done it for a year and a half. I'm gonna need some space. I'm sorry, Ben."

"But..."

"And don't pretend you care that much about the band—you're terrified! You don't have to lie to me. You never had to."

"What? Jake? What do you mean...? Of course, I care..."

"You need help, Ben. Casper is at your beck and call, but I know you don't need me anymore. Maybe you never did."

"Jake, please. Stop this. Why are you saying that? Of course, I need you." My chest constricted, and I was struggling to breathe.

"I've tried to ignore it for so long; I can't take it anymore."

"Jake! Please, Jake... please..." I was choking, my vision blurring.

"I love you, Ben, and I wish you all the best. Look after yourself."

He stepped back up to the pavement and stormed into the leaf-buried path as I reached for him one final time.

Interview excerpt: Date unknown, presumably late 2015

INTERVIEWER: So, are you guys on good terms? Have you spoken since?

Ben: I wouldn't necessarily say 'good terms,' but they're not bad, either. I have no anger towards him at all, though. No matter what, I will always consider him a friend. We went through a lot together, and you can never undo that. I just think he needed space, and back then we decided it was best if we just didn't really see each other anymore.

Now please, don't misconstrue what I say. Don't go harassing him or asking him questions. He's living his life now, and he's happy. I'm happy that he's okay, and yeah, we do check in with each other from time to time. You don't really need to know anything else. I don't mean that in a rude way, either, I'm just... ahh sorry.

[Ben signals to his manager to cut the interview short]

Unsolicited paparazzi interview with Jake Walters, stopped on the streets of Leeds city centre: January 2016

PRESS: Jake! Jake Walters! Just a quick word. Are you and Ben Audley still friends?

Jake: *[ducking his face below his arm to get past swiftly; a woman around his age holds on to his other hand]* You heard that interview leak, right?

Press: Yes, and...

Jake: Then you heard what he said. Listen to Ben. Leave me alone.

Press: Yes, but...

[*woman with Jake pushes past the journalist, and the two disappear into Trinity shopping centre*]

Casper

That night was horrible. I knew they had stuff to talk about, after all, they'd been friends for a long time, and I wouldn't understand everything between them. But even though Ben only gave me a vague summary of what happened, seeing the state he'd gotten himself into that night was something I'll never forget.

I was nearly sick with tears when I found him.

Ben was slumped outside the door to my bedroom, barely conscious, with dark coloured vomit down his front and an expensive, empty bottle of whiskey at his side. I roused him slightly, propping his head against the wall to ensure he was still breathing. I checked his pulse, which was dangerously low.

"Ben! Oh please, Ben, answer me."

He groaned, his head flopping to the side. I opened the door and lifted him inside. I was always aware of Ben's thinness, the medication he took for his blood, and how he could hardly handle his liquor, so seeing him like this heightened my fears tenfold. Millions of questions fired through my mind—how many hours had he been drinking? How long had he been alone? Had anything happened to him? Had anyone harmed him—spiked him? Why had he lied and texted me, saying everything was fine? He told me they'd gone for food.

I turned the light on and propped him up against my bed. His eyes wouldn't meet mine; he could barely keep them open.

"Ben, I need you to listen to me. I need you to tell me what happened." I gently moved his head from side to side, but it was no use.

I should have called an ambulance or had someone check him out. I was so close to calling for help, but then he finally opened his eyes, mumbling something. Something about the riverside.

"Ben, Ben, can you hear me?"

"Hear... hear you," he muttered.

"Good, good. Okay, Ben. What have you taken? Can you breathe properly?"

It was then that Ben vomited, and I had just enough time to step out of the way before it projected across the hardwood floor. He leaned forward, tucking his knees up beneath his chin.

"Ben. Ben." I moved over to support his head, which was pressed between his knees. His body was shaking, and he was crying—wailing. Truly broken.

"I'm sorry. I'm sorry. I'm sorry," he chanted, rocking, playing with the hem of his trousers.

"Hey, hey, Ben." I came back to his front and shook his shoulders gently. His dark hair was completely covering his eyes, the curls kissing his cheeks, slicked down by sweat. I brushed it back, exposing his forehead. He was burning up.

"I..." Tears dripped down his beautiful face.

"Oh, Ben." I gave in, pulling him in for a tight hug. A moment passed before his shaking arms wrapped around my back, his grip weak.

He cried into my shoulder, struggling for breath.

I pushed him back gently and faced him once more, his eyelids drooping. "Ben, you have to tell me what happened."

"I'm... I'm a mess."

I nodded, patting his back. "Let's get you changed then. Come on. Can you stand?"

He nodded as I helped him up, taking his full weight on my shoulder. I moved him over to the bathroom and turned the shower on, seating him on the floor beside the bath and helping him to undress.

"I... I can smell it." He gagged, and I thought he would throw up again, but he didn't. The room and mirror steamed as I lifted him up, getting the last of his stained clothes off him. I let him lean against me as I undid my own shoes and climbed into the tub with him, not caring where the water hit me, so long as I had hold of him.

I sat us down gently and washed his hair and body, kissing his crown when we were done. He didn't say much but let me move him about, and once we were done, he whispered his thanks. My chest ached for him. He was so fragile in my arms.

I dried us off and helped him into some fresh pyjamas, letting him lie on what had long since become his side of the bed. I ensured he kept himself propped up and awake, while I grabbed him a glass of water and cleared up the vomit. I sat right beside him, pulling the covers over us both. Finally, he told me everything.

To be honest, I wanted to punish Jake—to scream and yell at him for what he'd done. But deep down, I had no real reason to. Jake couldn't help how he felt, and he needed some space, but all I could think of at the time was what he'd done to Ben. I wanted Jake to know that by saying what he did, and how and when he said it, he'd sent his best friend into the deepest, darkest spiral that could have killed him.

Of all people, Jake should have known how best to talk to Ben.

I didn't think about how the band would move forward, or what this meant for our future. To be honest, I didn't care. That night, my only concern was keeping Ben safe. I got very little sleep, but it was only because I refused to move from his side. I would not let go of his chest, ensuring I felt the rise and fall of his breaths, and the steady recovery of his beating heart.

He was alive. That was all that mattered. That's all that has ever mattered.

<u>Solo interview excerpt with Casper, Louisiana USA: July 2018</u>

INTERVIEWER (LOUISA FORBES, 'Goths in the USA' – Fall 2018. Excerpt redacted from public release.): Casper, has there ever been a time you feared the band would break up?

Casper: Oh, definitely.

Louisa: Care to elaborate?

Casper: Not really, but I will say there were a few not so pleasant moments, especially towards the beginning of our career.

Louisa: Ben had a few medical incidents, didn't he? Drugs and ill health? Could that have been due to tensions in the band?

Casper: Where the fuck did you get that information?

[*redacted*]

⁂

"PERHAPS WE SHOULD DISBAND for a while. Give us all a break." Fran rolled her cigarette whilst we sat outside a café. I sat beside Ben, who had been notably but expectedly quiet.

It had been five days since Jake had left. Neither of us had heard a peep out of him, other than to finalise payments for his share of the house, but we believed it was necessary to give him time. He was clearly going through a lot himself, and we didn't want to push. Ben had barely eaten over the past few days, but he was improving. I stayed by his side always.

"There is nothing stopping us from going on hiatus and taking the summer off maybe? Just having some time for ourselves," I suggested, looking to Ben.

"I don't want that." He stared at the saltshaker as he spoke. "I don't want to stop."

"It might be what's best for us, you know. It doesn't have to be a permanent thing," I tried.

"But then that's just another thing to change. The band is everything to me, our music, the four—*three* of us. We're a family; we make music. I don't want to stop... ever."

I looked to Fran, who turned from Ben to cast me a worried look.

"Ben, it only has to be for a short time—a few months max to let things settle. It would be good for us all," she said.

"But..." He gave up.

WE WERE KIND OF ALL in agreement in the end. But that night, we got a call from Beck.

We'd just been invited to perform at Reading and Leeds Festival.

"WE'RE DOING IT. We're doing it. We're doing it, right?" Ben was grinning, and it was the first time I'd seen his face that bright in a long time. It hurt a little.

"We need to think about this properly," I said.

Fran looked at me, undecided. "It's Leeds fest... that's like a really big thing over here. An insane opportunity."

"But I thought we all decided we needed a break? We literally just arranged that this morning. We're nowhere near prepared for something like this." I paced the room, trying to keep my mind clear. I knew how much of a big deal this would be, but the vision of Ben on my bedroom floor would not leave my mind.

"I mean, we can be. We're gonna need to fill Jake's space, obviously, but I think we'll manage." Fran was balanced in a crouch on the sofa, knees pulled under her chin. Mind made up.

"We managed as a three before," Ben pushed. "We can make it work."

"But we never played as much then; our pieces were super simple. Now, we need extra people."

Ben refused to let his optimism drop. "I've got my mixer; we can just prerecord stuff—every artist does that! I can sort it all on my synth; I promise we can make it work!"

"But we'll need to practise *a lot*—this is a big thing. It's not just some gig in a dingy cellar. You know how many people could potentially be there? And it's just next month... I don't even know if we'd be ready, regardless of the circumstances." I really wanted to do it; I wanted to do it so badly, but I was trying to be the bigger person. We needed to stay grounded to ensure we didn't push ourselves to burn out and risk the band crumbling completely.

Ben's face finally fell, the brightness dying from his widened eyes. I blamed myself for that, even though I spoke with reason.

"I mean... We *could* try. It's only a small pop-up stage. We could use this as experience, and it's the perfect chance for us to get *noticed* and make it big. Isn't that what we've always wanted? Are we gonna let Jake's departure take that away from us?" Fran had edged slightly towards Ben, and I could tell she'd already made up her mind by then. She wanted to do this too.

I began to chew at the inside of my mouth, gums sore. I didn't know what to do; I couldn't decide what the adult decision would be.

"This is our perfect chance to show the world what we've got," Fran pleaded.

"Okay," I finally said, nodding at myself and the decision I'd made. "Call him back. Tell your dad to confirm."

Ben beamed.

I BOOKED Ben and I a few nights away in Edinburgh. Neither of us had ever been, and I thought it would help take his mind off things and help us unwind before we focused on our festival setlist. It was a beautiful trip.

"So, do you reckon they just dug a hole through the cemetery for the trains or do you think this was empty land regardless? It sure is an odd shape for church grounds." Ben tucked into his chocolate ice cream as we sat on the grass in Princes Street Gardens. I was just glad he was eating.

"I have absolutely no idea. Good question, though."

We trailed the old town, scouring music shops and second-hand stores to enhance our wardrobes. I took him up to the castle and got a beautiful photo of him peering down onto the city below. Ben hates photos of himself—don't we all, especially when someone else takes it—but even in that moment, he winked. "That's a good one. Thanks, Casper."

We left it a few days after we got back before throwing ourselves into the project, but it was Ben who brought up that we should start.

"I wrote some bass lines I liked, and I thought we could maybe incorporate them into our setlist? I dunno, maybe add some vocals, and get the rhythm going with your drums?"

The three of us sat outside a café in Newcastle city centre while crowds of people bustled by in the heat. Fran smiled and looked to both of us as Ben spoke.

"Well, you know I'm down for this. I've been ready since..." She cleared her throat. "Sorry."

Ben waved his hand. "No, you can be honest. It makes sense, you barely even knew him a year."

"Do you reckon he'll come back?" Fran questioned.

Ben shrugged. "Doubt it. He made it very clear to me, and if Jake is one thing, he's a man of his word."

I nudged Ben's shoulder. "We will make this work," I promised.

Of course we would.

Ben

I was good at shutting away my mind. Dangerously good at it. I said yes to the idea of Reading and Leeds before I really processed what that would entail, but it had to work out, I'd considered no alternative.

Casper took me away for a few days, and my mind switched off entirely. I lived and breathed, and my jaw ached from smiling so much, then when we came home, Fran booked tickets for me and her to see this theatre production I'd always talked about wanting to see, and I was so overwhelmed at the love my friends shared with me. How was I so deserving of this?

"You're the most interesting guy I've ever met," she said over dinner before the show. I knew she didn't mean this romantically, there wasn't a single moment when I could make this confusion between the two of us.

"Charming? Incredibly good looking?" I played into it as a joke, taking a large sip of my rum.

"Oh, darling, you're the man of my dreams," she faked a whimsical voice, acting out her words by pretending to faint backwards in her chair, hand over her eyes. "But no, seriously. When I first met you, I thought you'd be one of those broody dude bros who cosplays as a feminist, but thinks himself too high and mighty for conversations other than 'what's your favourite movie?'. A dickhead basically."

I felt offended for a moment, but her tone was soft and in jest, so even before she continued, I relaxed.

She took another bite of her overstuffed burger, the contents slipping out onto the plate in a sloppy mess of tomato relish and red onion. "But…" she finished her mouthful and wiped her mouth, "literally the second you opened your mouth I was like 'protect this puppy at all costs.'"

At my raised brow, she snorted, nearly dropping her burger. "Oh my god, that came out really weird. I think I've had one too many doubles. That sounded completely innocent in my head, I swear."

I just burst out laughing. Then Fran followed suit and started hiccupping. "I'm going to need the toilet in a second. I don't want to break the seal. I'll miss the show."

"Fran, please stop, you're…" I cut myself off with laughter again.

It took a moment for our hysterics to fizzle, the alcohol burning away in our brains. Everything suddenly seemed hilarious. I had to keep looking away and covering my mouth, struggling to swallow the bites of my own burger.

"What I meant was…" Fran composed herself, sort of.

"Fran, stop while you're ahead." I had to suck in my cheeks to hold back the tears.

"No, cos like, I was talking to Maddie about you the other day, and she reckons you're like a golden retriever. But like, the goth version."

"I don't even know what you mean but I'll take it as a compliment."

"It's definitely a compliment. Everyone loves you, Ben."

They do?

"I mean it. You're the best."

Home video filmed by Fran: July 2011

[Local tattoo parlour, Fran and Ben are sat receiving tattoos, Casper stood watching]

Fran: [*waving at camera, angling it towards Ben behind her*] Say hello to the camera!

Ben: [*pulling a comical pain face and showing a thumbs up, his arm outstretched on the chair*] Helloooo. [*then, quietly to Casper*] She's not sending this to anyone, is she?

Fran: We're getting tatted up, I'm a terrible influence. We need this though.

Ben: Post-Punk therapy.

Fran: [*laughs*] Indeed. Clothes shopping doesn't quite cut it anymore. I'm going to run out of room by the time I'm thirty.

Casper: [*putting his head in his hands, looking towards Fran's tattoo artist*] Sorry about this.

Artist: [*laughing*] Oh no, it's no problem. Fran, can you stay still for a second please.

Ben: [*distantly*] I'm definitely not going to regret this. [*looks at Casper sheepishly*]

Ben

MY MUM CAME up at the end of July, and we spent the day together, just the two of us. She took me for pizza, and we chatted about life and future plans; I showed her my room and my guitars (of course, we had the student loan conversation. "No mum, I did not use my maintenance money on a Precision Bass."). She asked me how I was coping with everything, and I explained bits and pieces, trying not to get emotional. Having her with me again made everything alright. My anchor. She asked me if I wanted to drop out, and I didn't exactly say no, but we came to the decision that I'd manage the final year. Just one more year until I could do this full time.

She stayed over in my room for the night, and I stayed with Casper. The next day, I took her to the cathedral before she caught her train home. She marvelled at its beauty and told me a bit about where she was currently with her faith. We had a few moments of silence, where Mum lit a candle but didn't tell me who it was for. Perhaps my grandad—her dad. Or maybe for me. I know, selfish, but... never mind, I didn't mean that.

We were really making things work as a three, though, and by the beginning of August, we were practically ready for the stage. I loved the summer of 2011... before the accident.

I was happy.

One of my best memories was our first double date. The four of us: me, Casper, Fran, and Maddie in an American diner booth, eating greasy burgers and loaded fries, laughing about childhood stories and silly encounters. I remember laughing so much that my sides hurt. Fran really knew how to trigger my sense of humour.

Then, as we were waiting for the bill, a girl came up to us— probably no older than thirteen. She had a napkin in her hand, and I clocked her mother and father in the distance, smiling with mild embarrassment.

"Hi," was all she said. Our conversation died out as our attention drew to her. She stepped back a little. We didn't mean to intimidate her.

"Hi," Casper said, I couldn't see his face; I was sat behind him, but I knew the tone well enough. He was grinning.

"I'm really sorry to bother you." Rehearsed, but sweet. "But I just wanted to say... Casper, that's you right?" Her voice faltered. I was stunned with her composure.

"Yeah, that's me. You listen to our band?"

She nodded really fast.

"You want to speak to me specifically, or..." He was trying to help her out, gesturing between me and Fran.

"You don't have to lie; you're allowed to have a favourite," Fran butted in, helping the poor girl who was clearly worrying over the question, not wanting to hurt our feelings.

Her face lit up. "It's Casper; I just wanted to say..." The napkin trembled in her hand; she looked as if she were about to place it on the table, but worried about invading our personal space.

I peered around Casper slightly. "Would you like him to sign something for you?" I suggested politely.

Another silent nod. "I'm really sorry to disturb you all; I really am. I know what it must be like being pestered. I just—wow. I just never would have thought I'd ever get to meet you in person. Casper, I just wanted to say how much I adore you, like not in a creepy way. I just really admire you, and you inspired me to start drumming, and I just wanted to say thank you. I know you're American, but you're a band from my home, and it means so much to me." It all spilled out as she finally handed Casper the napkin.

I genuinely think he was awe-struck. He did not breathe a word but took the napkin slowly and glanced down at the blank canvas before him. None of us spoke, all a little taken aback.

Fran spoke first. "Wow. That was so cute," she said.

Then Casper looked back to the girl. "What's your name?"

"Angelica."

"Wow. What a beautiful name, Angelica. Are those your parents?" He gestured to the watching adults.

"Yeah, sorry. They told me I should leave you alone, but I said I was going to go anyway."

Casper laughed and then waved over to them.

"Well, Angelica, you just made my day. In fact, no, you made my *year*. I'm... wow. I'm speechless. What you just told me meant the world. I had no idea I'd ever inspire someone, let alone have them come up to me for an autograph. Wow, thank you. You are amazing. I'm actually going to get emotional here, I..." Casper briefly glanced at me, lost for words. He tried to smile it away, but I knew how much that moment meant to him.

"Casper is the soul of the band," I said, and I meant it. I've always known that. He started it, and the band could never continue without him. Casper was Forever Red. My Eternal.

He signed the napkin and left a full message. I didn't intrude on reading it. He thanked Angelica again and again and wished her all the best. She skipped back to her table, instantly showing the napkin to her parents.

"You are so sweet," Fran said, sipping her milkshake.

"I'm stunned, that's what." Casper kept looking at me, wide-eyed.

"You're gonna have to get used to it," Maddie piped up with a wink.

I gently squeezed Casper's thigh under the table. "I love you," I mouthed.

"I love you, too."

Tortured your ink
black heart,
Said you left it
by the tree,
Ho[...]ts you
now[...]ell me,
can yo[...]rust me

PART THREE
'IN SICKNESS AND IN
DEATH'

2011-2012

Casper
August 2011

Jesse flew out to watch our test run for Reading and Leeds Fest. I wangled it so he was listed as part of our crew, so he watched from the side-lines and gave his creative input. It was a hot day; I remember the four of us decided to grab some fancy drinks in a cocktail bar in the city after the rehearsal. We didn't have a whole entourage at that point, but Fran's dad made it look like we did. He chauffeured us around in his black van, and we felt like royalty.

"You guys are insane." Jesse couldn't stop smiling.

"Well, we know where Casper gets his talent from," Fran joked, sipping on her cocktail.

I feigned being insulted.

"Hell yeah, if it wasn't for me..." Jesse said, joining the wind up.

"Hey!" I couldn't stay mad, though. We were on the top of the world.

"Can you believe it's nearly two whole years since you started this band, Casper?" Jesse nudged my shoulder.

Ben's eyes widened. "Gosh, has it really been two years already?"

"We've come a long way." I smiled. I was proud of us—proud we didn't give up.

Fran took another sip of her drink then spontaneously asked a passing waiter if they could take a photo of us, whipping out a disposable camera and handing it over.

Ben looked stunned at first, but I nudged him and whispered to him, saying we would just keep the photo for us. Fran said the same, out loud.

We smiled in the booth as the waiter took the photo, the flash almost blinding me.

We didn't develop it for a while because Fran was really picky about what she used the camera for, but once we got them back, I asked to keep it. I scanned it in and made it the background on my laptop. It was such a happy photograph. My brother and my partner, with Ben's eyes squinting with real joy.

WE PLAYED on the tiny stages we were allocated for the two festivals and were amazed at how many people turned up. Despite all the big acts on that year, people actually chose to come and see *us*.

We had our first proper recorded interview, where the guy said Fran was much better as the lead guitarist, boosting her already strong sense of confidence.

We were living in the moment, having the best time and not once did we think about university or the fact we were getting closer to our final year. We were rockstars... well, in our own way. We felt like it.

. . .

THROUGHOUT THE WINTER of that year, a lot changed for us. We had to rethink our schedules to make more time for our demanding courses. We moved into a different house—much smaller this time, but closer to where we needed to be. It was a stressful period, but we managed to produce some of our best work in that time. Maybe the rumour is true—we worked better under pressure.

We had a bit of a shift in genre; Fran really pushed the boat out with her riffs, giving us the confidence to try new things. Ben started being more open with me about how he was feeling, like when he was feeling down, and I did everything in my power to help. He was smiling a lot more, and getting more hands on with *everything,* the music included. I'd never seen him this light. It was a good time for us. We didn't look back. Ben produced our song— *his* song—Moon Brats by himself, all parts included, and I wished I could listen to it on repeat for the rest of my life.

ONE NIGHT, perhaps mid-November, I opened a strange email, claiming to be from two fans. Immediately, the wording made me think 'SCAM.' I didn't think much of it, filtered it to spam, then went about my evening. Me and Ben had a reservation at a new pizza place, and I wasn't going to be late.

I would have completely forgotten about the email, but a few days later, another one popped up. This time, it detailed information about me that *shouldn't* have been public knowledge: family stuff, hobbies, and interests I kept between close friends. They even mentioned things about Ben that made me uncomfortable, and it came across as quite threatening—the 'fans' demanding hush money. I was so baffled as to why someone cared that much about us, but again, I brushed it off as something we'd have to get used to dealing with. They had nothing detrimentally harmful on us.

But this time, the thought lingered.

And two nights later, I had my first encounter.

"Murphey, right?" A voice called out from behind me as I left the university library. It was a cold, rainy evening, and with a series of deadlines approaching, the library had become my new home. It was dark and too quiet at this time of the evening, so there was no mistaking it—they were talking to me.

"Y'all okay?" It just came out of my mouth, a defensive and sure tone. It was two young men, it seemed. Nothing stand-out about their looks.

"Yeah, Casper. We're big fans. We thought you could do us a favour."

I nearly laughed at their monotone demeanour, but my head had started to throb, and my words just slipped out: "What can I help you with?"

I don't remember the meetings, but they must have visited me for months, getting into my head and forcing things out of me that I can't even recall. I thought they were somehow drugging me or using some sort of weird hypnosis technique at first because I was waking up in places I didn't remember going to sleep in, not being able to recall large gaps in my memory; adamant I was losing my mind. I blamed it on stress from uni and the band. Told myself to take some time off to rest. But in reality, it was much more compli-cated than that.

Perhaps they saw me as a puppet, a toy to play with. Pure entertainment. But they must have started turning up to our shows, too, because Ben kept pointing out how I looked distant and confused, yet I could never explain why because I *didn't know.*

But when I learned the truth, my whole world changed.

I have no idea why they chose me *specifically* to prey on, but sometimes, people don't need a reason. I say 'people' loosely; let's not beat about the bush; they weren't human.

Yeah, this next part is where things start to get a little complicated.

Ben
February 2012

WE FINISHED our first gig of the year. Normally, we would all meet for drinks afterwards, but Fran had to rush home for something family-related, so Casper and I decided to take a slow stroll back to our apartment and order a takeaway. He'd been jittery all night, zoning out of our conversations and peering off into the crowd, wide-eyed. I presumed he must have been drinking, but that wasn't really what Casper did, so a quiet walk was the best time for me to broach the issue. It wasn't the first time I'd noticed him acting like this recently. Casper usually had to deal with *me* being the difficult one, so I wasn't used to this side of confrontation.

We turned left off the path towards one of the city's many cemeteries, where the pavement narrowed, and the trees hugged you a little tighter. It was dark and misty, so it was automatically creepy. It took a lot to scare Casper, but I'll be the first to admit I'm scared of most things. I huddled just that tiny bit closer to him.

"Who were you looking for?" I asked him, linking our arms together and increasing our pace.

"Hmm? What do you mean? When?" Casper turned to me with genuine confusion. He didn't seem to be hiding anything.

"Oh, I just thought something had caught your eye during the show. You kept looking off to the side and into the crowd. Was someone supposed to be here for you tonight?" I scrunched my nose.

Casper returned his gaze to the dimly lit path ahead before peering up at the sky. "Was I? I dunno. Huh." He shrugged.

An answer like that wouldn't have phased anyone else, but Casper always had his reasons for everything. He never hid anything from me, so this immediately felt *off*. It was only two days ago when a similar thing happened; he'd lost focus and wandered off. When I finally caught up with him, he told me he hadn't the faintest idea why he was there. So, now, I was growing significantly more concerned.

I chewed at my lip for a moment before we reached the cemetery gates, and Casper turned to me, blocking my path, and holding my shoulders steady. His eyes pierced mine.

"What?" I said, startled.

He didn't say anything for a few seconds, but his expression morphed, a grin spreading across his lips. "Cemetery walk?" he suggested, one brow raised.

I swallowed the lump in my throat, my heart pounding. "Not today."

Casper's gaze lingered on mine until he dropped his arms. "Okay. Not today then." He continued to grin, though.

Instead, we stuck to the road and walked alongside the cemetery wall.

"You know, burials are becoming a lot more popular again," was Casper's next sentence. He almost didn't sound like himself saying it, either. The words felt forced. Odd.

"Hmm." A shiver coursed down my spine. You couldn't see the cemetery from this part of the road as the stone wall was too high, but soon enough, we would reach the open fence, and I'd have no choice but to stare at the tendrils of mist seeping through every crack in the headstones, and the moonlight silhouetting the statues of stone angels. In the day, it would have been peaceful, but

I don't think anyone, no matter how brave, would willingly spend a night alone in the centre of one. I believed I would faint at the slightest sound or sign of movement.

I was a horror kid. At twelve, I begged my dad to buy me a Stephen King novel, and every night when my mum was working, he'd let me watch scary movies. (Nothing involving the devil, though; even my dad's lenience ended somewhere.) He told me that if I didn't tell mum, I would be allowed to watch 'The Greats,' like Poltergeist, IT or Halloween. I realised rather quickly that I preferred gore to psychological horrors. I enjoyed the extreme thrill, not films where strange emotions and questions lingered long after the movie finished—those were too much for me. By that age, I had acquired a too inquisitive and fixating brain, convincing myself of unimagined horrors, like eyes at my window or a screaming woman with a hanging jaw and arms bent in numerous places. I would create mental horrors I'd never witnessed in any movie before, and would bury myself under the covers, face down, as soon as I turned off my light. My mum found out one night when I woke my dad up, dripping with sweat and shaking. She was distraught. "How could you let him watch this sort of stuff, David? He's just a kid. He has a hyperactive mind. He sees things; he makes things up in his head. He's terrified! Look at him!" she shouted. She was furious at my dad then, but I didn't blame him. All the other kids at school were watching these things, too, and they were allowed to watch much worse, unsupervised.

My mum sent my dad to sleep in my room and let me get into bed with her, where she held me tight all night long, stroking my head and calming my breathing.

Eventually, I grew out of creating monsters out of clothes piles and shadows in reflections, but even as an adult, if I stay awake too late or eat certain foods, I get rather paranoid.

"Stop," Casper suddenly said, pulling me from my thoughts. He thrust out an arm to prevent me from stepping any further and peered over the fence to the graveyard.

My heart pounded again. "What is it?"

Casper snapped around and pressed a hard finger to his lips, shaking his head.

"What?" I said, quieter but firmer. He was acting so strange; I just wanted this evening to be normal and safe and—

"I saw someone," he said confidently, body turning to face the cemetery.

"Who? Casper, please stop messing with me; you know I'm a wuss." I tried to stay calm, but my mind wouldn't let me.

I didn't want to follow his eyes, but I needed to know who he was looking for.

"Cas—"

His actions cut me off again.

Pitch blackness surrounded us; I could barely see in front or behind me; I felt like I was going to wet myself in fear.

"Please don't play with me," I aggressively whispered.

"I'm not, not this time," Casper promised before doing the thing I feared most. He stepped up to the gate and wedged his foot on the railing, preparing to climb.

"Casper!" I part whispered, part shouted. "Please, don't... Casper, leave it. It's probably nothing."

"No, I need to. I remember now. It's the person I was looking for. I need to speak with them. I'll be quick."

He's lost his mind.

"Casper, have you heard yourself? You need to meet a random person in the cemetery at eleven o'clock at night? Are you on drugs?" I was aware my last comment held no standing, especially as I myself had taken pills before the show. They were wearing off now, but Casper would have had a perfect counter. But he didn't know, did he? I never told him...

I promised Casper I'd not taken them since sixth-form. But that became a lie once I reminded myself of how free they made me feel. I wasn't addicted, I just needed a little escape sometimes. *I'll stop. I will.* Why am I like this? I know it's silly, immature, pathetic. I just...

"Wait here. I'll be back in a second, I promise." He began climbing. He didn't look worried or scared anymore, which maybe he thought would reassure me, but it didn't. If anything, it made me more terrified.

"Casper, please! Can we just go home? We're not far—" It was no use. He was already over the fence. I was frozen in fear. He looked back at me one last time and *winked*, but my legs wouldn't move.

"Two minutes," he said before disappearing around the bush and into the mist.

I was beginning to feel faint; maybe the drugs hadn't worn off as much as I thought. Perhaps this was a side effect... I'd never hallucinated on this one before, but... What was happening? It didn't make any sense. Something was seriously wrong with Casper; I couldn't just stand there and let him get into trouble. *Why did you take the pills when you vowed to stop?*

Gathering all the courage I could muster, I started back down the path to the main cemetery gates, my heart pounding in my ears. I soon realised my stupidity; of course, the gates were locked, and the cemetery had cameras. The second it processed, I ran back up the path to where Casper jumped the gate and forced myself over it with great difficulty, muttering curses the entire time and scraping my hand on metal and wood.

I landed in a heap, catching my coat on the twigs and weeds lining the fence. I was blindingly dizzy at that point and felt moments away from dropping down unconscious. *Had I taken my iron tablets this morning? Wrong pills, Ben.*

The moon had moved from behind the clouds, gazing down upon the tombstones, casting a silver glow that did little to mollify my fears. It was deathly quiet. I wanted to shout for Casper but had no energy for the words. I stumbled into a run, heading in the direction I saw Casper go, but there was no sign of life anywhere.

All the while, a million questions fired in my brain. Who was Casper meeting? Who was this person? Did I know them? Who were they to him? Was he hiding something from me? No, that's not Casper. He wouldn't do that. He wouldn't.

Movement caught my eye. A brief blur of red jumped into my peripheral and startled me cold. My hands were starting to seize like when my iron levels were messed up. My heart thudded harder but slower, despite my fear. *It hurt.*

My breaths plumed in the moonlight as I crouched, resting against a stone archway to catch my breath. Casper was in danger. I just knew it.

It would be my fault if anything happened to him. *Stop being a baby, Ben.* I slowly stood and peered at where I thought I'd seen movement. Nothing. It was hard to make out most things in the light, but I knew I'd seen something poking up from behind a headstone.

My limbs were liquid, but my fingers refused to relax from the position they were stuck in—I was going to be sick. Taking heavy breaths, I closed my eyes before charging forward. I needed to find Casper—that was all that mattered. I needed him. I needed to take him home.

My footing was uneven and askew; breathing shallow and depriving my brain of oxygen. The moon was blinding despite the dim and murky night sky. I was exhausted. The drugs had fucked my system. God, I was so stupid. *Never again, Ben. Never again. You're above this.*

"Casper," I called, but it was far too quiet. There was no way anyone would have heard me. But my body was shutting down, and I was *terrified.* I was starting to see movement everywhere, but I found nothing. My mind was playing tricks on me... it had to be.

"Casper!" I cried out this time, envisioning the worst. I caught my foot on a rock and tumbled face-first to the ground, catching myself and scuffing my hands on the cobbled pathway.

Tears welled in my eyes, and I called myself an idiot, a wuss, a baby. Pathetic. I needed to keep focused. I needed to find Casper.

Then, I heard a pained but inaudible mumble—noise coming from the same area where I thought I'd spotted the first movement.

I ran. All other thoughts evaded me as I threw myself up and ran towards the sound. I didn't even notice my leg and palms were bleeding. I got to a clearing and glanced behind me to see if I was in the right place, but I couldn't see anyone.

So, I shouted. The adrenaline rushed straight to my brain.

"Casper! Casper, are you there?" My voice was shaky, and my throat burned with the strain.

No movement. I turned around in all directions to make sure I was in the right place.

"Casper!" I shouted it as more of a plea that time. I was so frightened.

I DON'T REMEMBER what I did in those last few moments before finding his body. I think I shouted for him again and looked around the headstones. All I remember is the exact moment my eyes found his muddy white trainers sticking out from the grass behind a large Celtic-style gravestone. I saw his shoes, then his legs, and without blinking, I finally reached him.

I just stared. I stood looking down at his mangled body, his arms unnaturally bent, and his head turned, his eyes wide open and *glassy*. Then, I noticed the blood, blood that coated his denim jacket that was half torn off his body and half glued to his side. Blood coated his torn shirt, too, and his jeans, his scarf... his beautiful face. Casper.

My legs disappeared beneath me, and I crumbled before him. It finally sunk in that this was no hallucination, and I *screamed*. I didn't think I could be as loud as I was that night. When I reached down to lift him to my chest, his head flopped back, his arms dropping to his side as I held him. His eyes were unblinking; his chest didn't rise. I held him tight as I screamed and cried. Blood coated my hands, and I rocked and rocked, cradling him like a mother would her newborn. I couldn't breathe or think; I just needed him to wake up.

"Please... please!" I wailed, snot bubbling at my lips. I was blinded by tears.

"Wake up, Casper. Wake up. Stop pretending." I was in denial. I refused to accept what happened.

I couldn't live without him.

I couldn't live.

I only survived when I stayed with Casper.

He kept me alive.

Then, anger set in. Someone had done this. Someone had targeted him, and perhaps they had for weeks. Who was he meeting with?

With trembling hands still gripping his body against mine, my vision cleared, and I looked around, searching for anyone—anything. I needed...

I'm not proud of what I did next, and I think the only sound thought entering my head was that Casper wouldn't want me to do what I had planned. But Casper didn't need to know. I just needed him. I needed to be with him.

My breathing slowed as I realised what I was about to do. I closed my eyes and told myself to be a man—to be strong and accept my fate. I was doing what I wanted. What I chose.

I was terrified, more terrified than I'd ever been before.

But I wanted this. I couldn't live without him.

"Please!" I shouted into the darkness, my voice echoing eerily across the stones. A bird flew out into the sky, its flapping wings the only reply.

Casper's body slowly slipped from my grip as I laid him against the headstone and stood to full height, opening my arms wide. My whole body was covered in a mixture of mine and Casper's blood.

I was afraid. My heart was dying.

"Please!" I shouted again, offering myself up to the dark. "Whoever you are. Please. Take me, too," I gulped, panting. "Take me. You can have me. I'm not going to run."

I'd lost my mind now. No one replied. No one was there. I dipped my head to look at Casper, who remained unmoving.

Maybe I was dreaming. Maybe it was the drugs. Maybe I should have stopped them a long time ago when I said I did.

Maybe. Maybe. Maybe.

I sank back to my knees and bent over to hug Casper close again. I shuffled into a cross-legged seating position and let his head rest against my stomach. I used my bloody hands to pull his newly loosened curls from his forehead so I could see his beautiful face. I kissed him on both cheeks, the way he always liked me to. My hands trembled, and I felt my body shut down. I was so cold.

I crouched to shelter Casper's head and passed out.

A MILLION HANDS grab me and hurl me backwards. I make no protest as they throw me to my back; I open my eyes.

THERE WERE FOUR OF THEM, their eyes glowing a veiny red and their teeth too long in their mouths. I couldn't think of anything beyond that. The grim reapers had heard my pleas and had come to take me home.

The first one bent down to bite my neck, and the second my wrist, tugging me towards them. The third and fourth went for my body and legs. They were *hungry*. I cried out at the pain, but I stopped eventually as the pain subsided. They tore away at my body, and I let them, blood bubbling in my mouth, clogging my airways. A smile formed on my face.

Wait for me, Casper.

Interlude

"Where are they?"
"Can I see?"
"Wait, who? Who did you say they were?"
"Marianne, what's the low down? Where were they?"
"Mars, get them out of here. Please."
"Wait, Forever Red?"
"ID says this is Casper Murphey."
"Casper? It is him. Forever Red."
"Who's the other one?"
"He might not make it."
"Which one?"
"Does anyone know who the other one is?"
"Please, let me see. I'm a fan of the band."
"Don't lift the covers. Just look at the faces. Do you know the other one?"
"Can anyone ID the other one? Please!"
"Everybody calm down."
"Hey! Stop!"
"Don't lift the—

"It's Ben. The blood, I—"
"Ben? You know him?"
"He's in the band. Is he going to be alright? How did his arm get like that?"
"I'm going to be sick."
"Please step back and let the process take place."
"Is he going to make it?"

"Marianne?"

"I'm not sure. He's not responding at all. We'll have to wait and see."

"Where did you say you found them?"

"I didn't. It was the new boy. He found them."

"New boy?"

"He's hiding. Lawrence, I think his name is."

"Never heard of him."

"BEN AND CASPER? Is it them? Really?"

"PLEASE! I NEED TO SEE THEM."

"Mars, please keep them all away; they shouldn't be here."

"Come on guys, nothing to see here."

"They're famous, you know. How will they keep this secret?"

"How long does it take for the blood to work?"

"Depends on the damage and how long they were left for dead."

"We got to them too late, didn't we?"

"Marianne?"

"I don't know."

"Thank you, Mars. Sorry. I didn't expect this. I've never heard of this band."

"I have."

"You know them?"

"I've worked with them. They don't know me, though. I've never met them in person. That's them, though. Casper and Ben. They're about my age, I think. God. It's so sick."

"I know. We need to speak to this Lawrence; he knows more than he's letting on. How did he know where they'd be?"

"I don't trust him. He's a rogue."
"He's young. We can guide him. There's still time."
"Ben's not going to make it, is he?"
"I have my doubts."
"What do you think happened? How did they even get in the cemetery?"
"I have a million questions."

Casper

I HAD WOKEN up in some strange places in my life, but I never guessed I'd wake up in what I first believed was a tomb, facing stone arches in some church-like structure.

I had no recollection of where I'd been the night before or how I'd gotten there. I couldn't move my limbs at first, but my eyes wandered to my right at the sound of voices. A woman sat slouched in a chair, her hair the colour of sunrise. Then my gaze wandered further, making out the blur of another person standing, guarding a doorway with their arms folded.

I couldn't speak yet, but sensations slowly returned to my limbs. Everything *stung*.

My movement was enough for the woman in the chair to bolt upright and have the other person running over.

"Ahh! Marianne!" They held their hands over the space above my face, making claws of victory with a grin far too ecstatic for my current mood. I remember thinking that perhaps I'd smoked one of Ben's cigarettes.

"Casper Murphey. So, we finally meet. How are you feeling?" the person continued. *Yup, definitely inhaled something.*

"Mars, please calm down. Let me see." The woman pulled the younger, East Asian person out of the way to lean closer and *inspect.*

Mars? As in, the Mars?

"Casper, love. Can you hear me?"

I could hear her—perfectly well, in fact—but when I opened my mouth, no sound emerged.

"Here, let me help you sit up." I strained to sit upright and grabbed her arms for support. Mars joined in, looking overjoyed to assist.

"I..." I was so confused. "Where?" *Where am I?*

"How do you feel first? Any pain? Do you feel different?"

I squinted my eyes and scrunched my nose; this woman made no sense.

"I don't..." I didn't think I felt different. I felt tired and exhausted, but I was still me. Or so I thought.

"Can you stand?" Marianne's voice was smooth and calming like she could have demanded me to do anything, and I would have. She was very pretty. I—

"BEN!" I shouted, head tipping to the ceiling.

The two of them stilled, eyes wide. The tone of the room immediately shifted, and I suddenly felt dizzy. I glanced down at my body, my legs covered in a cloth blanket, and my chest bare, wrapped in bandages...

"Wait, what happened?" I grabbed at my chest and tugged at the bandages, frantically searching until my eyes wandered to a table on my right... *Ben.*

I dove without thinking, but the woman shot around and grabbed me, holding me against the table as my feet slipped against the cold, hard floor. She held me with such force, her brow tense and breath held. I remained transfixed on Ben and only Ben. He wasn't moving. His eyes were shut, and scratches marked his face. *He's not breathing.*

I used all my force to try and pull my arms free so I could move to see him.

"LET GO!" I screamed. Why wouldn't she just let me out? *Where the fuck am I?*

"Casper, please!" the woman pleaded. She was so fucking strong.

"Marianne!" Mars shouted from behind—they seemed scared.

The woman's breathing grew heavy, her hair slightly misplaced while her eyes remained fixed on me.

"Casper, listen to me. Please. Sit back down. I can explain." My muscles weakened with her words, and I felt compelled to do as she said. My breathing eased and I stopped my struggling, slowly sinking back onto the stone.

She looked me in the eyes, sorrow painted across her face. When she spoke, she told me everything.

She spoke of things that couldn't be true. Things that couldn't be real. I sat in denial as she explained the existence of immortality, manifesting as a parasitic and permanent infection of a human host. A host who would be reborn with a taste for blood and a distaste for silver. *Vampires*, for lack of a better word.

I told her to shut up, to stop reciting a story we'd all heard before. I even laughed a few times, because it just could not be true.

"I think I'd like to wake up now, please," I said through a scoff, but Marianne only lowered her gaze and smiled in pity.

Surely this nightmare wouldn't last much longer, I thought. Now that I was aware it was a dream, that would force me to wake up—that's how it works, right? I'd wake up in a panic, but Ben would be beside me, breathing softly in deep sleep, his curls draped across his face like silk, and I'd let my heart settle as reality flooded back in, and I would tell Ben the story in the morning over coffee and our favourite cereal.

I'd wake up soon.

"Casper, darling. I'm sorry but you have to listen to me. I know it's a lot to absorb, and we will be there for you every step of the way, but you need to take this in. You're not dreaming." Marianne reached out to squeeze my hand in comfort, but I pulled away.

She sighed and looked to Mars beside me. I didn't hear them speak.

Then Marianne continued. And finally, it all started to piece together.

"You've been experiencing some memory loss, I'm assuming?" she looked at me quizzically. She already knew my answer, so my nod affirmed nothing.

"One of the most useful, but most dangerous traits of our kind is our ability to Manipulate. From gentle persuasion to fully grown mind control. All in the form of an undetectable scent. You, my boy, have fallen victim to what we like to call the 'Turned'. Greedy monsters with little humanity left. They're vampires who use their skills to a selfish and evil advantage; not caring what they do or how they do it—they only care about satisfying their *hunger*. Their lust for power, entertainment... murder. All because they know they can get away with it."

I drowned her voice out as flashes appeared in my mind. Suddenly I'm in a graveyard, with dirt beneath my nails. There's a buzzing, muffled moan all around me and the trees start spinning. It's dark, so very dark, and I'm falling. So much dirt...

"... Ben's injuries were a lot worse than yours. They'd probably already overdosed on you, so Ben will have sent them insane. The Turned don't care who they harm or how much. We got to you both as quickly as we could, but sometimes it doesn't work. I'm sorry, Casper. We're trying. He might make it, but he might not. It was a miracle that you yourself survived."

My ears were ringing, and a tear trickled down my cheek. I glanced over Marianne's shoulder to where Ben rested.

I—

"Marianne," Mars said again, and I startled, facing them. They stood almost silently throughout the whole explanation but looked just as concerned.

"I know, Mars, I know."

Know what? Why were they talking as though I wasn't there? Why did I feel weak?

Ben.

I shot up faster than Marianne could catch me, throwing out my arms to hold Ben. His head snapped back loosely as I tried to lift him, the covers dropping from his body, exposing his limbs and torso. *No.*

I held him like a porcelain doll, yet he wouldn't rouse. Then, like slow motion, arms hauled me back; Mars moved around the slab and caught Ben before he slammed against the table while Marianne pulled me away. Both their voices were frantic in my head, but I couldn't make out what they were saying; it was like my brain had stopped working altogether.

"Casper, please. We need to leave him be. There's still time. We can't disrupt anything. I know you want your friend to be okay; trust me, I know how that feels, but—

"He's not my *friend.*" I ground my teeth. Then, the implications of my words hit me. We'd kept our relationship secret for a reason, and I nearly let it slip.

"Is he your partner?" Mars asked, no judgement in their voice.

I looked at them and slowly nodded. I was weak. Defeated.

Mars pursed their lips and turned away as if processing the information. Eventually, they turned back and said, "I will sit with you, and we can wait for him to wake."

Marianne didn't protest. In fact, she smiled. Her grip on me dropped as she straightened.

I looked at her in a plea of silent approval. I did not know this woman, but I knew she held great power. She had been alive for a long time, longer than humanly possible.

I didn't process what I was straight away, but I understood, rather calmly, that there was a small possibility Ben could return to me, even after what we'd gone through. The understanding of my immortality came to me in pieces, but that was the furthest thing from my mind as Marianne left, leaving Mars beside me as we waited, waited, and waited for Ben to wake.

We sat for hours.

I thought about prying for more questions, playing along with the idea that I now was a vampire, despite still not fully believing it. I just needed something, anything that I could do to help save Ben.

"You want me to prove it to you?" Mars asked after a long while of us sitting in complete silence.

I didn't turn to face them; I only had eyes for Ben, lying before me in this *shroud.*

He's just resting. He'll wake soon.

"Prove what?" I said in a trance.

Mars sighed beside me, and I felt their hand feather over my own in my lap. I almost protested their grip, but their gentleness and inviting manner relaxed my muscles and I let them take hold. I followed our hands as they raised it up to their mouth and they curled up their top lip, exposing unnaturally long canines. My eyes widened but I let them press my fingers to the tips of them. It was like a pin prick, a brief sting of discomfort, then nothing. They pulled my hand away and looked me in the eye.

"That's it," they said. "That's all it is."

I flitted my gaze down to my hands and rubbed at the finger I thought was injured, but there was nothing there. Not even a mark.

My brow tensed and I once again turned to face them in confusion, a million questions on my tongue.

Mars smiled. "Oh, that's a cool trait too. We *heal.*" They fluttered their fingers in the air and winked. "Bet you didn't think you were trading with a *vampire.*"

So, it was Mars. *The* Mars who'd helped us design our logo, who walked dead among us the entire time.

"You..."

Mars grinned. They had such a kindness to their face that I saw in very few people. I felt comfortable with them. *But are you just being Manipulated? Don't let yourself be fooled again.*

What the hell is going on?

"How much longer do we have to wait?" I asked, changing the subject; legs restless as I pushed away the fact I was almost about to believe them. Ben hadn't moved an inch.

I asked them a few times over the course of the next few hours, and Mars' responses were said with less certainty each time. "Not much longer." But the more they said it, the more I realised they weren't implying he would wake; they were implying it was not much longer before we'd know the outcome—before he would be gone forever.

They had to restrain me, but only once, in what was possibly the fifth hour of waiting. I wanted to hold Ben. His face had grown ashy, and he looked so cold. I wanted to hug him, warm him, and keep him safe. I couldn't. We had to wait. We had to...

At some point, Marianne returned with a mug for each of us and forced me to drink in front of her. It was so sweet and nothing like I'd ever tasted. It took a while before the revelation that vampires existed *truly* sunk in, despite the evidence I'd been given, and it took me even longer to process the fact I'd died and come back as one. I'd not yet thought about what that meant for our future or how we would return to our normal lives, or how I would hide it from Francesca, from my family.

I just needed Ben.

Marianne came back a while later and told me it had been seven hours. No one had been brought back that late, she said.

Ben was dead.

I had to say goodbye.

Two people I didn't know moved around his body and covered his beautiful face with the sheet, hanging their heads low. Mars squeezed my hand. My limbs stopped working, my head dropped; I couldn't think of *anything*.

I was gently escorted out of the room in a slow, static blur. Marianne stood at the foot of Ben's table, the only person left in the room before the door closed, and I could no longer see him. I stumbled backward down a hallway and was taken into another room, only a single thought prevailing in the mush that was my mind.

He was gone.

Interlude

"Ben. If you can hear me. Drink this."
"Please."
"He's waiting for you."

Ben

I WAS HAVING the strangest dream.

I woke up smothered in sheets and shot up in a panic. I couldn't breathe.

I bolted upright, but the room I was in was so dark I couldn't see a thing. Eventually, when my eyes adjusted, I could make out a slither of silver cast from a high window. I was in a church, or maybe a chapel. I felt around with my hands and learned I was lying on a cold slab of stone.

My first thought was that I was in purgatory, awaiting something. I didn't feel awake, though, not entirely. Nor did I feel alive. Very quickly, it dawned on me that I was not in proper clothing. In fact, as I felt around my body, I realised I was covered head to foot in bandages. Nothing else. I pulled the tight bandage off my forehead and tugged at the one on my neck, my arms aching and sore. My eyes had adjusted further then, and as I tore away the bandages, my skin beneath stung; dark patches were scattered across my body. Old wounds, scars.

Perhaps I was in hell, then.

I grabbed at my chest for the warm comfort of my crucifix, but it was gone. *I've sinned too much.*

I wracked my brain for any sort of explanation as to where I was. After a few minutes of exploring my body, I concluded I must have had a serious accident, or perhaps I was hallucinating, comatose somewhere in a hospital bed.

Or maybe this was some sick game, like an escape room, where I had to find a key to get out.

I stumbled off the gurney, wincing at the sharp, icy stone beneath my bare feet. My legs jolted slightly as I planted my feet firmly onto the ground, knees nearly crumbling beneath me, but after gripping the table behind me to steady myself, I stood and slowly let go, wandering aimlessly into the darkened room like a wounded deer.

My teeth chattered. I needed to find something to cover me.

I limped around the room, half-awake, only managing to focus on the simple task of moving.

I tripped over something on the floor and fell to my knees with a clatter, my mind dizzying for a moment. I gathered myself again and squinted, focusing on a white sheet dangling in the distance. As I drew closer, I realised it was two white garments hanging side by side over a wooden chest. I reached for one and immediately understood what they were: hospital gowns. Smeared with blood.

Blood.

My mind shot open, my senses heightening at the smell of iron. It was dried to the cloth, yet I craved to touch it. To taste it. *What?*

I shook my head vigorously and staggered back, clinging to the garment. I needed warmth, and although it was hardly hygienic, I didn't care; I couldn't feel my fingers. So, I threw it over my head, where it hung loosely over my body. It was better than nothing.

I wandered around again, my panic and fear increasing. Was this some sort of test? Was I being watched? Had I been kidnapped?

I decided to return to the chest; it was the only thing I thought might have the answers to my questions. A large padlock secured it, but after lifting and twisting it, I realised it wasn't sealed. I ripped it off and heaved the lid open.

Again, it took my eyes a moment to adjust, but then I began to discern the sharp metal tools. Medical equipment. Bandages, like the ones I was wearing. Dressings and vials.

What happened to me?

I pulled more of my bandages until the one on my arm unravelled, and I saw the extent of the damage. I touched my fingers to the tendons at my wrist and winced and—

The cemetery.

"CASPER!" I screamed into the darkness. Casper. Oh, Casper. "Casper!" I tried again and again. But there was no answer.

Then, my eyes flashed back to the table I'd been lying on, and I finally noticed there were two. I knew—I just *knew*—he had been on the second one. But it was empty now, not even a cloth in sight. *I'm being punished.*

"Casper!" I cried again before falling to my knees, tears arriving like a flood. I cried and cried until my throat was raw, and my body weakened. I leaned against a pillar just to keep upright.

Then, I smelled it, stronger than before.

Blood.

Sweet and metallic.

I glanced to my side and noticed two cups, one tipped to its side, where the remnants spilled into a pool on the ground. It had mostly dried, but some freshness remained.

I didn't even think. I bent down and *licked* the inside of the cup.

My eyes rolled back as the taste trickled down my throat. I felt momentarily weightless before reality drew me back down and I tossed the cup against the wall, shattering it into tiny pieces.

I was in Hell.

This was a test.

And I had failed.

Interlude

"The parasite blood will slow the deterioration."

"The room was cold enough, he'll be okay. We'll bury him soon."

"I'm so sorry, Casper. I'm so, so sorry."

"It's perhaps best you don't follow me in here."

"I know, Casper dear, I know."

"We will make it special; I promise."

"Please wait there, we will take good care of him."

Casper

MARS DIDN'T LEAVE my side all night. I didn't even know them, yet they were the closest thing I had to a friend in that place. They kept me talking and let me tell them everything about Ben and how amazing he is—or was. They smiled and nodded, keeping me focused on the happy things to distract me from my terror. I was in some weird underground castle labyrinth filled with *vampires*. Nothing made sense.

The next morning, Marianne came to speak with me calmly and sympathetically as she explained the process she took with the people she couldn't save. I had no choice but to accept it. She told me more about our skill of Manipulation and how it worked as a 'free pass' in some everyday situations. Marianne had a contact, a local funeral director, who could make this happen as quickly and as smoothly as possible. She informed me of the correct way to break the news to our friends and Ben's family, preparing me for potential situations or questions that could arise as a result of the news.

I wanted to see him, just one last time. To properly say good-bye. Marianne explained he might look a little different because of the parasite blood in his system, and that it would be best if she handled the next step alone. She promised I could visit him after they prepared the body for burial.

But it wasn't enough. I needed to see him right then, no matter what he looked like.

Mars held me back as Marianne unlocked the door, and the oak swung on its hinges, revealing the slightly dimmer room. It took me a delayed second to realise what Marianne was screaming about until the figure on the other side of the door jumped up and screamed too.

Ben.

He was alive.

He was there. Standing, breathing... with blood on his mouth. His eyes were bloodshot and his teeth... his *teeth*.

I didn't care. I yanked my arm out of Mars' grasp and dove down the steps, wrapping my arms tightly around a startled Ben and hugging him close, breathing in the scent of his hair. His arms didn't return the hug immediately, but after a moment, they slowly closed around my back. His breath hitched.

He was alive.

"Oh my days," Mars exclaimed behind us.

Ben abruptly pulled back and stared at everyone, his eyes searching.

"What am I?" he begged, lifting trembling hands to his face as he touched his canines in horror. "Why do I feel like this?"

I pulled him in for another hug. It's all I ever wanted to do.

"You're okay, Ben. I've got you. We're going to be okay."

"I thought you were dead." His voice shook. "Am I dead?"

"No. No, Ben, you're not. You're alive. Look!" I held him out at arm's length and cupped his face, pressing his lips to mine, ignoring the iron tang to his lips. Ben savoured it for a moment, then jerked backward, eyeing our company again.

I turned to face Marianne and Mars, who simply stood frozen in shock. I knew Ben was afraid of kissing in public, but even if they didn't accept us, our kiss was the least of their worries. Ben had been dead for over a day. Marianne had explained that it had never happened before. He shouldn't have made it, but he did.

He made it.

"It's okay, Ben. They know, and they're like us."

"Yeah, where's my kiss?" Mars piped up.

Ben still looked lost. He was dressed in a bloodied gown, one I instantly recognised as the one they must have put him in, the blood stains matching his more severe injuries, which were now mostly exposed from the torn bandages.

"Where are we? What happened?" he asked breathlessly. "Why do I feel like this?"

"We can explain everything to you, Ben." Mars stepped down to join us at eye level. "I'm Mars, by the way. Yes, the Mars you've worked with. I'm not artificial intelligence, after all." They briefly glanced at me. Okay, yes, I admit it. I had suspected they weren't a real person, seeing as though they were so private, and Jake had neglected to share any information about them other than the fact they were 'hot.'

Mars' introduction did little to calm Ben.

"What's happening, Casper?" He cowered into me like a frightened rabbit, seeming so small at that moment, his body ice-cold from being trapped for so long in that room. How long had he been awake? Had he been calling for me? He seemed so scared; he'd essentially woken up in a morgue.

"It's okay." I kept kissing the top of his head.

"Casper, why do I keep thinking about blood? What happened to me?" Ben kept his eyes fixed on mine, searching for answers.

"It's going to be a long explanation, but I'm here. We're going to be okay; I promise."

I waited for him to nod, and eventually, he did. Taking his hand, I helped him step out of the room.

"You're a strong one," said Marianne finally, her voice less gentle than it had been, but more... youthful. She stepped forward to get a closer look at Ben, and I moved to the side to let her, still gripping one of his hands. His wounds had mostly healed now, but the deep scars remained.

"I can't hear anything... If you don't mind, I need to check a few things first." Marianne mumbled, directing the last part at me but quickly glancing back at Ben. "This has never happened before, and I need to make sure the process happened properly."

"What are you talking about?" Ben shuffled back a fraction, and I gripped his hand tighter as he looked to me for reassurance.

"She's the one who saved us; she just needs to check you."

Ben still looked frightened; his hands purple.

"It won't take long." Marianne smiled.

"Stay with me?" Ben asked quietly. I nodded and the three of us re-entered the room, Mars guarding the doorway.

The first thing Marianne did was turn off the air conditioning, before pulling up a chair and asking Ben to sit. I stood by his side.

Marianne reached into the giant, open chest—perhaps Ben had been in there—and pulled out a stethoscope and a thermometer.

"How do you feel, Ben?" she asked as sweetly as a nurse would.

"Weird. Not fully awake." He looked distant.

"Did you touch the blood in that smashed mug over there?" She gestured to the ceramic fragments near the two stone slabs. The mug I'd drunk from the day before.

"I drank it. I don't know why. Why did I do that?" Ben kept looking at me instead of her.

She took his temperature and asked to check his gums, putting on rubber gloves and rubbing his canines, which had since retracted to normal size.

Then, she pressed a stethoscope to his chest and listened, asking him to breathe in out and announcing his lung function was fine. She pressed fingers to the side of his neck, and only then did I realise why. We had no heartbeat. I felt for my own and was met with painful silence.

Once she was done, she let Ben take off the remaining bandages by himself and then turned to me. "He's perfectly fine. We did it." She looked as if she was about to cry.

It was a miracle.

OF COURSE, we had to put the band on hiatus for a while. We were in our final year of uni anyway, but this was the real kickback. We couldn't tell Francesca what happened, which hurt, but Marianne and Mars helped us plan out how to assimilate back into our normal lives. I took the whole thing surprisingly well; I didn't question much, just accepted what I was told. I'd gone from believing it was all a dream, to 'hey, you're a vampire now. Okay. Cool.' But I think it was mostly because I felt like I had to protect Ben, who came back into this world in a much worse condition. I brushed aside my burning questions and told myself I just had to get on with it. I needed to be there for Ben.

It hit me rather abruptly about a week later. I woke up laughing maniacally one night and saying what I believe Ben recited as "I want to suck your blood." It was utterly insane. We were *dead.* But not. We had to drink blood morning and night. We were going to live forever. It was impossible.

Marianne caught the people who did it. She'd been looking for them for a while, and finding us was the last piece in the puzzle. Because they attacked Ben so badly, they ended up attacking each other; high on our blood and losing their already corrupted minds, and left too much evidence behind at the scene–making it easy for a vampire as experienced as Marianne to track their scents.

It was the guys who kept talking to me after gigs. I'll never find out why they chose me, but I suppose it didn't matter, because as Marianne said, they were 'no longer going to be a problem.'

It wouldn't have taken a genius to figure out that they had been Manipulating me and called for me that night in the cemetery. Ben must have been caught in their Manipulation, too, hence how they got us both.

Ben didn't like talking about that night; he said he didn't remember anything, but sometimes, I saw a glint in his eyes that told me he wasn't being entirely truthful. I didn't pry, though. He'd tell me when he was ready.

We sort of, unofficially, joined the group Mars had aptly named "The Thorns." I tried not to laugh at the dramatic effect of the name, but then Marianne said I could judge all I liked. She didn't care what they were called, as long as they could successfully do what she wanted: keep humanity safe.

Oh, and the final change? Mars asked to become our manager. It was only right—we were in this world now.

We clued Fran in on who Mars was (the cool artist who designed our first logo, nothing else) and she loved the idea of hiring a local 'up and coming' manager. While her dad had filled the role nicely until that point, it was about time we got something a little more official. Mars had the power of human charming persuasion, on top of the occasional innocent Manipulation technique. It worked a treat. We signed with a label two months later. After Ben and I handed in our dissertations in the summer—essentially refusing to have anything more to do with the institution—we were freed into the outside world to start recording our next single since the hiatus.

It was hardly an easy task sneaking away to feed, and would probably always be a fear in the back of our minds, especially on nights where we worked late and fell asleep on the couches, waking up specifically aware of Fran's and sometimes even Maddie's *life source*. Ben had to fake a stomach bug some mornings, I had to take up long morning runs through the forest to 'get into a healthy routine', as I scrounged for wildlife big enough to make a few days' worth of meals from. It wasn't fun, it never will be, but we did what we had to do to survive. Would we get caught? Did the government know we existed? How many people would we have to Manipulate in our lives to hide who we are? These were all questions we asked each other daily. But we'd manage. We'd make it work. We hid enough from people as it stood, so what was one more thing to add to the list? The humans in our lives wouldn't suspect a thing.

The Thorns made everything so easy. Life could go on as normally as it could. Everything fell into a routine and just *worked*. Sure, those first few months were like a fever dream, and sure, we didn't do that well with either of our degrees, but none of that really mattered anymore. We were free. Forever.

The car's ablaze,
psychadelic
carnival
He's running
from life, like
ing
end
com
ngh
urr

PART FOUR
'A THORN IN HIS SIDE'

2012-2018

<u>**Interview excerpt: December 2012**</u>

INTERVIEWER (GRAHAM HOBBS, 'NEXT BEST STRINGS' – January 2013 Issue): So, boys. You came back stronger than ever post-hiatus. What did you do in that time that helped you?

Ben: Well, we had a lot of sleepless nights with uni, but we really immersed ourselves in music. We lived and breathed it. It was the only thing keeping us alive for a time.

Graham: And you think that was the main booster? How you got picked up by a label? Congratulations, by the way.

Ben: Thanks! And yeah, I suppose it was.

Graham: Now, it was reported you both had some ill health during this time? Fans were pretty concerned, but it seems you came bouncing back!

Casper: Yeah, that's sort of private though.

[*redacted*]

Graham: So, you gained a new member as well! Lawrence Marigold. Now, that kid has a crazy life story, doesn't he?

Casper: Yeah. I can't act like that's not public information. The kid could have a movie written about him. He's a wonder.

Graham: That he is. I can't wait for him to start joining you in interviews; I would love to ask him some questions.

Ben: Wouldn't we all.

Ben
April 2012

So, we joined The Thorns. We had no choice, really. Becoming a vampire was no easy feat, and we had to essentially 're-learn' how to survive: when to feed, what was best for us, and how to go about life like normal. I struggled—we both did—but at least we had each other. I can't believe how easily it eventually took over our lives; as far as living off blood, we convinced ourselves to treat it like a normal dietary requirement, so we made it work. We worried we'd lost our minds for a time, but no, we *were* dead: immortal hosts for a potentially alien parasite. We didn't really know the origins of our kind, but it was dangerous to search for answers. I didn't want any more attention drawn to myself than I already had. Being in a band that was beginning to actually 'make it' was hard enough with the rumours, the questions, the spotting. All I needed to do was remind myself how much worse it could be.

Casper was always protective over me, but things changed after we came back. He was even more cautious and wary around me, though I couldn't blame him. I shouldn't have really made it, but by some miracle, I did. Maybe my faith had something to do with it.

Had I continued believing real vampires were agents of the devil, instead of a parasite routed in science, permanently infecting our bloodstream and acting as its own silent pulse, I would occasionally consider that perhaps I had been saved by something other than a god. Or perhaps I was meant to be reborn like this. I don't really know, but at least Casper was the same as me.

The hardest part was hiding the truth from Francesca. It shouldn't have been, and it didn't have to be, because the only thing different was we didn't have to eat normal food as much so would often skip lunch. We drank our blood in private; we didn't have to avoid the daytime or cower away from garlic, fire, or pointy wooden things. We weren't too different from humans if we accustomed to our surroundings. But every time I got close to someone I knew, I felt like I was going to be sick. I would overthink every action and be constantly on edge.

Much to our luck, Fran was a big talker and didn't always pay attention to others, so it worked out fine. She didn't suspect a thing.

Mars became very friendly with us, helping us with marketing ourselves after the break and promising to always help with design and poster promo. I learned very quickly that they had little to no experience managing *anything,* but with Beck's lingering assistance, and our moderately successful image, we comfortably sailed through the indie scene. We never wanted to be *big* stars, just important enough to be remembered by people who enjoyed our music, so our setup worked just fine. All we needed now was one extra player to help with our more complex songs.

We'd talked about it many times, how to go about replacing Jake. There were some Thorns who played instruments but had no interest in our style or genre. We asked around the uni, but it was a terrible time; it was dissertation season, with both Casper and I in our final years. No one wanted to do anything other than *get that bloody essay done.*

Marianne remained mysterious, only ever showing up to monthly meetings. I knew she had a story to tell; after all, she'd lived for so many years but never opened up about anything. She struck me as someone who lived in the now, never dwelling on the past or wondering about the future. Maybe that was a good way to be. Or maybe it was all an act.

Everything was sort of *normal.* We adapted. We survived.

In our first month as vampires, The Thorns caught the group that killed me and Casper. One culprit apparently begged for us to help, while the others were too proud of their actions to be saved. Marianne decided for them. We never did find out what happened to those ones, but no one dared ask.

A week later, the final one began showing signs of aggression, and I witnessed my first act of violence within The Thorns. I shouldn't have been where I was, but curiosity got the better of me as I followed a stressed-looking Mars down into the darkest and most narrow parts of the hideout. I'd heard shouting and wished to investigate. I waited until they were far ahead of me before sneaking behind them. Luckily for me, they'd disappeared behind an old wooden door made of vertical panels that had weathered over time. When I pressed my face up to the cracks, I could see into the room perfectly.

There, in the middle of the room, stood Mars, Marianne, and two other bodies. The Turned was already shouting and waving his hands.

"I swear it's just who I am! I'm aggressive; I lash out. I didn't choose this life!" he shouted. He sounded sincere, but I couldn't read his face.

"You hurt people; you killed people. If you were mortal, you would be in prison for life. You see how I'm struggling to see this as an excuse?" Marianne sounded *harsh.*

"Yeah, but it's different, those boys survived, right? You turned them."

"That holds no weight," Mars inputted, hands on hips.

I was trying to make out who the fourth person was, but the angle hid them from sight. But the Turned spoke again.

"Come on, Lawrence. Back me up here, kid. You followed us for months. Did you see us kill anyone?"

"Just because I didn't see you do it doesn't mean you didn't!" Lawrence threw his hands up. *Lawrence. I've heard that name. What does he have to do with this?*

"Lawrence can't act as a witness." Marianne's tone was blunt. "He also joined us and proved he could change. He's just a kid, no offence."

Lawrence shrugged as if to say, 'none taken.' I glimpsed his face then and pieced together that he was the person Mars had described to us before, the young vampire who roamed the streets, getting into bother. They brought him back to the Thorns and figured out he wasn't from around the area. He needed guiding— lone vampires found it very easy to fall into the wrong crowds. I gathered he must have encountered these Turned creatures who attacked me and Casper.

"So, you *are* a spy then, fucking faggot. I should have known." The Turned lashed to his side and pushed Lawrence backward. The words themselves hit me right in my soul, and I flinched, thinking back to my school days.

Mars was quick to react, pushing the Turned to the floor. "Say that again, and I'll gut you," they spat.

Marianne was at Lawrence's side and helped him up, his face flushed and stunned.

"At least I'm not a fucking killer!" Lawrence yelled; his face scrunched in anger.

"You could have been. We could have taught you; you can get away with anything when you're like us," the Turned gloated whilst Mars pulled him back, keeping him from Lawrence who was back on his feet.

That was enough for Marianne to snap. She went straight for his throat, yanking him out of Mars' grip and thrusting him against the wall. "I knew you were lying. There's no helping people like you."

The room burned red with rage. Lawrence and Mars posed to

attack, yet Marianne hardly moved a muscle as the Turned lashed in her arms.

"I nearly got you, though. Go on; admit it. You considered letting me join you." He winked, grinning to expose his fangs. So, this is what happened when evil melded with the parasite. I shivered. This person had a part in killing Casper.

"Believe it or not, I have major trust issues. Happens when you get to a certain age," Marianne admitted, cocking her head to the side. "I give people a chance, but people like you don't want that. No prison could hold you; no intervention could mend you. You are the devils of the earth."

That should have knocked him, but his smile only widened.

"I got away with so much," he laughed. "You'll never catch us all."

I think he had accepted his fate and wanted to get the final word in. To try and shake them. He turned to face Lawrence as much as he could with Marianne's hand cutting off his airways. "This what you wanted then? Little tranny. You snitch on your mates to get new ones? Happy now? Freak." He turned back to Marianne. "You talk about having trust issues; do you even know if that's a boy or a girl? Can you trust someone who can't even be honest about what they are. I killed a few humans, yeah. But they were gonna die anyway. Mortals are pathetic. At least I'm not *delusional*—"

He didn't finish. Mars was like a flash, thrusting a blade straight through the guy's chest, silencing him as Marianne backed away and watched his body slip down the blade that had embedded into the wall. A second later, Mars dropped the blade and jumped back, arms flying up as if they'd touched molten lava; they covered their mouth in shock, fingers trembling.

"I... I didn't. Oh, Marianne. I'm sorry. I didn't... I couldn't."

Eyes wide, Lawrence stood as he bit the back of his hand.

Marianne didn't look directly at Mars as she addressed them, but her message was clear. "Don't apologise. You haven't even killed him. The heart doesn't mean anything to the parasite." Then she stepped forward towards the Turned, who still grinned despite losing a lot of blood, his smile hauntingly wide.

"Nice try, little girl," he said, watching Mars.

"Oh, shut up." Marianne pulled out her own blade and slashed his throat, deep enough to sever the nerves and arteries. His head flopped to the side and—

I gagged and pulled away from the door, cursing myself for making a noise. A moment later, the door swung open, and Marianne hauled me up, eyes blood-red. I let her pull me to a stand while awaiting my own death. But all she did was stare at me, breathing heavily.

"Ben?" I heard Mars' voice, and a second later, they were at Marianne's side in the doorway. "Oh god, Ben. I'm sorry you had to... oh god." They pulled me from Marianne's hands, and she let go. Mars embraced me, holding my head tightly to their chest and pressing a kiss to my forehead—which felt rather odd, but after what I'd just seen, I don't think any of us were thinking straight. Mars' protective instincts kicked in.

"Get him somewhere safe," was all Marianne said. I don't know who she was talking about, me or Lawrence, but I must have passed out because the next thing I remember was getting home, rushing up the stairs, and jumping in the shower.

Casper was in the living room, working on his essay. I didn't tell him anything.

The next day, news spread that Lawrence had run away.

Casper

"We're going to look for the kid then?" I said, discussing the disappearance of Lawrence with a fellow Thorn, Elise.

"He's technically an adult. I think he just died young. Pretty sure he said he was nineteen."

"Still a kid, though. And he's on his own." It was a few days after Marianne reported him missing. No one knew much about him; he'd only been taken under her wing a couple of months prior. He was barely newer to the group than we were.

"He was kinda weird and didn't talk much. I think he preferred being alone. Also, people said they think he was actually a girl. He had girly features."

"Is that so?" I looked at her, stunned at the words that had left her mouth. "And his gender matters because?"

Elise shook her hands in defence. "Oh my god, no; I didn't mean that. I'm not transphobic or anything. That's just what people said. No one really got to know him."

"Riiight..." I let my eyes roll visibly before turning away from her. It was the typical ignorance I encountered way too often. People needed to learn when to keep their mouths shut.

I went to join Ben, who was sitting with Mars, playing cards. He'd been quiet the last few days, but whenever I asked him about it, he brushed it off.

I comically leaned on the back of Ben's chair. "Whatcha doin'?"

"Trying to get him into a money free game of poker," Mars jested.

"And I am failing miserably," Ben added slowly, eyes focused on his cards.

"I wouldn't even know where to start," I admitted.

I figured I was interrupting, so I left them and headed back to the house, where Fran lounged cross-legged on the sofa with her girlfriend's head in her lap, slowly curling her fingers through Maddie's hair. I poked my head around and greeted them with a silent wave and nod—I think Maddie was asleep.

Now, I'm not a conspiracy theorist. I don't *generally* dwell on things out of my control, but all I could think about was Lawrence and how I was going to find him. I had very little to go off, only a vague description compiled from multiple sources. I'd probably seen him around; this familiarity was in the back of my mind that I couldn't shake, but where could I begin? He wasn't from around here, so as far as we were concerned, he might have gone home. But Marianne was adamant that finding him was quite important; she said he was vulnerable. I thought about how I'd feel if I'd been turned in my first week of getting to the country and how scary and terrifying it would have been, not to mention how daunting it was anyway in a place like this. I didn't know anything about Lawrence, like his age or hometown, but I wanted to find him. Call it a gut feeling.

I had to try.

My first port of call was our favourite pub, where we sometimes gigged. Everyone seems to know everyone in these places.

I sat at the end of the bar; the building was empty at this time of day. I started with a soda then pulled the bartender, Gary, for a chat.

"You're gonna think I'm insane, but if I describe someone to you, can you wrack your brain for me?"

Gary laughed but promised to try his best.

"Young white guy, about five-seven, maybe a little taller in boots. Long brown curly mullet, lots of scarves, and coloured pieces—

"A nar who you're talking about."

It definitely shouldn't have been that easy.

"You do?"

"Yeah, you doubt me, Casper." Gary winked, then put down the glass he was drying. "New to town, I think. Came in a few times, once with a group of seedy-looking blokes, and the rest of the times alone. Sat in the corner. Ordered tap water. Definitely would've ID'd him; he looked about twelve."

"So, you know him? Lawrence?"

"Couldn't name 'im from Adam, but I remember him. If the clothes weren't enough, his order was. Nee one gans into a bar, orders tap water, then sits alone unless they want attention. Why are you asking anyway? He a mate of yours?"

I shook my head. "Nah, I just heard a few things and think he might be in trouble."

"Ah, a see. Gimme two secs."

Gary disappeared, and I downed the rest of my drink. A few moments later, he returned with a woman.

"Tracy might be able to help, says she's spoken to the kid."

"Aye, threw the little bugger out the other week, asked for ID, and he got all cocky as he weren't drinking, but we have to kick kids out by nine—licensing laws, ya nar." Tracy tilted her head, chewing her gum. "He alright?"

I shrugged, still getting used to the mackem accent. "I don't know; I hope so. Did you speak to him at all?"

"Oh aye, proper Manchester kid. He tried to tell me he didn't need to show me ID as if he were in charge. Sneaky little bastard."

"Ye let the lad stay though," piped up a guy from the other end of the bar.

"Ah did not." Tracy got all defensive, but her mask slipped slightly. She avoided looking at Gary.

"Sorry. I shouldn't get involved." The guy returned to his pint.

"Ah swear ah kicked 'im out." She finally turned to Gary, but he just laughed and shrugged.

"As long as ye didn't serve 'im, I couldn't care less."

The tensions had risen but I kept silent. I had all I needed, because when Tracy told me her story, a light bulb went off in my head. Lawrence had Manipulated her.

I was a vampire too.

"You've got cameras?"

"Aye."

"What was the date when this happened?"

. . .

THAT WAS my first attempt at getting my way, and despite the initial guilt I felt, I was doing it for the greater good. I wasn't even doing anything *wrong,* per se. I did what I felt was necessary. Gary took me up to the office and showed me how to work the CCTV playback. We went to the night in question first, and then I asked him to leave. He didn't question me.

I had to zoom in and slow the recordings. It took me a while, but I found him sitting exactly where Tracy said he'd be. He wandered over to his spot and sat down, back half to the camera, and crossed his legs on the booth. He wasn't *doing* anything but sitting and looking around.

I skipped forward to the part where Tracy went over, and I watched the interaction closely, trying to see if I could make out the Manipulation through the camera. It was a hushed and brief conversation but then Lawrence seemed to get more defensive, raising his arms. He looked like he was going to get up and leave but stared her down and tilted his head. A second later, Tracy patted him on the back, smiled and walked away. *There. That part. Gotcha.*

But it wasn't over. I needed to know who he'd been in with before. Who were the 'seedy' people Gary had mentioned?

I replayed days of footage but decided I would have to Manipulate once again if I wanted to keep my sanity. I called for Gary and asked if he could remember what day Lawrence came in for the first time. He really had to think back to figure it out, but we landed on a rough date and time.

I had a gut feeling but didn't connect the dots at first.

Of course, he came in with my killers.

I watched the footage of them all entering and felt like I was watching a scene from Lost Boys. Lawrence trailed after them like a puppy, and after they all got served by being loud and boisterous, they sat in the same booth and drank. Lawrence didn't seem to open his mouth once, at least not at first. He glanced around as if scared someone would see him. Then, I watched one of them slip something into their drink and take a swig, offering the glass to Lawrence, who refused at first, but they persisted. The three of them were on the other side of the table, all goading him to drink. He gave in eventually, and I watched him cough and splutter at the contents. The three laughed and aggressively tapped him on the back.

He wasn't *with* them. He was a runaway who fell into the wrong crowd. That was clear.

My final date to look at was *that night*. The night we gigged at the venue, and the Turned followed us. I didn't want the reminder but needed to know if Lawrence was there, too.

I spotted the Turned rather quickly; after all, I could remember where they always stood. Lawrence was not with them, and I believed I was simply at a dead end. Of course, he wasn't with them; he was a Thorn by that point.

But then, I found him.

It was a 'blink and you'd miss it' moment, but there he was in the shadows. Arms folded and back against the far wall beside the toilets, his eyes flitting from the stage to the Turned and back again.

He knew something.

I pulled my seat closer to the computer screens and leaned forward, catching every detail. What if...

I watched the three of us pack up and wave goodbye to Fran, who left in the opposite direction; then when Ben and I decided to leave his guitar there overnight before leaving through the fire exit door around the back.

Lawrence had disappeared by that time, as had the Turned. But then I saw them—all three of them—laughing and egging each other on. They followed us, and two minutes later, Lawrence left through the exact same door. I paid close attention as his face flicked to the camera, as if he was worried about being followed. He looked *terrified*.

He knew what was going to happen.

I needed to find this boy.

Everyone said Marianne saved us, but she wasn't in the cemetery.

Lawrence was.

Why didn't he tell us? Why didn't anyone tell us?

Interview excerpt: March 2013

GRAHAM HOBBS: Let's not beat around the bush. Lawrence Marigold. We are honoured to finally talk with you. You've given us permission to ask you whatever we want—no topics off-limits. So, let's begin with this. What's it like being a missing person for years, only to come back the way you did?

Lawrence: Hmm, well... where do I begin?

Casper

August 2012

"TELL ME AGAIN: why did we pick Manchester as the place to show our faces?" Fran was in the back of the van, holding a compact mirror before her. I sat in the front while Ben drove; Mars and Maddie were squished in the back, along with the instruments and amps. We were definitely going to get pulled over.

"I just thought it would be nice. We've not been for a while, and we seemed to have quite a few fans here." I was partly telling the truth, but the other reason? I believed Lawrence was back in his hometown. It only made sense. Of course, Ben knew the real reason; there was no point in hiding anything from him. He agreed we should find Lawrence and take him back to the Thorns where he'd be safe. Mars figured it out the second I suggested the location. There was no need to discuss the details; they filled in the blanks.

I'd googled missing persons in Manchester and the surrounding area and figured because of his age and the fact he was alone, he might have been reported missing.

But boy, did I get a shock.

One of the first articles that popped up was one from early 2011: the unsolved disappearance of Lauren Marigold, the troubled seventeen-year-old who ran from their adoptive auntie. The plea that stood out the most was from the teen's birth mother, who, in nearly every sentence, used the word 'she' or 'daughter' or 'little girl.' It was obvious then, and as I dug deeper, the whole story unfurled.

Lawrence was kicked out of his home when he was twelve. His mother was abusive, an alcoholic, who had a string of partners whom neighbours and friends all described as 'terrifying.'

His auntie took him in and got custody of him, helping him begin his journey as a boy. The facts about Lawrence as an individual dwindled after that. Still, schoolteachers reported him as a 'rowdy kid,' who struggled to listen and make friends, often getting into fights and even being suspended once.

Lawrence ran away not long before his eighteenth birthday and had not been spotted since.

His auntie begged for his safe return; his mother begged for attention.

You see, the thing was, all the publicly available photos of the kid were old school photos of an awkward teen, forced into feminine clothing with near buzzcut hair. No one would recognise him now, but despite everything this kid had been through, I smiled. He'd done exactly what he wanted to. No one was ever going to find Lauren because Lauren never existed.

I'd shown Ben the articles and he understood how serious it was that we find him.

"You're so sure Lawrence ran back home, after all this? Why?" he asked.

"I just am." Though really, I had nothing else to go off.

"Hey, we were in Manchester when he disappeared, remember?" he said, scrolling through the article.

I actually hadn't linked the dates up, but he was right. We had been. Huh.

But here we were, back in Manchester, playing our first gig since the beginning of the year, and I was going to save Lawrence.

"WE CAN TAKE a shortcut through this street to get to that café, I think." Ben held his phone like a map, turning the whole device north. We'd dropped our kit off at the venue then left Maddie and Fran to explore the city whilst Mars wandered off to an art gallery. Ben wanted to go to a queer coffee shop and buy gay coffee that robbed you blind. (I sort of wanted to go as well, honestly.)

"Yeah, I think that's just the roads; we're on foot, so can cut through that alleyway." My sense of direction was rubbish, too.

We got to the café no quicker than the route we initially decided to take, but the scenery was enjoyable enough for us not to care. We weren't public with our relationship yet, but this city was one of the places where I felt safest just sitting close to Ben, slipping my hand in his under the table. It was the little things that made all the difference.

It was a lovely day. Calm. Freeing.

Well, almost.

I didn't tell Ben; I didn't want to worry him, but I'd had the weirdest feeling we were being followed ever since we'd left the venue. Every time I turned, there was no one there, but call it instinct—heightened senses or whatnot—there was something, and I couldn't shake it.

I was right, though. He knew we'd be here today. Lawrence. So why did he run?

We left the café, following the sound of a commotion around the corner, until we reached a side street filled with waste bins, the type you see in downtown cities between tall buildings with fire escape stairs. The perpetrators threw something, the victim cowering away.

I could not believe the coincidence. I'd come all the way here to find him, and there he was, waiting, following us. But lord did I wish we could have found him in a safer scenario.

"Pin it down; get it!" Two of the attackers held Lawrence down by the arms, leaving no room to struggle, whilst the other one dove down to straddle him, yanking at his top to rip open the fabric.

Ben was already on the attacker, his arm over his shoulder, pulling him back until they lost balance and fell into the wall behind them. I moved next, pushing the other two away and growling at them to leave. They ran in an instant, leaving their victim on the floor in shock.

I looked at Lawrence, who didn't speak a word, but his eyes told me he knew exactly who I was. He looked terrified and held the torn fabric of his shirt up to his chest. I saw the scar, though. One long scar spanned the width of his clavicles and made a sharp turn all the way down to his left nipple. A wound.

Fuck.

I remembered.

The alleyway.

The figure.

The blood.

Of course, Lawrence followed us. He'd known us this whole time.

I staggered back, struck by the memories. I'd forgotten about the third attacker, but Ben made quick work of twisting his arm and sending him away with no memory.

I feared maybe I was losing my mind. Everything happened at once.

"Lawrence!" Ben ran over to help him up, but Lawrence ignored him, watching only me.

He stood at full height and stepped closer, brushing Ben off.

"You followed me," he said.

"You followed *me*," I managed to reply, also finding my feet.

Lawrence cocked his head and took a deep breath. "Okay, you got me." He held up his hands in surrender and let the remnants of his t-shirt fall with newfound confidence.

Ben moved to stand between us. "What's going on?"

"Lawrence has been following us this whole time. He came up to Durham to find us. I'm right, aren't I?" I looked to Lawrence, who only then let his smile fade.

"I came up to Durham for a holiday," he asserted.

"On your own, with no plans, after running away from home and being marked as a missing person?"

Lawrence clearly didn't know how much research I'd done. He hesitated.

"Lawrence, it's okay now," Ben moved in front of him and shrugged off his shirt, handing it to Lawrence and leaving himself in nothing but a thin vest top. Lawrence slowly accepted and covered himself up, though I could not take my eyes off his scar.

"Thanks for helping me," he said, looking at the ground.

"I think we all need a drink. You've got some explaining to do."

WE HEADED to the nearest bar and made our way to the quietest spot we could find, where no one would notice us.

Lawrence threw himself in the booth with his back to everyone, leaving the seat opposite free for me and Ben. Lawrence sat under a spotlight that highlighted how young he looked.

"I'm a man, if you were confused," he said harshly, reading into my stare.

"We weren't confused," Ben insisted. Lawrence shrugged. He had a very defensive aura, but I couldn't blame him.

"What do you want to ask me then?" He rested both arms on either side of the booth in feigned confidence. I adjusted myself for comfort.

"Well, to begin with, we wanted to make sure you were okay."

He nodded slowly. "Happens all the time. Drug crowds and stuff. A lot of bad business."

I looked at Ben as a reaction to how nonchalant Lawrence had been. I paused before asking my next question.

"I then wanted to ask you why you came to Durham. And I want the *truth*."

Lawrence inhaled deeply, then looked away as if he didn't hear me.

"It's okay, Lawrence. We're not mad. We want to protect you," Ben tried.

"I don't need protecting," he snapped, glaring at us.

"That might be true, but you ran away for a reason," I said. Ben shifted beside me; I wasn't sure why. Lawrence also noted Ben's movement.

"I do not belong with those people," he admitted. "I'm not a saviour, protector, or guardian. I'm just myself, and I don't need a group to watch over me."

"Clearly." I didn't mean the bluntness.

"I prefer it here." He changed his answer.

"Where you're legally declared missing?"

Lawrence smirked at that, an unhinged look in his eyes. "They'll never find me."

I was running out of ways to get him to talk. It seemed he wasn't one for sharing.

Ben leaned forward. "You brought the Thorns to us then helped catch those Turned, didn't you?"

Lawrence swallowed deeply, then sucked his bottom lip. "I wasn't going to let them get away with it," he deadpanned.

"But you saved so many people because of that. You could do so much more with us!" Ben beamed.

Lawrence's face didn't change. "I told you, I'm not a hero."

"That night when we—

"Stop!" he shouted it loud enough for me to stop anyway, but I sensed the attempted Manipulation in his voice. *Why won't he let us thank him? Why would he let Marianne take all the credit?* His eyes burned holes in mine.

Lawrence cleared his throat. "I'm not coming back with you if that's what you were hoping."

I felt the disappointment sink low in my gut. I had hoped we could maybe bring him back, to let him start anew and have a safe life with us all.

"You live on the streets, don't you?" My last attempt.

"I get by."

"But you get into fights; you get into crowds that put you in danger. You're vulnerable."

"I'd prefer it if you didn't insult me, Casper Murphey." He raised his brow, but I refused to back down.

"But I'm not wrong. There's no shame in admitting that."

"I don't want your life!" Lawrence shouted. He slammed a fist into the table, drawing attention from the surrounding tables.

I took in a deep breath and quietened my tone. "You knew we were going to be here today, though, didn't you? You were following us. You clearly want something from us."

"I..." He didn't finish.

"Can I clear these away from you, gents?" A bartender slipped around the corner and took away the two empty glasses already on our table. We looked at them and smiled in thanks, waiting until they left before continuing the conversation.

"You what?" I tried. I didn't mean to be this forward, but I'd waited months for this meeting. I needed to understand him.

"I like your music." He looked only at me when he said this.

"Oh." He was being honest; I could tell. Ben sensed it, too.

"I found your stuff on YouTube, bought your first single and played it on my aunt's hi-fi. I came to see you. The first time you played here? I was there. Front row. You guys were incredible. I followed you up to Durham because I wanted to hear you play again. Plans changed. Those guys found me and thought they could use me, but I wanted nothing to do with them. I knew they were Manipulating you, Casper, and that night, I had a bad gut feeling. I like you guys."

I was stunned but pleased he was telling the truth. Before I could open my mouth, he continued.

"And I know you're going to want the missing details; I suppose I owe you that much. A few nights before my eighteenth birthday, I was out getting drugs or whatever—not important— but I was set up. It was a trap. The fuckers got me and turned me. Poor little Lawrence left in a gutter. I woke up the next morning believing I'd overdosed. Then, I realised rather quickly that I was dead. There was blood all over my body. I had no desire to return home to my auntie, so, of course, being the idiot I am, I went looking for the guys who turned me. I found them two days later, on the day I became a true adult. They were dealing at a house party, and then I watched them head over to a pub. I followed them, and they found me, but instead of helping me, they attacked me and left me to bleed out in an alleyway, holding my entire chest wall in my hands. Yes, Casper. It was me. I didn't want you to remember... I'm sorry."

Well, shit.

"I can't ever let my auntie know who I am. She doesn't deserve that. It's too late to run back to her now; I've been dead for over a year."

I was lost for words.

"But no, I'm sorry guys. I will not be returning to Durham with you. I saw you there and got into way more trouble than I'd hoped. I'm not a good person."

Ben shook his head faster and faster until I spotted the tears in his eyes. "Don't say that, Lawrence. You saved our lives. You are not like them."

Lawrence laughed. "I wish."

A beat of silence passed.

"You need a community, Lawrence. We can give you that, keeping you on the right path," Ben insisted.

"I wish it was that simple, Ben. But it's not. I don't belong with the righteous."

"Will you at least let *us* help you, me and Casper? Here..." He pulled a pen from his back pocket and began writing on the napkin. "Here's my number. Will you call us if you ever need help? We might be far away, but we're always there to talk if you ever need us."

Lawrence accepted the napkin but didn't say a word.

"Will you at least think about it? We're in the city for another two days," I said.

Lawrence slowly nodded, chewing the inside of his mouth.

We talked some more, and while the conversation was limited, it wasn't a complete failure. We thanked him for what he did for us, but he kept brushing it off and changing the subject. As the chat drew to a close, Ben stood to pay the tab, while I went to the bathroom. I knew Lawrence would leave without saying goodbye, but I only hoped he would listen to our offer and reconsider.

"Surely his aunt deserves to know he's alive?" Ben pushed as we headed back into town.

Yeah, I suppose she did. But that wasn't my place. I barely knew the kid; he clearly had a complicated relationship with *everything* and definitely wasn't going to listen to us.

"It's a shame. He helped the Thorns; he knows what's right. Why is he continuing to run?"

"I don't know." I looked at the sky. "I really don't know."

I HAD a friend called Danny back in middle school who ran away from home. No one understood why, and it wasn't until the police finally found him that they began an investigation into his home life. The school never suspected anything; no one knew what he was going through, including me, but everything changed the day we all found out. He was a quiet boy, a shy but friendly kid. We weren't best friends, but we got on well in class. The services got involved and he ended up being transferred out of state I believe. I never heard from him again, but teachers told me he was in a better place with a family who would love him. You see, if you didn't have their address or home phone number as kid in those days, you had virtually no way of contacting them. It was as if they never existed at all.

I wish I'd spoken to Danny about his life. I wish I understood before it was too late.

I wish I could save Lawrence.

"YOU GUYS GET LOST OR SOMETHING?" Fran was already on the stage with her guitar, messing around with her amps for the sound check. "You said four, right?"

Ben pulled his 'oops' face, then hopped onto the stage, tying his hair back into a low, loose bun. Hot, but extremely irrelevant to this story.

We ran the soundcheck and tweaked a few things here and there, but decided we were happy and right on schedule. We headed out for some more drinks whilst the venue was getting set up.

All evening, I couldn't erase the image of Lawrence in the alley

—both times. The *creature* I saw last year, yet brushed off as a reoccurring nightmare, was real. And it was Lawrence. He followed us. The kid was *afraid,* no matter what he said or did.

I couldn't leave the city without him.

THE SET WAS ALRIGHT. We didn't sell out, but we didn't expect to. We hadn't been on hiatus for anywhere near as long as it felt, and plus, we weren't *that* big of a band. We were still finding our feet as a three piece.

Of course, I scanned the crowd for Lawrence—how could I not have? He said he liked us and wanted to hear us play. It was no coincidence he was attacked right beside the building we were in. Manchester was a big place; I don't believe in coincidences *that* large. So, why did he act like he didn't want our help? The kid made no sense.

Ben kept turning back to me during the show, winking or smiling in reassurance. He knew what was on my mind and how invested I was in saving Lawrence.

AFTER A DAY of sightseeing and drinking, we lay in bed the following evening while I tried to keep my mind off the subject of Lawrence. But knowing we'd be leaving the city the next morning *without* Lawrence cut deep into my chest. I just wanted to show my appreciation for what he did. I wanted to help him find a family, as we were beginning to ourselves with The Thorns.

"We will come back as soon as we can," Ben said, gently rubbing his hand over my chest. He leaned in close, a comforting embrace. He read me like a book.

"He's just a kid," I said, staring at the ceiling.

"He's nineteen, at least," Ben half-joked with a distant laugh.

"He's lonely and takes drugs from strangers on the streets. I don't care if he's like us; he's not going to live much longer living that life." My honesty frightened me, but there was no point holding back now.

"We'll save him, I promise. Whatever it takes," Ben reassured me.

Save him like he saved us.

MARS, Maddie, and Fran met us for breakfast the next morning before we loaded up the rest of the van. I walked with Ben before we left, trailing through the city centre without a destination in mind.

"I just don't want to leave him," I kept saying.

Ben reminded me that he had given Lawrence his number, even though we both understood Lawrence didn't strike us as the 'getting in contact' type. He couldn't even let his aunt know he was alive.

It was no good. We were chasing dead ends. Lawrence wouldn't magically show up; if anything, he would be deliberately hiding from us. He made his intentions very clear.

We reluctantly headed back, a little later than scheduled, but it couldn't be helped. Our journey home was less enthusiastic than the way there, and I knew it was because of me. My negative energy really choked out the inside of the van. The saddest thing was, we couldn't even explain anything to Francesca; she couldn't know.

Not yet, anyway.

Ben
September 2012

WHEN MADDIE ENTERED her final year at uni and Fran moved in with her, Casper and I found a house with all the money we'd saved—and a little extra from Marianne. In the meantime, we did... relatively nothing. We had our first proper long-winded argument—nothing important, in the grand scheme of things—and I don't even remember how it started. I think it was just a snowball of emotions until one of us snapped. I tipped things over the edge, which I was getting rather good at. With everything sinking in, like my immortality and my ever-lasting need for animal blood, I think it just got a bit much, and I caved. It's ironic, really, since I chose this life for myself, but we always love to blame ourselves for things we can't change. I suppose that's human nature. Something I'm glad I still understood.

We argued about the band, too—petty stylistic things we normally agreed on. I went in a huff, stormed out of the house, but then stormed straight back once I realised how selfish I was to the person I loved the most.

The Thorns really helped us with our teething problems, but we'd essentially settled into our undead life as if we'd always been like that—dead. We took small supplements morning and night and found our cravings never grew during the day. Marianne showed her face slightly less than I'd hoped, but Mars always assured us she had too much to deal with, and sometimes preferred to be alone, which I needed no explanation for. I understood.

WE GOT TO KNOW CARMEN; Marianne's human adopted daughter. No one ever explained the full reason why she was part of The Thorns or why she was still human, but Mars summarised it as 'a horrific accident that Marianne could never forgive herself for,' which was enough for me to stop prying. She reminded me a bit of Fran, the way she carried herself and made it clear she would always win an argument, but she was almost as reclusive as her mother. I hoped maybe one day I could get to know the pair of them better.

I spent a lot more time with Mars alone, learning about their life before The Thorns. They often visited their parents, who lived just outside the city. They shared their art and fear of academics, their stubbornness to comply to expectations. They also spoke at great length about figuring out their pansexuality, and it brought me great comfort to understand how *not* alone me and Casper really were. Fran always had this confidence about her preferences that I could never embrace; maybe hers was just a front, too, but the way Mars described their journey flicked a switch in me.

I met their sister, Poppy, when she came to visit for the day, and remembered finding it so odd they were actually related. They were polar opposites. Where Mars was outgoing and bubbly, Poppy was shy and reserved and could never keep eye contact. She spoke little, but Mars spoke highly of her, embarrassing her a few times with the endless compliments. She was sweet, and she meant a lot to Mars. She also had a tree nut allergy like me, and her extensive allergy list was another explanation as to why she didn't like going out a great deal. I wasn't sure if my allergy still stood now, but I hadn't dared to test the theory.

I wished I'd grown up with a sibling, someone to share my life with—a shoulder to lean on when things got too much. Poppy was 'the best sister you could ask for' and was planning to study medicine: 'the brains of the Rosario family,' Mars insisted.

When Casper wasn't around, I would go to Mars with the things plaguing my mind. They were just so natural to talk to, and I felt comfortable confiding in them. We were in safe hands.

Life was beginning to feel so *easy*.

Life was going to be okay.

Then, one night in late September, there was a knock at the door.

. . .

"Who the fuck is calling at this time?" Casper shouted from the living room. I was reluctant to answer at first, but when the bell rang twice, I felt like it was probably something we should answer.

I was right.

I opened the door slightly, still attached to the chain, and there, stood drenched in the rain, was Lawrence Marigold, shivering with nothing but a sodden canvas backpack hanging from his left hand.

"Can I come in?"

"What the hell? Jesus Christ!" Casper was right behind me as I beckoned Lawrence inside. Casper slammed the door shut behind us to keep the heat in while I ushered Lawrence into the living room, taking his bag and noting his scent of cold air and cigarettes. His face was flushed bright red, his nose a frozen purple. I sat him down on the couch without speaking a word and knew Casper was already running upstairs for towels and clean clothes.

Lawrence fidgeted a few times to get comfortable, but once he did, he lowered his head into his hands and sighed.

I didn't really know what to say. I was stunned.

"Sorry," he muttered. I didn't properly hear him at first, but then he said it again, louder, and tipped himself back, relaxing into the chair.

"It's... okay. You don't need to apologise." I didn't even have to think about my response.

"Nah, I do, especially because of what I'm about to ask you."

"What?" I sat back, stress rising within me.

Lawrence looked at me with heavy eyes and lowered his head, his brows disappearing into his fringe. "Wait for Casper."

I nodded and rubbed my hands down my trousers in awkwardness, still shocked by his sudden entrance. I definitely wasn't expecting it, but at the same time, I was massively relieved. The kid was alive and well. Not dead in a back alley in Manchester where the police would find him, identify him, and go to his aunt with the cruel news. (I'd imagined that scene playing out numerous times.)

"Right, I brought a few different things for you to choose from," Casper appeared at the door with a towel and a bunch of *my* clothes.

"Oh, thanks." Lawrence stood and took them from him, sitting back down with the heavy pile, seemingly waiting for permission to go and change.

"If you need to stay tonight, we have a spare room," was the next thing Casper said. It seemed too soon to offer, but I would have eventually asked him.

"Oh, well... actually, that's what I wanted to talk to you about."

We were all ears.

"I need somewhere to stay for a while."

Casper nodded slowly and silently with his arms folded. He sucked in his teeth and looked up. "I was going to offer that, too." *'But I should probably confer with Ben first,'* was what he didn't add but was definitely thinking.

It made me look like I had no choice but to agree, though I would never have said otherwise. Lawrence would have refused to return to The Thorns. We were essentially his only option.

"You're staying in Durham, then?"

Lawrence looked away when he nodded. "I suppose I am."

"What happened? What made you change your mind?" Casper went straight to prying. I always admired his bluntness; any words lingering on my tongue were long out of his mouth.

Lawrence took a deep breath and then flopped back onto the sofa, his eyes shut and his lips turning up into a grin. "You guys smoke?"

"What's that got to do with..."

I cut Casper off by extending a cigarette packet to Lawrence, whose eyes widened as he pulled out his lighter. I brushed past Casper to grab my ashtray from the bench in the hallway and mouthed a 'just this once' promise to him, then I went to lift one of the windows up.

Lawrence pushed the clothes to one side and lit up, taking a long drag. "That's better. I ran out on the way, and everywhere's closed on a Sunday night."

We sat in silence for a beat.

"But yeah. You'll want my story again." Lawrence cleared his throat. "I'm kind of a wanted man."

"Weren't you always?" Casper said, quizzical.

Lawrence snorted. "Well, technically, yeah. But now I can't Manipulate myself out of this situation. Big vamps. Lots of contacts. I may or may not have pissed them off. *Big time.*"

My eyes widened; Casper spoke for the both of us. "You weren't followed here, were you?" he asked, stress levels rising.

Lawrence took another drag of his cigarette. "I'm not stupid. I am, however, in need of a little bit of shelter for an unknown amount of time while the heat cools off and I can return home. If you don't mind." He cleared his throat again.

"You can stay here for as long as you need to." I felt it was important that statement came from me then, to clear the air between me and Casper.

"And we can get The Thorns to sort out your problem. They're good at that," Casper added, but Lawrence's face dropped at the mention of the vampire group.

"No," he said, anger tainting his voice.

Realising his mistake, Casper nodded and cleared his throat.

"I want to get this clear," said Lawrence. "I came to you two cos you said I could always contact you. I found your home and decided you were my best option. We're kind of similar, in a way, and I like you. But if you think for a second that I will set foot in that place once more, you are seriously mistaken. I'm not a Thorn, never will be, and I will leave this place without ever coming back if you even *think* about telling *Marianne* that I'm here, you got it? Capeesh?"

"Understood." We said in unison, slightly taken aback by the kid's shift in tone. I needed to stop thinking of him as a kid—he really wasn't.

Casper broke the silence again by offering Lawrence time to get changed, showing him to our spare room (thank the lord for fully furnished houses) and bathroom. He shouted for me to turn the boiler on, and I did, flicking on the kettle, too.

I stared at the wall for a while. Everything I'd planned for the evening had all gone down the drain.

I went back into the living room with two mugs of tea and caught Casper with an aerosol disinfectant spray in hand. He spritzed it around the room like he was trying to catch a bug.

"Sorry about that," I said in the doorway. I think I startled him slightly, but his shoulders instantly relaxed.

"I figured it would be the only way he would have talked. The boy's stubborn, I'll tell you that." He spoke quickly, with an edge of stress. I waited for him to sit before handing him his tea. I was successfully weaning him off coffee and onto the good stuff.

"I'm still trying to process it all. He just figures out where we live and rocks up at eleven o'clock at night? It feels like he's put a chip in us or something," Casper half laughed, still visibly stressed.

"I'm aware we barely know him, but we want to help him, Casper. He's *alive*," I voiced our thoughts aloud; Casper nodded in agreement.

"I just keep thinking about how I would have felt if this had happened to me when I first arrived in the country, like what could have happened, and how scared I would have been. Lawrence has been doing it for years, and he's only now admitting he needs help. He's crazy." Casper played with his lips, an anxious habit of his.

"He's strong is what he is," I said.

"We are gonna have to do something about those 'big guys,'

though. Kid can't hide forever. And if they are who he says they are, it will literally be *forever.*"

"Yeah, I don't think he thought that through, did he?"

"The Thorns will sort it." Casper stared into the unlit fireplace.

"I think we can work on him, you know," I said.

"What, with The Thorns?"

I nodded. Lawrence would learn, in time. I had faith he would. He was a good kid; I could see it in him.

"And then he can lead The Thorns right to them himself; we won't have to hide anything from him."

Casper considered my proposal. "It's gonna take time, but maybe you're right."

"I'm always right." I winked.

"WHAT DO you guys do for blood around here? I can't really be bothered to go out hunting tonight but I'm feeling a little peckish." Lawrence appeared at the door about half an hour later, his hair freshly washed, wearing my tartan Christmas pyjamas, the legs a little long on him. He smelled of chamomile.

"Fridge, straight ahead of you as you enter the kitchen. If there's no bags in there, try the freezer in the utility room, you'll have to heat it up," Casper directed, but Lawrence was already on his way into the other room before he had a chance to finish.

We listened for a struggle, but a minute later, he was joining Casper on the sofa opposite me with a half pint glass of blood, sucking it from a straw. We watched him in silence as he gulped it down. He was *hungry* and so very casual about it. This was normal to him then.

"Finished?" Casper raised a brow, trying to keep a straight face as Lawrence put down the empty glass with a satisfied gasp.

"Bit dry, but it'll do. Bird blood, right?" Lawrence sat back and lifted his leg, resting an ankle over his knee.

I think I just point-blank laughed at that point—the absurdity of it all. We were still getting used to normalising blood drinking. Every time we went hunting for animal blood, I tried to trick myself into believing we were just playing a game and that it wasn't real life. It was easier that way.

"So, you guys are fucking, right? Or are you just incredibly close?" Lawrence blurted. Casper choked on air.

"We—well…" I felt my palms sweat. I'd never had to admit this before. It scared me still, but it was clear Lawrence was like us—one of us—whatever that meant. He would understand.

"Yeah, we're together," Casper spoke for us. I felt the weight rise off my chest.

"Cool." Lawrence went to picking at his nails. "I mean, I knew that. It's pretty obvious if you spend more than five minutes with you both, but I just wanted to check." He looked like he was smirking.

"We don't—you know, we haven't really made it public," I said, my voice oddly quieter than usual. *Are we really that obvious?*

"Oh, guys. Please. I'm not a monster. Your secret is safe with me," he promised comically. I still felt a tad uneasy.

"I mean it," he added, much more sincerely.

"Thanks." I gulped. Hard.

Lawrence winked. "Anyway, everyone thinks Ben and your other lass are hooking up. I like how you're letting it ride. Spicing things up a bit, you know?"

"Are you always this abrupt?" I snapped, shocking them both.

Lawrence sat back and grinned again. "Sorry. I don't normally sit down and talk to people for longer than it takes them to hand me a bag of coke. I can't stay put for long." Lawrence flinched as if he'd been slapped by a ghost. "Wow. That's really sad, isn't it?"

I let out an awkward laugh. "Maybe."

"But you know we can help you, right? We promised you can stay here for as long as needed," Casper said.

"I know. That's why I'm here. I suppose I can admit now that you were both right and that I do need people to be around. Friends. I sort of decided it was you two I needed."

"You're safe now, Lawrence." Casper nudged Lawrence's shoulder. My smile was ever so slightly delayed.

A FEW DAYS WENT BY, with Lawrence keeping to himself. He refused to leave the house, which was understandable yet frustrating, leaving Casper and me to supply more blood to him, elongating our trips around the forest and back lanes. When we'd return, it was obvious he'd been around the house, helping himself to things and leaving trails, but when we'd shout for him, he'd be in his room again, like an antisocial teenager.

"Should I go and speak to him, do you reckon?" I asked Casper as we emptied the grocery bags.

"And say what?"

"I dunno; I just don't want him to think we're ignoring him."

At that, Casper raised his eyebrow. "Us ignoring *him?* You really think that?"

"Well, no. I just..." I didn't know what to say.

Casper sighed, stopping for a moment, and resting his palms on the kitchen counter. "I'll go and speak to him in a bit. Offer him to come down for tea since we're both staying in tonight."

I nodded and finished off unpacking.

As it turned out, Casper's charm worked, and Lawrence agreed to join us for food. We obviously didn't eat much, but every now and again, we'd enjoy sitting down for some small plates, simply to retain some normality. We each had a glass of wine mixed with blood, and we actually *talked.* Albeit forced at first, we eventually ended up having a few interesting conversations—regular, human chit-chat.

But after we cleared the plates, he was back upstairs.

"I'd call tonight a mild success," Casper snorted.

"Mild," I laughed.

Our next thing to deal with was Fran, who was due to join us at our house for a jam session like we did every Friday (though we cancelled the last one for... *reasons*, so we felt bad asking to postpone it again). We saw Fran a lot anyway, but our weekly sessions were a must for our band, the glue keeping us all together.

"Okay, so how do we explain him?" I pointed upstairs after we'd heard some concerning banging noises and heard a shouted apology. "We can't exactly kick him out, and it's not like he'll go unnoticed."

"Your cousin? You look like you could be related... kinda," Casper was clearly only half serious, but I considered it.

"But then I'd have to keep it going for ages and come up with a backstory, too, which I'd be terrible at sticking to. Can't he just be a student or something?" I wasn't sure where I was going with that last suggestion.

"Or we could just tell her everything," Casper said bluntly. I stared at him, open-mouthed.

"What? No. Of course, we can't. We can't let ourselves be known like that." I was panicking.

"We will have to tell her eventually, though. Marianne said we could."

"Did she?" I was clearly not present for that conversation.

Casper turned away from me slightly, his hands on his hips as he chewed his gums. "Well, sorta. She implied it."

I rolled my eyes. "So, no then. She didn't say that."

"Not exactly."

But our solution came to us on a silver platter the very next day.

The day Lawrence joined the band.

. . .

IT WAS MID-AFTERNOON. Casper was out, catching up with a few of his mates. He'd managed to keep in touch with some of the people from his course while I'd shut myself off. The orchestra was always going to be an acquaintance-based thing anyway, and I stuck out like a sore thumb.

He said he wouldn't be back late, but for some reason, I think Lawrence presumed I went with him. I kept myself quiet for a while until I heard him leave his room and head downstairs. I debated what to do; I wanted to talk to him and properly break the ice between us.

But then, I heard it—very faintly, at first, but the sound was unmistakable. He was in our back room, playing my acoustic guitar—beautifully.

I slipped onto the landing and peered over the staircase to where the door was pushed ajar. I heard it properly, then—a song, one I'd never heard before. It was incredible.

I snuck downstairs, scared in case he heard me. I didn't want him to stop.

I got to the door; the music so beautiful I could feel it in my core. I was grinning internally, so strongly my organs ached.

Slowly pushing open the door, I saw him, sitting cross-legged on the floor by the window, his long hair covering his face as he concentrated on the strings. I memorised the melody, already configuring the bass parts in my head, and since he didn't even stop to look at me and just continued as the tune got more rhythmic and hard-hitting, I thought it was worth a try with me joining in.

I walked over and lifted my bass from the stand, sitting opposite him and joining in where it felt best. And we just played. We played for ages—no words—just two boys and the music. And when he finally stopped, we sat in silence for a while and put our instruments aside. I didn't know what to say or how to break the moment. I didn't need to, though, because a second later, Lawrence finally looked up, his eyes full of tears. Leaping forward, he pulled me into a hug. I was startled at first, arms flying out in shock, but then I eased my arms around him and pulled him closer, letting him sob into my shoulder. It was entirely unexpected; I actually felt my chest constrict.

Through his sobbing, he mumbled into my shoulder, "Thank you. I need you guys. I'm sorry it took so long for me to listen."

The emotions rose in my face. I didn't know what to say or how to respond. I didn't pull back; I just waited for him to calm down, giving him as much time as he needed.

He finally looked up and loosened his grip, meeting my eyes as he rubbed his puffy, red face. "If I couldn't Manipulate, I'd have been dead a long time ago. You were the only people I had to turn to, and you were just *there* when I needed you. You listened. I...."

I'd never seen this side of him; he was so human and... afraid. He was scared and finally showed it. Through whatever power, whether it had just been building up or whether it was something to do with the music, he was finally letting his guard down and being *honest*. It shifted something in me until I only had one thing left to say.

"Join us. Join Forever Red. Stay with us," I said.

His face dropped as he processed my request, but then his mouth turned into a half smile, one of disbelief. He sat back slightly. "What? What are you saying?"

I smiled sincerely, feeling my own eyes well up. "It's simple. I want you to join the band. You *get* it. You are so talented; you have a beautiful style and way with sound. You're our missing piece."

"Really? You want me to... no. You're joking."

"I'm not."

"But I'm not a musician... I can't read music; I don't..." He shook his head, confused, but I knew deep down he wanted this. He would work brilliantly with our band. I *knew it*. It clicked. It made sense. He was meant to be with us.

"You are a fucking brilliant musician. And fuck sight reading. I can't do it for shite, either." I laughed as if nothing else mattered. Casper called it my unhinged laugh.

"You're serious?"

"Deadly."

And so, it was simple. We talked to Casper later that night; Lawrence played for us; we played together, and then we introduced him as our fourth member the following day. Technically, we didn't have to lie about anything. We kept the facts the same. Lawrence liked the band, moved to the northeast for a fresh start, and we met with him. It's not too dissimilar to how Fran joined us. We let him stay with us while he found his own place, and everything else was unimportant. Fran loved him instantly.

Our only issue now was how to tell Mars, Marianne—oh, and the rest of the world—that Lawrence Marigold was alive.

Casper

December 2012

We released our first single with Lawrence in the band, which really kicked off the beginning of our *real* career. The long-term one, this time. We were a real band now, one out in the open. Of course, the months leading up to it were rocky. Lawrence joined the band, and after a few weeks of hiding him, we brought Mars back onto the scene and made it clear where he stood. He was one of us now but refused to re-join the Thorns. Marianne immediately sent people to neutralise the threat in Manchester but never spoke about it again. Lawrence didn't need to know the exact details, only that he would be safe to roam freely again. No hiding.

He continued to isolate himself when we weren't in the studio or rehearsing, but we didn't mind. After all, he was allowed his privacy.

At some point in November, he brought a woman back to the house—a much older woman, I noted, though I wasn't there to judge his tastes. She stayed the night, while Ben and I spent the entire time biting our bottom lips, waiting for her to run away screaming. She didn't. Nothing happened. She didn't stay long, though. A few days later, she left the house and returned to her *husband,* as it turned out. So it was Lawrence we should have been worried about instead.

I fell out with Ben over something stupid; all our arguments were. They were never anything serious. I brushed it off as us 'hitting that part in the relationship,' as by that point, we'd been together a few years, and of course, when you properly start living together, you get a little more agitated over the small things. It was to be expected. I think this argument started when I caught Ben snorting something in the bathroom with Lawrence. I nearly threatened to kick Lawrence out for being a bad influence, but then I re-evaluated. Ben was an adult; these things could no longer kill him; they just made him a bit different for a few hours. I think I just didn't like the idea of it. Eventually, Ben admitted he'd used drugs a handful of times over the past few years, before breaking down and apologising, owning up to his stupidity. While I was mad he'd hidden it from me, I confided in Mars and Marianne, who promised there was no evidence of drugs harming our kind. He was immune to their detrimental effects, so I didn't really have a leg to stand on. I just wanted him to be himself and stop hiding from me. He kept going through periods of opening up and then shutting down.

Lawrence said some weird things, too, acting like some sort of prophet with random bouts of wisdom at peculiar times, but I figured it was just his eccentric nature. I don't think he even understood what he was saying half of the time.

Fran really liked Lawrence; in fact, at one point, I could have sworn they got up to something when they thought we weren't looking. Maddie was there, too… it was, well, none of my business. Lawrence had this charm, an air of mystery that I suppose some people liked.

We discussed different ways to publicly introduce Lawrence, you know since he was quite literally presumed dead by half the nation. We'd discussed with Mars if there was a way we could softly Manipulate things for a while so the police wouldn't be on our necks, but any plan we did have crumbled the day someone spotted him with us in Durham—someone who just so happened to know who Lawrence was. The blurry image was posted online, as they always are, and before long, we got wind of it all and started receiving questions. 'Who is the person seen with Forever Red?' 'Lauren Marigold, dead or alive? See the footage here.' You know, that sort of journalistic crap.

Lawrence was unbothered by the reprise of his dead name making the rounds. He laughed whenever it was pointed out, seeming to have already figured out his plan.

"I'm just going to announce myself as publicly as I can and get it over with," he said. "There's no point in pretending. This was always going to happen. It's time, I suppose."

And despite our protests about planning a safer way, Lawrence created a social media profile and announced himself. A PR nightmare. He went from wanting to hide and avoid everything, to being the most talked about person of the day; he even trended on Twitter. Lawrence Marigold was alive and well and had joined a band. He very openly shamed his mother, denounced any relation he had to her, and got in touch with his auntie, inviting her up to talk. I probably would have suggested he didn't introduce himself so abruptly to the only woman in his life who always cared about him, but they must have settled things, though, as she ended up staying with us for a few days. They kept everything on the down low before she travelled back to Manchester, kissing his forehead proudly in our doorway before leaving for the station.

We were heckled by reporters. I think Lawrence knew it would happen, but maybe he thought it would help with the publicity of our band. He wasn't wrong. Our CDs sold more; we gained thousands more followers; it was frightening, but we were on the rise.

Of course, with the harmless media came the more serious one. The police contacted Mars, who came up with this insane but believable story. We were questioned, but regardless of whether we could Manipulate or not, nothing could tie us to his disappearance; it was all his own doing.

<u>Interview excerpt December 2012</u>

GRAHAM HOBBS: Wow. It's been a year for you both then? How are we feeling about the new year? Confident? You're the talk of the music world right now.

Casper: It's all because of Lawrence.

Ben: Yeah, we didn't even have to do anything.

Graham: Lawrence Marigold, the boy who vanished and resurrected as a god.

Casper: That's one way of putting it.

Casper
July 2013

THINGS GOT REALLY crazy at the start of this year when our band saw success like never before. It was quite intense at times. I'd kind of always wanted it; I was proud of us and felt like we had something important to share with our music, but it was probably not the 'boom' I'd expected we'd ever get. I don't blame Lawrence. After all, we invited him into the band, knowing what we'd have to do. The media coverage died down quickly, probably thanks to Mars, but the fans stayed and continued growing.

We recorded our debut album 'Dead World' from December 2012 – May 2013, when the band was at its all-time-high. We gelled so well as a four; Lawrence and Fran worked seamlessly with their riffs and solos; Ben took up a lot more keyboard playing as we experimented with more synth and abstract sounds. He created the most moving soundscapes, where you could *feel* the music right in your very soul.

Everything looked great on paper, but what no one saw was what went on once we left the studio and finished recording—a hairline fracture in our reality, slowly beginning to grow.

Ben's dad cancelled on him more and more, which was beginning to take its toll on Ben. It put him off wanting to do things and halted his pretty smile; his dad's selfishness infuriated me. No matter his excuse, he should have gone above and beyond to ensure he was there for his son, regardless of whether they were biologically related or not. *What was his problem?*

On an increasing number of occasions, I found Ben taking drugs with Lawrence in our home, in alleyways behind bars, anywhere you could think of. I confronted him about it; he broke down and promised to stop, but I'd known him far too long by now to know he didn't mean it. I suggested therapy or counselling —a place where he could vent and speak his mind if he wouldn't open up to me. Ben refused, insisting there were people who needed it a lot more than he did. It was then that I finally understood what the rockstar life really entailed, and it ate away at me bit by bit.

"So, if he promises to clean up, do you think marriage could be on the cards? You know, if this law ends up getting passed. Real traditional marriage. It's looking hopeful, you know. It really is," said Fran.

Fran and I were at one of our weekly meet-ups. It was an important break for us. Whenever we were alone, we could avoid bringing up the band and just be ourselves, talking about normal, mundane things. From my side, it felt important to keep Fran in the loop, ensuring everything was 'normal' to avoid suspicions. From Fran's perspective, I think she liked that we could relate to each other in more ways than we originally believed. We were both stubborn, forward, and from musical families. We were the youngest of our siblings and viewed fame the same way. She even joined the same gym as me, which I was nervous about at first because I hate feeling like I'm being watched or judged when I work out, but she ended up being a great gym buddy. She was insanely strong for her height, and even taught me a thing or two about patience. It was great how well we got on, and a nice change for us both, away from work and relationships; we were just two good friends with similar interests.

On this day, though, we were talking about Ben. We had to.

"I dunno, I mean, I'd want to marry him regardless. I don't ever want to be apart from him, but marriage has always kind of scared me, even before I realised I wasn't straight." It was my truth. I would marry Ben in a heartbeat if I could, but reality stung like a bitch.

"He'll clean up; this is just a blip," Fran promised.

I sipped on my coffee and looked out of the window.

"Hey, Casper, I mean it." She reached out to squeeze my arm; sympathy in her eyes.

"I know. I just don't like it." I gritted my teeth.

"Ben's not...he's not daft. I know him well enough now to be able to say that with confidence. I can try and talk to him, if you'd like?" Fran smiled, trying to get through to me.

She could, but I didn't want her to get involved. I couldn't tell if she actually meant what she said, or if she was lying just to comfort me, because as far as she was aware, this habit could kill them any minute. Of course, this wasn't a usual case though. Ben and Lawrence were vampires, it was a completely different situation, but I would do anything in my power to avoid her getting closer to the truth, for her own safety.

"Do you think it's been since Lawrence joined and the world really started to learn who we are? Maybe it has affected him somehow?" Fran asked.

"Maybe." I returned to staring out of the window, mind distant.

"Or is it Lawrence? Do you think Lawrence is the problem? Cos I can talk to him too... I'm very good at getting through to people, it's my speciality." Fran winked.

"I dunno. We both knew what Lawrence was like when he joined. We knew what we were getting ourselves into." *Dangerous territory.* "He told us, he was very open about his habits right from the start." *Nice save.*

"He's not a bad lad, I just think he needs a bit of guidance. He's already come a long way since he started. I've noticed how much more relaxed he's become. He's young, he'll grow out of his habits the more he stays with us. Ben will be fine, I can make sure of that. Lawrence will straighten out eventually."

Then she laughed into her tea. "Well, you know what I mean. There's nothing straight about this band."

She said it quietly enough for me to break my stoic expression.

⚜

"If they pass the law, would you consider marriage?" I asked Ben the same night, the thought having played on my mind all day.

Ben was the most himself that evening, completely sober and jolly. I was so happy to see him like that, so I thought it was the perfect time to ask.

"Maybe," he said, though it wasn't really the response I'd hoped for. I worried that perhaps I had done something to upset him suddenly.

"Maybe?" I pushed, my chest feeling suddenly tight.

Ben couldn't look me in the eye as he opened the fridge for a blood bag. "I just think marriage is a scary thing, and I haven't really had a great experience with witnessing its effects."

"Hmm." I couldn't blame him for his perspective.

"Plus, we have eternity. We don't have to rush anything." He half smiled, ripping into the sachet and pouring a glass. He handed the first one to me before pouring his own. "We're technically already married." He winked, raising his glass to mine to clink.

Hmm.

⚜

Our song 'Stars for Alex' ended up hitting a mainstream chart, making number 9 on a top radio station, and gaining us the interview of our dreams. If only we'd all remembered it.

Ben barely spoke during the interview, and at one point, he looked seconds away from falling asleep. I prompted conversations about the interview afterwards, making up questions to try and catch him out. It worked.

"Ben, what have you taken?" I closed my eyes, sighing.

"Erm… I—I'm not sure," his eyes rolled.

I stormed away to confront Lawrence and give him a piece of my mind once and for all, but Mars was already there.

"You're out of the band if you keep this up. You do realise the whole country will be listening to this, right?" they said to a disgruntled Lawrence, who was slouched in a comfy chair.

Once within earshot, Mars looked at me, raising their arms as if to say, 'this is hopeless.'

"I'll stop getting Ben involved if that's your main concern." He watched me, his eyelids heavy, but his voice was direct enough.

I didn't know what to say. It was a start, but would it be that straightforward?

HE KEPT HIS WORD, though—quite intensely, too. He actively refused to give Ben anything and even convinced local dealers to refuse him service. I worried that Ben might have been addicted enough to Manipulate the dealers, but as it so graciously turned out, Ben listened and cleaned up almost entirely. Playing him the interview might have also had something to do with it; he was *embarrassed* beyond words. He brought it up and apologised almost every time we were alone. This went on for *weeks,* but I knew he meant it this time.

Fran suggested I ask him to marry me again, but I brushed her off in a panic.

As for Lawrence? Well, Lawrence was Lawrence. He'd been living in the underground world for long enough that his body sort of acclimatised to it. It was bad, but at least he could function during sessions and gigs. He was just a handful to deal with afterwards.

We thought about asking him to leave, even just temporarily to clean himself up, but that was when I realised how much this band meant to him. This was the best thing that had ever happened to Lawrence, and time and time again he promised to never ruin it for any of us.

Ben decided to see his mom for a whole month, all on his own, and when he returned, we were the strongest we'd been in a long time.

Rumours resurfaced that Ben and Fran were dating again because of a demo they released together, yet there was no photographic 'evidence' this time; people just really wanted the rumour to be true.

"We're going to have to tell them at some point, aren't we," said Ben. He turned to look at me, gritting his teeth. It was wintertime, and we'd just lit a fire for the first time that year. We sat in the front room with the TV on, and Ben was on a cushion on the floor between my legs, scrolling on his brand-new smartphone while I played with his curls.

"We will when we're both ready. Are you ready?" I didn't mean for it to sound condescending.

"No. I don't think I am."

I kissed his crown. "Then we'll wait."

Casper
2014

This year all went by in a blur. We looked like we were on the top of the world; we did so many magazine interviews, had our biggest national tour to date, and our music was getting *recognised*. However, we couldn't absorb any of it because we stopped looking after ourselves. The fame was all well and good until we woke up drunk on a couch in some random storage room and went straight back out there, performing again the very same day. Rinse and repeat. Trying to handle the attention was becoming a struggle for us all.

Ben had sworn off drugs, but the four of us began to *drink*. At every venue, we were handed bottle after bottle, pint after pint, and it became our fuel. I remember thinking, was this what being a star was? Is this what it had to be? Was it inevitable?

Mars scolded us on multiple occasions, saying we needed to 'clean up our act,' but even they ended up joining in. We were all so young, still.

Then the rumours got worse.

'Young and Audley, what's the deal?' 'Dark indie rock sensations Forever Red: How close are its members?' 'The gothic romance you always needed.'

I didn't know how much longer I could take it. I wanted to scream how wrong everyone was from the rooftops. How could they be so blind?

Ben did very few interviews and appearances during this time; he hid away from it all, spiralling into his old self. I held him close some nights and promised everything would be okay. On other nights, we were both too tired to speak a word.

It was hell.

We were everywhere and nowhere at once. Our music was insane; we were losing our minds.

I pulled Ben close to my chest one night. "We need to talk."

"I know; I just can't," he said.

I genuinely didn't know how we could continue. There was no end in sight.

Yet, on one mild summer night, I found Ben lying on our porch, blood foaming from his mouth.

Lawrence held him in despair, looking equally dishevelled, but at least he was breathing and sober enough to realise something was seriously wrong.

We pulled him inside and forced him to be sick. He'd drank so much he'd bitten his tongue. When he regained consciousness, he couldn't figure out where he was. This was just as bad as the drugs; only this time, we were all involved. Fame had blinded us.

We were falling apart.

Interview excerpt, Whitby Goth Festival: April 2014

INTERVIEWER (ANIYAH FAY – "It's So Dark in Here"): Catching up with you guys is becoming a challenge! But I'm glad we could get you all here; everyone has such busy schedules these days!

Fran: We're just too popular.

[*everyone laughs*]

Aniyah: Seriously though, you've really taken off these past few years! What's it like?

Lawrence: [*yawns*] It's crazy, really.

Fran: It's great; it's what we could have only ever dreamed about.

Casper: [*looking spaced out*] We're having so much fun. We're living the dream, as they say!

Aniyah: It seems like we couldn't have caught you all in a better location, too—just look at the four of you! You'll have to walk us through the ensembles! [*gestures to the band's outfits, specifically Lawrence's top hat and Casper's platform buckled boots*]

[*redacted*]

Ben: We feel right at home! [*loses his balance and Casper catches his arm to keep him from falling, but then Casper also trips*]

[*redacted*]

Aniyah: So, I hear you're booked to support quite a big artist in October? Care to share how that came about?

Casper

"I HATE IT. There we go, I've said it. I hate this fame, and I want it to stop. I want to go back to what it was like before, with small venues and people barely recognising us." Ben sighed and climbed off me, rolling beside me on the bed. It was August. The band had been spiralling for months at this point, and we were just waiting for one of us to say it.

Hearing it from Ben was a bittersweet feeling. This was the first time in a long time that he'd spoken his mind so deeply; I just wished the reality wasn't as bad as it had become.

"I don't know where we can go from here. Bands like us aren't meant to be big and popular. It's not a pop genre. We go against the grain, so why does it feel like we're assimilating?" he continued. "People just want the eyeliner and our absurd outfits. I bet they don't even listen to us outside of concerts. It's the aesthetic, isn't it? We're just an aesthetic."

"They want their emo lovers," I said, more resentful than intended. We had, after all, agreed to let this rumour ride a while longer.

Ben looked at me, his brows knitting together. "I hate that, too."

"Then we should do something about it." I brushed a hand over his bare shoulder. "I think I'm ready to tell the world." I was relatively sober at this point, too, so I knew I meant it.

Ben tipped his head back, as if he'd expected me to say that. "Hey world, I'm gay," he said to the ceiling.

"I know it's much easier said than done, but I think it might help us."

"But he can't be gay; I wanted to marry him!" Ben mimicked a high-pitched voice, brushing his hands through his freshly cut hair, the sides buzzed to the scalp.

"People will get over it, it's all just fantasy, anyway!" I rubbed his bare thigh in comfort. "I genuinely believe it will be okay. Lawrence is fine; he's very public about everything, and yeah, people talked about it at first, but now look, he's just accepted. And we will be, too."

There was a pause while I stared at Ben. He sighed.

"Lie back on your front. We'll talk about this tomorrow."

I sighed, wishing we weren't putting off the conversation, but I wasn't about to turn down what he was going to do.

We ended up cancelling the big support date lined up for October. Collectively, we agreed to take some steps back and save ourselves before something irreversible happened. We'd get those opportunities again; we were still young and forever would be. It was probably the first adult decision we'd made this whole time.

We said we'd stop the drinking, clear our heads, and get back on track. But the thing was, we were making our best music in years, and we *believed* it was because of the drink. We immersed ourselves so much that we no longer cared about the outside world. We were just *the music* and nothing else.

But the band wouldn't last with the way we were going.

By the end of this year, after one of our smaller, local, but sold-out gigs, me and Ben headed back to our house in our varying states of drunkenness, Lawrence in tow, and raided our secret fridge for blood, making a serious mess and just laughing at the state of the kitchen. Lawrence passed out on the couch, Ben started dancing *in* the blood, spreading it further and further around the house, and I just stood and watched it all unfold, completely carefree.

The next morning Fran rang the doorbell and I'd never hated myself more. *How could we have gotten to that stage?*

I became hyper aware of everything in seconds, diving around the rooms trying to hide the mess. I didn't want to Manipulate her, we'd never really had to, so I made a swift decision and went out for a walk with her, praying like I'd never prayed before that Ben and Lawrence had cleaned up by the time we got back.

It was a nightmare.

Casper
2015

PEOPLE SAY it's hard to clean up from excessive drinking. That's an understatement. We had to remould ourselves out of dried-up clay, alter our entire schedules, and cancel countless events for the greater good, but we did it. It took a while, but the strain was worth it.

By mid-March that year, we were virtually back to how things were before. We didn't quit drinking completely, but we tried our hardest to learn our limits. We had our ups and downs—and would do for a long time coming—but we were never going to return to the previous year, most of which we agreed was now a blur.

Our music production slowed during this time, too, but we didn't care. We had so many great things in the works, and we could be patient; we knew the wait was for the best. Fran and Ben slowly worked on a single they hoped to release, but that was it.

"BEN, HAVE YOU GOT A MINUTE?" Mars called. We'd just returned from a walk and decided to hang in the Thorns' hideout for a bit. Mars seemed like they'd been holding something in all day, but I couldn't place what.

"What?" Ben sounded panicked. He'd not spoken much on the walk.

"I just want you to come with me for a bit." Mars' tone remained calm and professional but they glanced briefly at me—a 'blink-and-you-miss-it' glance.

Ben looked like he was going to protest going alone, but his eyes widened, and he decided to follow Mars. They were gone for hours. I didn't worry, though. I knew Mars told Ben things they didn't tell the rest of us, and I appreciated how much they trusted Ben.

I waited, climbing into bed but keeping my bedside lamp on, listening closely for the door. When Ben finally returned, he slipped quietly into the bedroom, probably not realising I was still awake. He made very little sound but once I felt his weight lower into the mattress, I reached over and turned off my lamp. We sat in silence for a moment, then I turned over.

"Everything okay?" I whispered.

Ben had his back to me, but after I spoke, he turned, lying down onto the mattress and staring up at the ceiling.

"Did you know Mars had a sister?" was all he said.

Mars had mentioned her a few times. I think Ben had met her before also. I knew she was training to be a doctor and Mars was close with her, but she hadn't been mentioned in a while, so it wasn't at the forefront of my mind.

"Poppy. It's a pretty name," he said sleepily.

We fell asleep not long after.

The next morning, I woke up to Ben frantically moving about. He tore clothes from his closet, throwing them in piles strewn across the floor; his makeup box was upended, its contents scattered. My head was still a little fuzzy, but I shot up a moment later and demanded to know what was happening. Ben looked startled, as though he'd forgotten I was there, but soon returned to his mess making, mumbling to himself. He said something about a clear out, then grumbled.

"Ben, slow down. Talk to me, what are you doing?" I'd climbed out of bed by this point, slipping on some shorts and making my way over to him. I pulled him in for a hug from behind. His shoulders tensed initially but then he dropped them and relaxed into the embrace.

"I need to start again," he said.

"What do you mean?"

"I just need a fresh start. I need... to be *me* again."

I took in a deep breath. What had Mars told him?

"What do you need to do? Is there anything I can do to help?" I said, keeping my tone calm.

"I need to cut my hair." Ben pulled out of my grip and stumbled into the bathroom. I immediately followed, concerned he was having a full-on breakdown. Instead of pulling out the clippers and giving himself a buzzcut, he pulled out the scissors he normally used to trim his bangs and began hacking at the length of hair growing down his back. The hair fell in chunks, some in the sink, some on the floor. I was about to stop him, but he knew what he was doing. He trimmed his bangs like normal but cut away all the length at the back. He looked younger and less tense. He turned to me with a sigh.

"I couldn't breathe."

I knew exactly what he meant.

We spent the rest of the day clearing out his closet and deciding what to keep and get rid of. He bagged up all his mesh, fishnets, and makeup—except for his eyeliner. I told him we'd hang onto things if he changed his mind. Watching Ben erase a large chunk of the past few years upset me, but he wanted a change.

Whatever he and Mars discussed, it had clearly impacted him. All I could piece together was that it must have had something to do with Mars' sister, Poppy. Had something happened? How did it link to Ben, though?

"I lost myself for a while. I think getting rid of the act will help me to find myself again—properly. Stop putting on a show and acting and dressing just to impress people I don't even know. It's the final step to being me." While Ben had calmed, he still looked like he had a bunch of things on his mind.

I nodded. "So, what does this mean then? For you? ... For us?" I dared to ask.

"It means I'm gonna clean the fuck up and stop being an idiot. Permanently." He looked me dead in the eyes. "I'm going to reset, and things are going to work this time."

"Okay."

"No more lies. I'm not going back to that place again. I'm over it."

"Okay." I really wanted to believe him this time.

"Will you join me?"

I nodded, pursing my lips. "I'd do anything for you, but yes. We're doing this. Properly, this time. The start of a new era for us all."

He kissed me, and that was the first kiss we'd shared in a while that just felt like it was between us two, with no thoughts or memories or drunken interference—no drugs, blood, or high emotions. Just Ben and Casper. Love.

Ben

I STOPPED DRINKING ENTIRELY in March. It was an abrupt and strict decision, but I figured it was for the best. Even before the 'rockstar' life, I'd always turned to drink and drugs to ignore the fact I was really fucking depressed.

My dad refused to see me; I drank.

I got stressed with the band; I drank.

I got overwhelmed by the fact that I still couldn't pluck up the courage and come out to anyone other than my mum and the band; I drank.

I spiralled, found my feet, then spiralled again.

Then Mars told me about Poppy.

Poppy was always someone I could relate to, even if it was mostly just through Mars' words. I didn't know her, not *really*, but the way she put 110% into everything and strived for greatness no matter what was comforting for me because I knew I did the same. Poppy was praised for it, which I thought was a good thing.

But then, the reality came crashing down when Mars pulled me aside that day. The second we were out of earshot, they burst into tears and grabbed me by the shoulders, pulling me in for a hug that only someone who wanted comfort would give. I hugged them back and held them, letting them explain what happened.

Poppy had taken her own life.

She thought she couldn't handle the world. She took on too much.

And no one even noticed the signs.

PEOPLE ALWAYS SAY traumatic situations force you to change, and I understood it in theory, but I didn't realise the truth of it until I put it into practise.

I didn't want to get into that headspace again. I couldn't. I had the best life. I had Casper, Mars, the band, my mum, my gran—even just passing friends I made at uni in the orchestra. I died once, and for whatever reason, I was chosen to walk the earth again, forever, if I so choose. It hit me like a gut punch how much I wanted to *live*.

· · ·

The following day when Mars didn't pick up their phone, Marianne called us in a panic, saying they hadn't been themself for two whole days. We went to her straight away. I hadn't directly told Casper what happened—I didn't feel like it was my place—but by how I acted that morning and the hints I'd unintentionally dropped, I figured he had a pretty good idea.

When we got to Marianne, she asked us if we knew anything. I couldn't lie to her. As the words left my mouth, it hit me all at once. I knew where they'd be today, and I needed to stop them.

I ran. Bursting out of the hideout, I bolted straight to my car, the engine still warm. Casper and Marianne were hot on my heels, and I let them in the back. "I know where they are," I gasped before turning the engine on and heading for the main road.

We pulled up to the hospital and Manipulated our way through to the morgue.

Oh, Mars.

We got to the room where Poppy's body resided and heard their cries before anything else. We turned the corner to find Mars, their back to us, sobbing in fits of hysterics and sitting cross-legged with their bloody hands by their sides.

Marianne dove first, throwing her arms around Mars and rocking them into a deep hug, quieting and comforting them as a mother would. I still tried to catch my breath and clear my head, but I finally absorbed the scene, noting the red handprints on the metal door in the wall, the one with the latch loose. *Had they—*

"I have to try. I have to. I need to!" Mars wailed. I'd never seen them so vulnerable and helpless, but this was the second time in two days. My chest burned.

Casper's hand gently and discretely found mine as we stood before Mars and Marianne.

"Mars, you can't. I'm sorry." Marianne continued rocking them in her arms.

Mars frantically pulled away and shuffled back on the floor, kicking out their legs against the ground like a drowning spider. Blood oozed from their mouth, their eyes a veiny red—they'd tried. Oh God, they'd already tried. My head darted to the holding wall.

Marianne didn't attempt to return to Mars, giving them space.

Mars' eyes were so wide and their breathing sporadic. "I NEED TO TRY!" they screamed.

"No, Mars. You can't." Marianne's voice was so soft it was as if she herself were about to cry.

"Then you do it!" they cried, flaying out their arms in frustration. "You saved Ben; you can do this. You must!"

The demand shook the room, I stood stunned. Casper's grip on my hand tensed.

Marianne had her back to us, but I could picture her face. She was still crouched to Mars' level, who now sat quietly, panting for breath. "I just need her back. I need to tell her I love her. I didn't get to tell her the last time. I didn't think to—" The plea shook through their voice.

The room was deadly silent for a moment, the smell of sanitation and blood mixing in my nostrils.

"Poppy already knew that. She always will. She knew she was incredibly loved." Marianne promised.

"But—but she... why would she..." The words died on Mars' lips, and the silent tears came.

I let go of Casper's hand and ran over to the centre of the room to Mars, bending over to hug them. They returned the tight grip.

"She loves you, Mars," I whispered into their soft hair. Casper appeared behind me, and Marianne did, too.

I held Mars for a while until they asked me to help them up. Facing us all head-on, their bottom lip trembled. We all still looked like kids, with none of us appearing any older than twenty-one.

"I should have known," they finally said.

"That's not your fault, not even a tiny bit," Casper reassured them.

"You're the best sibling anyone could hope for," I promised, and I meant it. I wished Mars was my older sibling.

Marianne closed the scene. "Come, Mars. Let's get you cleaned up."

WE PROMISED Mars they could take as much time off as they needed.

They ended up going home to their parents for a while, flying back out to the Philippines. We didn't hear from them for *days*, but when they came back, it was as if no time had passed at all. They admitted they needed to return to normal life otherwise they'd never feel better. It made sense.

They entered a stage of serious creativity, producing art piece after art piece, pouring their heart and soul into it. They submitted their work to exhibitions and succeeded, even receiving commendations. I was so very proud of them. Mars was the greatest.

TOWARDS THE END OF APRIL, Lawrence asked to move in with us again, albeit temporarily. He said the flat hopping wasn't good for him and that he was tidier and cleaner when he stayed with us. We couldn't say no.

Francesca, on rocky terms with Maddie, also started spending long periods at our home, and once again, our bond as a band deepened. We argued and fell out, but it was always from a place of love and passion. Our band was evolving into something grand—I had such high hopes for our future, especially now that we were more focused on the creative side, pushing boundaries and exploring new avenues, no longer caring if we'd sell or whether people liked our new stuff. We stopped creating for other people and returned to the core values of the band. We were goths, after all.

Casper

IN THE MAY of that year, Jesse flew back over to record some extra parts for our planned upcoming single, he stayed for longer after and me and Ben took him to Edinburgh, showing him our favourite spots. Ben had since started smoking a lot more, very easily managing a pack a day sometimes, and I remember even my brother started commenting on it, but I told myself it was a small price to pay for his complete sobriety.

A month later, Fran broke up with Maddie in a really heated nightclub where it was revealed Maddie had been cheating on her for the better half of six months. Horrible, and we couldn't blame Francesca for the way she reacted. The pair were kicked out and we followed straight after, comforting and supporting Francesca as best we could. The three of us decided to take her to her favourite bar and made the rest of the night on us. We were like family now.

Fran and Lawrence later found an apartment to share, it only made sense.

Home video from Ben, Casper and Fran: June 2015
[Sat in Ben and Casper's living room, Ben lying with his legs over the side of the chair, his head in Fran's lap. Fran crossed legged playing with Ben's hair. Casper beside them, adjusting the camera before sitting down and pulling out his laptop]

BEN: *[laughing and kicking his feet, staring at Casper]* haha this is so staged. It doesn't have to be a serious interview.

Fran: No, no, I want to do this. It will be good practise. I don't like being put on the spot in interviews.

Casper: Okay, how did it make you feel then?

Ben: Woah they won't be that blunt!

Fran: They might be! Urgh, I just wish I'd not been so public with everything I did and the people I'm out with. Then this wouldn't happen!

Ben: It doesn't have to happen, if you don't want it to. You don't have to answer *anything*. It's not like you made the *relationship* explicitly clear, it was only ever mild speculation. I mean look at... we're not posting this anywhere, are we? No behind the scenes documentaries in the future? Forever Red, raw and uncut?

Fran: [*laughing, ruffling Ben's hair*] No, this is just for me, I promise.

Ben: Okay, then just look at me and Casper, we've been together five years and still no one *really* knows.

Fran: Yeah but... that's different.

Casper: How?

Ben: [*flapping his hands*] You've been open about your sexuality from the start. I get it.

Fran: See! I'm on display, people are interested in my life! Sure, I chose this, but there's no going back now.

Casper: [*focused on his screen*] Well they can't be that interested, at least a third of our fans still think you're dating Ben.

Fran: Okay, true, but they only look at the big picture. Heteronormativity is still *rampant* and Ben's my best friend.

Casper: [*feigning offence*] Ouch, I thought I held that title.

Fran: [*pointing comically at Casper*] No, you're my big brother, Ben's my best friend.

Ben: [*sticks his tongue out at Casper*]

Casper: [*grabs Ben's ankle and pulls him down the chair, everyone laughing*]

Fran: No seriously though, they only see us on smoke breaks and go 'ahh, *les amants*' and make weird video edits. They don't know anything about our *actual* relationship, [*putting on a silly* *voice*] but if they did, then they'd ship us more. [*leans down to kiss Ben's forehead*]

Ben: [*in a sing song voice*] I love you, my dear.

Fran: [*matching the voice*] and I you, my... god I can't think of a silly pet name. *Gumdrop!* My sweet gumdrop!

[*everyone laughs, Ben snorts*]

Casper: Ben's right though, you don't actually have to tell anyone.

[*redacted*]

Fran: We should do more of these. Home movie style. Ooh we should get a proper old camera and make it all nineties.

Ben: For the documentary?

[*video cuts*]

Casper

TWO HUGE THINGS happened for us that August—two things that forever changed the way we moved forward.

On one sweltering evening, Ben and I were lying in bed (or on top of the bed, to be more accurate. I'd lived in England a long time and shamefully picked up many elements of the northern accent, but one thing I never got over was the lack of air-con and the duvet sheets being thicker than the mattress), and we heard the front door banging *loud*. It was about 2am, and I was turning to liquid, but Ben insisted we checked it out in case it was important. We dressed and hazily made our way down the stairs as the banging persisted.

"We're coming!" I shouted, slightly annoyed.

We unlocked the door and swung it open, faced with a dishevelled-looking Fran, eyes wide, and blood leaking down her neck.

Oh, shit.

"Either of you care to explain to me why Lawrence fucking Marigold just went full Dracula on me and bit my neck? I'm not afraid to admit I like a bit of force in role play, but the bloodshot eyes and fangs were a little advanced to be a spur-of-the-moment prop. He fucking *bit me!*" She stormed into the house.

Oh, shit.

Of course, we'd had many conversations about how to eventually tell Fran, who would have to know in time; we couldn't hide it from her forever. We had never needed to Manipulate her in any way, but Lawrence had been so well-behaved when it came to our immortal antics that we thought we'd have nothing to worry about. We went through great lengths to protect her.

"Where is Lawrence now?" Ben asked, stunned.

"Well, I knocked him out. He's probably still lying in a pool of his own blood. Or do creatures like that heal super fast? Is he allergic to garlic? No, that wouldn't make any sense. Sunlight? No. What the fuck *is* he?"

"I think you should probably sit down for this," I said.

We told Fran everything.

She took a lot of convincing, despite her first-hand experience, but once we showed her the evidence, she had no choice but to accept the truth. It's an insane thing to offload onto someone, but if we didn't tell her in that moment, the lying game would really have to start, and she didn't deserve that deceit.

We then cleaned up the mess. Lawrence was sitting in the window of their apartment living room, smoking a cigar, completely naked apart from a bedsheet toga, covered from head to foot in what was most likely 90% of his own blood.

"Ahh, guys," he hummed. "Hmm, yeah. About that..."

I ran over to him and hauled him up to a stand; he didn't protest, leaning over to extinguish the cigar.

"Are you *that* stupid?"

"I'm sorry," he said. "I don't know what came over me. I'm not on drugs I swear." He held up his hands, his grey eyes flashing in fear.

He could have killed her. He could have killed Fran. My tight grip remained around his body.

Then he clocked her, head darting towards the door.

"When I said bite me, I meant the human way," Fran shouted.

He swallowed down his heavy breaths. "You know then?"

Fran stepped forward, making the dressing on her neck obvious. "Of course, I fucking know. I... urgh!" She went over to the window and pressed her head against it. "What the actual hell is going on. I've lost the plot! We all have. We're insane," she shouted against the glass.

"I'm so sorry Fran, I..." He tried to pull away and move towards her, but I pulled him back.

"Please," he begged. "I haven't drank in a while, I've never done this before, and I swear I wouldn't have gone all the way..."

"That's not really good enough though, is it? You bit her, which not only exposed who we are, but also could have *killed* her."

"I... I wouldn't have... I swear. Please." He really did sound sincere, he was never very good at Manipulation, even if it was harder to work on our kind anyway. I couldn't just let this slide though. We needed to do something about it. Make sure he would never let himself do something like this again.

"We're sending you to Marianne." I decided.

"Oh no. No, no. Not her. Please. I'll do anything. Anything you want. I'll quit the band if you want, I'll leave town. Anything..." He *begged.* I felt his whole-body tremble in my arms, his eyes swimming with terror. I've never seen him so small and so frightened since... well, since he was attacked.

"Lawrence, please don't make this harder than it should be.

She'll help you, we'll explain everything," Ben said softly. He was the only one of us who didn't seem mad.

It didn't help though, Lawrence's breathing was erratic. "She'll kill me," he said, his voice quiet in defeat.

"What?" Fran perked up and walked over with her hands up. "What did you say?"

Ben spoke before Lawrence had a chance to respond. "She won't Lawrence, I promise. You're not like them." He sounded so sure. It was rare Ben came across as the most confident person in the room; it startled me. I felt like there was something I didn't know. Something only Ben and Lawrence knew.

"Woah, woah. Marianne? I thought you said she was good?" Fran said abruptly.

"She is," I said, though I wasn't so bold when I said it. I let go of Lawrence.

"So, everything will be fine then. Right?" Fran said, looking between me and Ben for reassurance. "She can help him and then we can put this all behind us and get on with our lives. I'll play along with things, I won't tell anyone anything, I'll act like I don't have a clue. You have my word."

I swallowed then turned to Ben. "Everything okay?" I asked, presuming the answer was yes, but Ben's face said otherwise. His gaze fixed on Lawrence, almost solemn looking.

"Please, Ben. Don't tell her what I did," Lawrence said, exhausted.

I kept my eyes fixed to Ben, realising he would be making the decision. Fran stood silently with her arms folded.

"We'll sort this ourselves," Ben finally spoke.

"What? Marianne will know what to do, she's our leader, this is what she does." Why was he saying this?

"We'll sort it ourselves. Come on, Lawrence. Get yourself cleaned up."

I was about to protest, but Lawrence listened to Ben like a dog following his master.

Fran also didn't protest, which concerned me at first, but after processing the way Lawrence reacted, something told me this was the right decision.

So yeah, Fran was now in the loop and naturally avoided Lawrence for a while. He never stopped apologising, even after Fran started turning the situation into jokes. He wasn't going to do that again. I knew that now.

Fran took her time properly coming to terms with everything, choosing to keep herself separate from The Thorns, but before long, it was as if she'd known from the start; like nothing ever changed.

Oh, and the second thing?

We went public.

Me and Ben.

We told the world.

Interlude
August 2015

Two months after the publication of the interview of Ben Audley and Francesca Young—in which the pair admitted they are definitely not a couple—Casper Murphey, the band's drummer and co-founder, released a post of himself and Ben Audley on holiday together, with Audley wrapped in his tight embrace. The photo dated back to summer 2010, and the caption read: 'My eternal. I love you, Ben.'

Audley, the band's bassist, responded with a '<3' emoticon, forcing the comment section to flood with speculation that the two were a couple, and had been for a long time.

'I knew it!' One fan wrote, claiming they'd guessed the pair were dating ever since they met the band backstage in a gig in May 2011.

Neither Murphey nor Audley have commented further, but it is safe to say this is big news for Forever Red fans.

Casper

I'D JUST GOTTEN off the phone with Jesse, who saw our announcement and rang me straight away. He'd known for years, as had my family, but he called to reassure me that whatever happened from thereon out, he would always be there for me. We mostly received positive messages from fans, but of course, we expected the onslaught of both the ignorant, religious, homophobic keyboard warriors who questioned why we needed to shove it in their faces, and the immature teens who were disappointed that their 'shipping' of Fran and Ben wasn't real. Somehow, that was my fault. I ruined their perfect little fantasies. *Tough luck; go write your fan-fiction. I get the real Ben.* It would take a lot more to phase me.

"So, I'm thinking we need to do something to celebrate," I said to Ben. He perched on the edge of the bed with a long, white towel around his waist, having just come out of the bath. His hair was wet, curls reforming, his face freshly shaved, and skin smelling of apples.

"Like what?" He pushed himself back onto his side of the bed, propping himself up with the pillows. "I don't really feel like going out."

"Is that because of the announcement or just in general?"

He shrugged. "Bit of both."

"Everything will be fine, you know. We're in a tiny village in the south for a reason—no one really knows us here. We don't have many pensioner fans," I joked.

"Oh, I know that. I just fancy staying in, mainly for comfort purposes." He stretched his arms and yawned. "And mostly because I can't be bothered to put nice clothes on."

I joined him on the bed, the two of us sitting with our hands in our laps, staring ahead. "Well, we could just order in and play video games. This place has a great retro selection."

Ben turned to me with a smug grin. "You read my mind."

WE ATE our pizzas on the bed; Ben still hadn't bothered to change. We blasted our favourite songs through the speakers and played random games that came with the cottage's Play Station. One of the games had a vampire character, and Ben and I exchanged glances whenever the character said or did something we could relate to.

I caught him yawning not long after, so we called it a night on the games and turned off the TV. I cleared the bed, shuffling down slightly and nuzzling closer to him.

"What?" he asked, noticing the look on my face.

I quoted a sensual scene from the vampire in the game, and it took Ben a moment to catch on, but when he did, his face changed. He gleefully moved his body down so we were lying side by side, facing each other.

"That kind of turned me on a bit, is that bad?" I asked, thinking back to the game, and how I'd pictured Ben in the character's place.

"What do you want me to do?"

"Whatever you want." The weight on my chest intensified as butterflies formed in my stomach and my legs numbed.

Ben smirked and moved himself lower to cage over me, the towel loosening as he did. "Okay then." He lowered his face to my neck and kissed me once, twice, three times. I grabbed onto his ribs as the towel slipped away. God, his body was a masterpiece.

My fingers danced over his back as the kisses intensified, and then I couldn't help myself, reaching down to pleasure him as his lips trailed my face and neck. He groaned in between kisses, and oh, how I adored that sound.

I loved it when Ben took control. He normally let me do all the hard work, but seemed all for it this evening. His turn was long overdue.

He started rocking his body against mine, and I needed to remove my pants before I exploded.

"Hang on." I managed. He stopped for a moment, lifting his hips so I could remove my clothes.

Once we were skin to skin, his mouth wandered down my body. He worked all the way down to my hips, then dragged his tongue up my inner thigh once before grinning and pulling me up; we toppled back, and then both stood upright, sweaty and breathless. He pulled me towards him and then turned us around, so my back was thrust against the bare wall beside the TV. He recommenced his kissing on both sides of my body before facing me, his eyes catching mine in wonder.

"Let's try something new. Something I've wanted to try for a while now."

God, I really, really loved it when Ben came out of his shell.

"Turn off the lights and grab a blood bag. Or two." He demanded before pulling himself free. He spread himself against the bed, propping up on his elbows as he stared straight at me.

"What are you—"

He shook his head to stop my questioning.

Okay... whatever he wanted to try, I wanted to.

I ran downstairs to the fridge and grabbed two blood bags, returning upstairs and turning off the light. Ben had turned on the far bedside lamp and now stood beside it.

"I want to bite you, then for you to bite me, and then we finish with the blood to satisfy any excess hunger," he said confidently, with only a hint of embarrassment. I could tell he'd kept this to himself for a while, so I wondered why he suggested it now.

A fellow vampire's blood alone would not give us enough nutrients, but that's what he wanted the bags for—for afterwards. We would undoubtedly grow extremely hungry in the heat of the moment, and this would be our precaution.

I'd thought about us biting one another before—many times —but I figured early on that Ben wouldn't be interested in it. Too violent or too intense, even. But the words left his mouth, not mine. So, now came the fun.

I set the bags down. "Where do you want to bite me?"

He cocked his head in the lamplight. "Let's keep it old school. I'm going to turn you."

I bit my lip. This was going to be fun.

"Where do you want me?" But before I could even finish, Ben leaped up onto the bed and dove for me, knocking me backward and leaving me fully in his grip. My arms flayed, and vision blurred as he wrapped an arm around my head and pulled my neck to one side, baring my neck.

"This okay?" he whispered into my ear, the two of us breathless.

"Oh, more than," I admitted.

I caught a glimpse of the way Ben slightly tipped his head back, allowing his fangs to protrude before sinking his teeth into my neck, holding me strong and tight.

It hurt only a little, but it very quickly turned into pleasure as I felt his grip tighten in my hair. *Why had we never done this earlier? It's been three years.*

Ben drank slowly for a minute. My body shuddered and tensed with the feeling until I felt slightly dizzy, tapping him on the back to stop. It took Ben a moment to realise before pulling back. His eyes were bright red, and teeth coated in dark liquid, indistinguishable in the light. My blood, of course.

I wasted no time in throwing him backward onto the bed. We

grinned at each other, and I could see his face now—his mouth was smeared in sweet red; his pupils dilated. He carefully reached for my neck wound and caught the remaining drips with the tips of his elegant fingers and—*oh lord*—smeared it down his torso before grabbing himself with bloodied hands and letting out a shallow cry. His lips were deliciously swollen, and my eyes fixed to the tenseness of his brows, every muscle in his face working tirelessly as he bit back groans of pleasure. Once our eyes met again, he finally let out a whimper that almost sent me crashing straight to my knees.

"Let me touch you," he managed to say, squeezing his eyes shut in ecstasy, head tipping back as his hand picked up the pace.

"I'm right here," I said, grinning, head still fuzzy from his drink. I leaned down to cage him and he propped himself up frantically, grabbing the back of my neck again and releasing his restraint into my ear. He peppered my skin with bloody kisses, exploring every inch of my body with his delicate hands. I will never tire of his touch. The vibrations it sends through my core will never falter, never weaken. He traced the lines of the muscles stretched over my shoulders and chest like a sculptor would his creation. I watched the jade in his eyes glisten as he analysed every inch of my skin, as if discovering me for the first time, calculating the contact of his fingers so precisely. As if we haven't done this a thousand times before. I forgot to breathe I was staring at him so intensely, focusing too much on the elation I was feeling. I never wanted these moments to end.

Ben's breathing settled as he homed in on the line of hairs below my belly button, his pianist fingers playing my core like his penultimate piece, the calm before the storm. He inhaled deeply and the corners of his mouth turned up into a grin, as for his grand finale, he stroked my tip in a gentle but teasing manner, and I had to shudder back a scream. A bead of sweat trickled and pooled in the fine lines in the crease of his stomach, mixing with the blood and causing it to stream to the side like a vein of rain on a car window, hitting the sheets below us. Ben frantically reached to catch it too late, peering down and gripping to his skin like fabric as his breath shook. In the dim light, with our heads almost touching, I could just about see the way he bit down on his lip, and he swallowed down another heated sound of struggling pleasure. He was in such a hot state and seeing him that way made me so *wild*.

This just wasn't fair, not one bit.

"My turn," I demanded, pushing him back down then prowling to him. I kissed his bloodied lips and tasted my own metallic blood, biting the same parts of his lips with my own teeth and drawing my first bout of blood, catching it with my tongue as it dribbled down his chin.

"Where do you want me?" I asked. He didn't need to make a sound; he just grabbed me by my crown and shoved my head over to the top of his leg, to the soft tissue of his upper, inner thigh.

"There," he panted, tipping his head back and arching his spine.

Oh, this was going to be good.

I breathed in and wet the area with my tongue before letting my mind take over. I bit down hard. His whole body jerked, forcing him to sit up slightly and grip onto my head with both hands. He released a cry before letting go completely, flopping back down onto the pillows. I believe he swore.

He tasted even better than I thought—thicker, sweeter. I took about the same amount, splaying a hand flat against his chest to keep him from jerking as I hit nerves and tendons.

I didn't want to stop.

Then, even when he tapped my head in surrender, I lost myself and bit harder, grabbing his body tight and holding him in place. He let out a cry of pain this time, and it wasn't until he called our safe word that I stopped and pulled back, panicking.

"Shit. Sorry. I got too into it." Stress marked my face, but Ben only leaned closer to me.

"It's okay; I didn't want to stop either," he admitted calmly. Clearly, he was still a little stunned, but when he reached to cup my chin, it proved he'd prepared for this.

"We'll get better at managing it. That's what the blood is for." He reassured me with a soft smile.

"I'm sorry," I panted, brow tense.

"Don't be," Ben whispered. "I kind of liked it."

He pulled away and stood, reaching for the bags with a grin. "Let's try not to make too much more of a mess. The owners don't need to know what went on in this room."

Ben
April 2016

THAT YEAR really became the year I grew up. It sounds silly, but I had finally begun to grow out of my teenage ways. I cleared out a bunch of stuff last year, amending my wardrobe and belongings— after all, I was nearly twenty-five now. I wanted to feel like it. I had ample time to reinvent myself; this didn't have to be the only chance. I was just getting sick of being viewed as the baby of the group, despite being older than Francesca *and* Lawrence. I tried to start growing a beard, which sort of failed, but it still made me feel grown up. I tried to go to the gym with Casper and Fran to try and bulk up, too, but that also failed. I blamed it on the fact I couldn't technically consume enough protein, not because I couldn't stick to a routine to save my life. Casper was managing just fine in that arena.

I also found myself spending more time with Fran. We were always close, but I think once we all let our minds clear up, and we could stop hiding from her, we started to prioritise the mundane time we all had together. Fran made life entertaining, and I missed the relationship we had before all of this.

<u>Home video filmed by Fran: April 2016</u>
[Ben and Fran in a supermarket]

FRAN: Okay, it's recording. Say what you said to the camera again.

Ben: [*laughing*] What? Oh God, you're actually filming on that thing.

Fran: It's vintage.

Ben: [*sticking his face in the lens*] I'll be all pixel-y.

Fran: And you'll go down in history. Only mysterious works of art make it on this camera.

Ben: Oh wow, what an honour. [*rolls eyes*]

Fran: Okay, okay, but just repeat what you said before I started recording.

Ben: [*holding back laughter*] What did I say?

Fran: You know exactly what you said. [*points to the lettuce section*]

Ben: What, that cabbage is the goth of the green veg category?

Fran: [*laughing hard, the camera shaking*] Care to elaborate?

Ben: [*putting his hands behind his back and staring back into the lens*] Nope, but to all the fans watching, if you know, you know.

Fran: For the documentary?

Ben: [*wandering down the aisle and pointing at different vegetables*] Have you seen the way asparagus grows?

THIS WAS the year Casper and I stopped arguing. No more big fallouts. We were back to how things were before the vampirism and drugs and drink, and I felt so *light*.

We sorted out our band issues despite it being the height of our careers. We had a couple of albums out by this point and did a few UK tours, even producing proper music videos—again, creatively directed by the one and only Mars, who, in the year since Poppy died, had almost become a different person. They remained strong, though, a ten-foot presence that made you feel safe, and the best manager we could ever ask for. Of course, I still worried about them, and checked in as often as I could in private, but that was becoming increasingly difficult with the amount of time they spent with all of us.

This year was the first time in a long time that I'd allowed myself to be in front of a camera, with everyone insisting I should be centre stage for the video of our latest single. Fran's 'vlogging' helped, but it was also because of the song choice; I'd written it myself as a sort of goodbye to my younger self, yet we masked the lyrics as a dark love song. Yeah, maybe that was it.

Then, somehow, we managed to get ourselves to the stage for a European tour, finishing off with some North American tour dates, specifically Louisiana for Casper. I think the highlight of my career so far was our stop-off in Paris. They put us up in this super posh hotel with balcony views of the Eiffel Tower. One day, the day after our concert, we'd been booked for a big interview in the afternoon, but our late nights had caught up with us—specifically, me. I remember that morning vividly.

We all had a lie-in after a late night, and though me and Casper woke up with plenty of time, we still managed to be late. We *really* made a mess of the hotel bed. You know, when in Paris...

Honestly, the interview itself was dull; it focused on our recent album, the music video and the things you could infer from it, and then, of course, questions about me and Casper. But we were done by two o'clock and still had the rest of the day and the following morning to have some fun, so the five of us went out for tea and a few of us got rather drunk. I allowed myself one drink and told the others to stop me from buying more. I felt fine, didn't crave more, and I grinned at myself for how far I'd come.

Home video filmed by Fran: August 2016

Fran: [*holding the camera down by her feet, speaking in a drunk French accent*] say hellooo Paris!

Lawrence: [*facing down towards the camera, grinning, equally drunk*] Bonjour, I've just been sick.

Fran: [*camera goes black, voices muffled*] Eww Lawrence, no one needs to know that.

Ben: [*voice distant*] You better not post that anywhere.

"TO THE UNDEAD RED," Lawrence raised his cocktail glass in a toast as we sat around the table. He always said that phrase, clearly proud of his rhyming skills.

"To the undead red," we all chimed in, clinking our drinks together.

It was the first 'wild night' we'd allowed ourselves to have in a while.

Fran disappeared in a bar and then returned with a pretty young woman, with whom she announced she would be spending the evening.

Lawrence managed to have a good time, too.

And Mars.

Sadly, some things get burned into your memory, whether you want them to or not.

We headed back to our hotel early the next day, and by that time, it was just me and Casper left, but we decided to knock for Mars to check everything was okay since they were the only one who hadn't answered their messages. The door was unlocked, which we found concerning, so I—being a tad naïve—wandered into the dark room, where I not only saw the frantically moving shadows of two people, but heard them, too. I backed away in a panic and slammed the door, turning my back to it wide-eyed.

"Lawrence was in there, wasn't he?" Casper pinched the bridge of his nose.

"Yup," I said, still forgetting to blink. I took off down the corridor, wishing I could bleach my brain.

So, yes, inevitably, Mars and Lawrence entered a—as I liked to describe it—*interesting* bond. Neither knew what they wanted, but they began spending significantly more time together. Unlike the brief period with Lawrence and Fran, this one actually lasted, becoming something more serious. It never seemed romantic, though.

Mars hadn't been with anyone for a while, not since Poppy died, so I was glad they were finding things enjoyable again and living their life.

We finished off the tour in New Orleans. It was incredible; I always loved visiting Casper's home state. We got to meet Jesse again and record some stuff. I considered maybe moving there with Casper if the government sorted itself out. Yeah, late 2016. Hmm.

August 2017

By this point in the year, Lawrence and Mars had broken up and gotten back together enough times for us to realise it was a very complicated situation, one we perhaps would never understand. One minute, they were arguing, and the next, they were best friends. They were like chalk and cheese, but chalk you could eat and cheese you could write with—their own little mess.

I think Leeds Fest was the last time the band considered breaking up. The situation wasn't too bad, either; we were all exhausted, wondering how much longer we could keep at this. We were hitting the ages where people started to question our skincare routines, pulling up side-by-side pictures of us spanning the eight years we'd been together. It was less of a falling out this time but more of a serious discussion about where the band was going. We'd already had one comment saying Fran had had a 'bad paper round' despite none of us having reached thirty yet, vampirism included. Lawrence suggested we broke up for a few decades and then re-emerged as our kids, but that garnered stupid looks from all of us, including Fran, who argued she'd be too old by then and would genuinely have to pass the role down to her kids, if she had any. She didn't want things to end. Lawrence jokingly offered to turn her, the first time he'd tried to make light of that bad memory, but he really wasn't reading the room and she responded with a direct slap to his face. We all agreed he deserved it, Lawrence included.

An article was published about us after the 2017 festival season, calling us the LGBT+ band of the century. It probably sparked from Lawrence shouting at the opening of our Reading set: "We are Forever Red, and we are dead queer!" But I broke down crying the night I read it, hugging Casper and saying: "We made it."

I was completely sober, it just meant the world to me that we were finally seen and accepted, and I wished we'd come out sooner; our band was *thriving*.

We just needed to plan the next ten years.

<u>Interview excerpt: September 2018</u>

Interviewer, (Paul Norris, 'That's Alt' – October 2018 Issue): So, where do you see yourselves in ten years' time? You've almost completed your first decade, think you can beat the likes of the Stones?

Lawrence: Oh, without a shadow of a doubt. I've only just started.

Fran: Nah, they'll probably outlive me somehow. I feel like I've got another decade in me but then I'd probably quite like to settle down. That's my plan, anyway.

Casper: I can see us going on for quite a while. We've got so much more to give.

Ben: I reckon another decade or so of new material, a few years of just touring, winding down, and then we'll all just go off and live normal lives. I know that's what I'd like, at least. [*looks to his partner, smiling*]

Casper: Of course, I'd love that too.

Home video filmed by Fran: September 2018

Fran: Okay, everyone budge up, we're not all in frame.

Mars: You want me in this, as well? I wasn't in the interview.

Fran: [*beckoning Mars over to join the four of them on the sofa*] Yes, come here, you're one of us!

Mars: [*stands behind the sofa, centre frame, adjusting their shirt*] Oh I do not like this camera.

Fran: You won't care in ten years' time, come on, everyone focus! [*clicks her fingers*]

Lawrence: [*laughs at Ben's startled reaction to the noise*]

Ben: [*squeezing his shoulders in*] We're a bit snug on this chair.

Fran: Oh, come on guys, it's just a quick video. Stick it out for five minutes!

Casper: [*smoothing his eyebrows in the viewfinder*] The quality is insane.

Fran: [*rolling her eyes at Casper's sarcasm*] Right, honestly, you lot are a pain sometimes.

Lawrence: [*stretching arm out behind Ben to squeeze Fran's shoulder, winking at the camera*] You love us really.

Mars: [*dramatically clears their throat behind them*]

Fran: Okay, so, I'll start. My name is Francesca Young, I'm twenty-six years old and I'm the lead guitarist and vocalist of the band Forever Red.

Lawrence: [*smirking*] Lead?

Mars: Shhh.

Fran: [*inhaling deeply, closing her eyes in annoyance*] I'm the *lead* guitarist...

Lawrence: [*quietly muttering to Mars behind him*] I was joking!

Fran: And in ten years' time I want to own a nice house in the south of France and hopefully be married with either two cats or two kids, I'm not fussy, I'll take what I can get.

Ben: [*looking to the floor*] Aww cute.

Fran: Okay, who's next?

Lawrence: [*raising his hand high*] I'll go. [*clears throat*] My name is Bartholomew George the third and...

Fran: Oh my god, how old are you?

Mars: [*to Lawrence, angrily*] Have you taken something?

Lawrence: [*tone more serious, straightening his skirt*] No, no. Sorry. Someone else do theirs. [*stands and walks off camera*]

Casper: Right, okay, I suppose I'll go next then. Hello future me! This is twenty-seven, soon to be twenty-eight-year-old Casper Murphey from Alexandria, Louisiana. In ten years' time I want to be living with my partner Ben [*leans forward to reach out and squeeze Ben's knee*] and I want us to have an insane record collection and have the money and free time to travel the world. And yeah, we could start a family. We could, erm. [*rubs his hands together*] I can see us getting a dog, yeah. I'd like a dog, someone to keep us occupied.

Fran: Aww, that's adorable. I can totally see you two with a dog. Ooh, like a German Shepard or something!

Ben: [*eyes widening*] Ooh no, too big. Something fluffier. [*trails off*]

Casper: We can talk about it! This is just random dreams that spout off the top of our heads, nothing serious!

Fran: [*turning back to face camera*] Okay, okay guys, I don't know how much battery is left on here. Quick, Mars, you go.

Mars: Oh, right. Well. Greetings nearly forty-year-old Mars. [*looking down at Fran*] Oh my god, I'll be forty. That's a scary thought.

Fran: Well, you don't age so...

Ben: [*panicking, standing to reach for the camera*] Cut that! We can't have that on record!

Fran: [*stopping him*] Woah, calm Ben! No one is seeing these videos except us! I told you these will always be private vlogs!

Ben: [*calming*] Okay, sorry.

Mars: Shall I start again?

Fran: No need, I'm not editing this or anything, it's genuinely just for us to look back on and probably laugh at how aspirational we'd been.

Mars: Right, okay, where was I? Oh yes, I'll be hitting forty and will most likely still be single, which is fine. I want to have won at least one proper art award, have my stuff immortalised, even if I'm only known as 'that quirky millennial' who made a few interesting pieces but who has small corners of the internet praising me like I'm the second coming. I want to do some more high-profile commissions too, no idea who would be interested in my stuff, but I'd love to maybe collaborate with fashion designers maybe? I dunno. Honestly, I'm just taking life each day as it comes. Ooh, I'd like to buy a house near my old home in Caloocan. Try and make a name for myself there too. That would mean a lot. Honestly, as long as I'm happy. I'm sure I'll accept whatever the next ten years throws at me!

Fran: Wow, Mars.

Casper: Yeah, these are proper aspirations that I can totally see coming true, you can tell you've been adulting way longer than us.

Mars: Hey! I'm not that much older than you all.

Casper: [*holding his hands up in jest*] Oh, I know. You've always just been more level-headed than the rest of us.

Ben: We're just teenage boys still. [*looks off camera towards where Lawrence wandered off to*] Some of us definitely are still teenage boys.

[*all laugh*]

Mars: Okay, but seriously, you think I'm being reasonable?

Casper: Completely. You'll achieve whatever you set your mind to. You're more stubborn than you think, and I mean that in a good way.

Mars: [*smiles*] Oh, right. Okay then. [*looks back at camera, pointing*] Forty-year-old me, don't let me down!

Fran: Ben? You want to do yours?

Ben: Yeah, sure. Hi, Ben! This is your younger self, you are twenty-seven, you made it to twenty-seven, and you're the happiest you've ever been. I hope you can speak a bit more Spanish by the time you look back on this recording, but honestly as long as you're just as happy as I am now, then that's more than I could...

Fran: Oh, shit, the battery is flashing.

[*camera cuts out*]

father always gets
me off the hook,
always such
an
...ous
...view
...u're ...gged
by a
...ne
the
...illside

PART FIVE
'THE ETERNAL'

2018

Casper
September 2018

WE WERE BACK IN DURHAM AT THE START OF
September, recording the last parts of our upcoming single. Book-
ings-wise, 2019 was a busy year for us, so we wanted to make the
most of our time before we began touring again. We met with
Marianne and The Thorns, who welcomed us back with open
arms. Mars and Lawrence remained relatively civil with one
another in public despite calling it quits towards the end of the
tour. Mars seemed to be better at letting bygones be bygones, but
Lawrence was a little more bitter; maybe being a permanent
teenager still had that effect on his personality. They never allowed
their relationship to get *too* serious—it was always more of a
'friends with benefits' type of thing. But Lawrence admitted he
liked the fact that they were both trans, and I couldn't judge him
for that, seeing as it was the main reason they hooked up to begin
with. There weren't many trans folks in the city—or any city, for
that matter—so it meant something personal to him, and maybe
to them both. Mars was a good role model for him and kept him

on the straight and narrow. In the long run, they just didn't work out.

I didn't worry about how it would affect the band. We'd been through a lot more than that and still came out strong. Our band's image had shifted massively over the decade, progressing into softer synth-rock in the last year or so. We'd performed at Leeds and Reading Fest for the past two summers and had travelled for what felt like forever—introducing more acoustics, which surprisingly went down well. I felt like our real fanbase had grown with us. The loyal ones had reached a stage where they claimed they'd listen and love anything we released, no matter how experimental. They just wanted to hear our creations.

Ben had long since hung up his fishnets and wild jewellery, toning down to a more 'subtle goth' vibe. On his twenty-seventh birthday in June, he said he wanted to be respected for his age, only for me to remind him that twenty-seven is still so young. Ben could rock that look for as long as he wanted; being 'goth' isn't a phase you grow out of, vampire or not.

Interview Excerpt: September 2018

Paul: So, tell us about your new image. We're coming up to the end of the decade, and fashion has changed quite a bit, hasn't it? How much of that has played into the band's image?

Fran: We've never really cared about what anyone else is doing. We've always just gone with the flow. I'll probably always bleach my hair and crop my shirts, but our image will be ever changing.

Ben: Yeah. I've traded in my New Rocks and lace for now, but who knows? I might bring them back. I'm going for a softer look now, though, it's just what I'm feeling. Casper calls it my 'grunge' era. All tartan shirts and oversized jumpers.

Casper: [*looks at Ben and grins*]

Paul: You all definitely still look young enough to pull off those aesthetics. In fact, you all look exactly the same as when you first started. How did you manage that? Any skin care tips for the fans?

Ben: [*shifts in his seat and clears his throat*]

Lawrence: Sleeping in coffins and gorging on blood.

Paul: [*looks startled but laughs it off*] Ahh, good one. Eternal goths, am I right?

Casper

25th October 2018 – evening

SINCE IT SEEMED we'd be staying in the city for a while, we decided to help The Thorns more. Marianne had recently implemented patrols again, making groups of us go out each night to keep the streets clean from potential attacks. Recently, it seemed like a bunch more Turned had arrived in the city and were causing unrest. Two deaths had occurred, and although they didn't seem linked to an ordinary outsider, to us, it was extremely suspicious. Apparently, the city had been quiet over the last year, but trouble is never far away when you know what you're looking for.

It was the day before my twenty-eighth birthday, and Ben insisted I left the house while he 'prepared things.' I had no idea what surprise he'd have in store for me, but he promised it would be good. I went on patrol with Mars and a few other Thorns, sticking to the central areas, especially the riverside. It wasn't a quiet night; people dressed in Halloween costumes roamed the streets, mostly drunk first years. Halloween is nowhere near as big over here as it is in the States, though. You know, everything my country does has to be bigger and better, almost like it's compensating for something... I digress.

I told Mars I'd stick by the riverside whilst they focused on the streets, and then we'd reconvene.

Despite how easy it is to turn someone, there were fewer vampires than you might expect. Throughout my whole time as one, I think I stumbled across maybe five, excluding The Thorns, so spotting one should have been easy.

Not long before midnight, I got a call from Mars. They'd found a body. *Shit.*

I legged it along the riverbank, shamefully pushing past people to reach them. A body. A young man, they said. He might still be alive, they said. Images of Ben lying on the stone slab entered my mind. *We must save him* was my only thought.

I got to the alleyway and saw the cluster of three Thorns all standing in a circle. Mars turned to me in the dim light, a wallet in their hands and tears in their eyes. "I have to try and save him," they said desperately.

I looked into their eyes and knew instantly who they were thinking of. Poppy. This was their chance to save someone.

Mars crouched as I stepped over to see the victim. He was very tall but young and had the same youthful innocence in his face as Ben. I gulped down my memories.

He had been freshly drained, and I barely even breathed my next question before Mars answered, "I think we scared them off. We heard a commotion, but by the time we got here, they'd gone." Their tone was one of feigned confidence, not willing to expose their emotions.

I nodded, trying to stay calm. "Is he alive?"

Mars only had eyes on the boy; they stroked his face and wiped away the blood on his neck. "I can sense a faint heartbeat. It's trying, but he's going to die if we leave him. If we ring the paramedics, it will be too late. I have to do this. I have to try."

"The kid doesn't have a say, though. You'd be changing his life forever," piped up one of the Thorns. There was always the moral dilemma of deciding to bring someone back from the dead, but

Mars seemed certain; they'd never done it successfully before and needed to prove they could. I thought back to the day we found Mars in the morgue and how badly they wanted to save Poppy, begging Marianne to help. They'd never had the chance to save her, but now they did, in a way.

"Do it," I said. "Try. Save him, Mars."

Mars looked from the Thorn to me and nodded, taking only a single breath before handing me the boy's exposed ID and wallet and pulling out a razor blade to their cut their wrist.

"Drink it, Arlo. Please," they said, leaning over the boy and parting his lips to let the blood trickle down his throat.

It had to work.

I'd never witnessed the process. Sometimes, it worked immediately, and other times, it took hours. For Ben, it was over a day.

Arlo woke up instantly, though I don't think he remembers that part.

Breathing loudly, his eyes shot open, his body arching. Mars caught him and held his neck. His breathing was strained, as though he had no air. He wasn't fully responsive straight away. His eyes rolled back, and his mouth hung open as his fangs grew in. His whole body shook and jerked, his legs kicking at all angles. It was extremely unsettling. I flinched and turned as Mars held his body, keeping him still. The process wasn't as swift as I'd hoped, but eventually, Arlo relaxed and collapsed into a deep slumber. I helped Mars carry him through the quiet streets, back to the hideout, where we let him rest and waited for him to wake.

WHEN I WENT BACK HOME that night, I told Ben what happened. He gave me a big hug and told me not to dwell on it, which was ironic advice from him, but it still helped. He'd cleaned the house, especially the guest bedroom, leaving me curious as to what he planned to surprise me with.

I got up early the next morning, and Ben had made me breakfast in bed before we headed to the hideout for updates on Arlo. Ben said that my surprise wasn't until mid-afternoon, something to distract my mind in the meantime.

"He hasn't woken yet," Mars said, slightly worried. They'd stayed outside the room all night, occasionally dipping their head in and trying to rouse him.

Ben joined the others in the main hall. Marianne had planned a morning meeting, so he went to catch up with some of our old friends.

"I'm starting to think I didn't give him enough blood. What if it only partly worked? He's breathing but only lightly, and—

"Hey, hey, Mars." I grabbed their shoulders. "Look at me. You did enough. More than enough! You put your own life at risk to save him. Whatever happens, it's not your fault!"

"I know, but I really had faith this time."

"Then everything will be okay." I wasn't sure of that, but I had faith in Mars. If anyone was going to manage to revive someone, it would be them.

As it turned out, Arlo was very much alive.

Ben

I HAD PLANNED Casper's present months in advance. I was never very good at buying presents as my mind always went blank, no matter how much I knew a person, but I was good at remembering people's feelings. I know Casper missed his oldest sister, who lived out of state; they hadn't seen each other for years. So, I called her and managed to arrange travel for her, her husband, Thom, and their two kids to fly over to stay for a week and surprise him. I cleared our guest bedroom and pulled out the futon. We'd been hiring out the house whilst we were out of the city, but I had a feeling it would be our home for a while longer with the new disturbances in the city. Regardless of our job, we were Thorns. We had a duty to protect.

Kathy wasn't due in the city until late afternoon due to train transfers, but everything was going according to plan. Casper would be thrilled.

But the night before his birthday was quite unpleasant for him. He didn't talk about it much, keeping a lot of details to himself; he was restless and couldn't sleep. I learned a long time ago that Casper was one of those people who kept most of his feelings to himself. He was an extremely selfless person who put others first no matter what. He acted confident and positive and optimistic, but I knew when something was eating away at him. That night, his mind was wholly consumed.

We headed to the hideout early the next morning, after a slightly rushed birthday breakfast in bed. (In hindsight, that was probably for the best. I couldn't cook for shit.) But we were there in a hurry for the meeting we all saw coming. Something was beginning to terrorise the city.

I left Casper with Mars, who looked distressed. It was clear neither of them wanted to share what they witnessed that night. I prayed the boy was okay, for both of their sakes.

It wasn't long before Mars brought Arlo into the main hall. The poor boy looked like he wanted the ground to swallow him whole. I knew the feeling. He was pretty, like an angel. Yes, I remember thinking exactly that. He was an angel. Something shifted in my chest when I first looked at him. I couldn't explain what; it was a weird sense of comfort. I wanted to get to know him more.

"I need to protect him," I whispered to Casper, who looked at me funny. After a moment, his face relaxed as if he understood perfectly.

"We will," was his reply.

Casper

AFTER WHAT WAS A FAR from comforting meeting, Ben drove us home and picked Fran up on the way; he said the three of us were going out for some lunch to kick off my birthday celebrations. Honestly, I've never been one for big parties; I can't really be bothered with them, but what I do love is spending time with those close to me, which is exactly what Ben treated me to.

When we got home, Ben left me alone and said he needed to pick up the surprise. I hoped he hadn't wasted money on something silly, but he only winked when I told him this. I should have trusted he knew me enough.

When I saw my sister's face for the first time in five years, I broke down. She came running at me and pulled me into the biggest hug. I was stunned and couldn't move, but the second it sunk in, I caved. Ben had planned this?

I lifted my nieces and spun them around like I used to when they were kids. The oldest, Adriana, was nearly a teenager and thus a trying weight on my arms, but I didn't care. I was overjoyed and overwhelmed but in the best way.

"Happy Birthday, Uncle! Why do you have to live so far away? I'm missing classes for this!" The youngest, Ila, pulled a silly face in jest, feigning annoyance. Glad to see she took after her Uncle Sam.

Adriana stood back more maturely, folding her arms and wishing me a happy birthday as if it were a corporate agreement, but then she stepped closer and smiled. "I've missed you," she said.

We had the best evening I'd had in years, with posh wine and a feast fit for a king. Ben had planned the whole week ahead, promising to take the girls trick-or-treating and letting them decorate the whole house as crazily as they wanted. I watched him chase them around the house in a Scream mask and thought about what a great dad he'd be. I longed to bring that up to him, but he wasn't ready. I know he was running from adulthood for as long as he could. He tried so hard not to show it, though.

"When are you guys finally gonna settle?" Thom asked from the kitchen table, sitting with my sister on the high stools with beers. They'd clearly caught me watching him, and I was probably grinning without realising.

"What, oh. We've settled. Sort of."

"Sort of?" Kathy raised her eyebrows, teasing.

"Well, yeah. We don't mind taking things slowly. We're still young."

"True, but you've been together for years. Have you even talked about it?"

"What's with the quizzing?" I asked defensively. I didn't mean for it to come out harshly or so *British,* but I was glad to end the conversation. Ben didn't want to get married; it was as simple as that. I wasn't going to push him. He had his reasons.

After the kids went to bed, the four of us stuck on a movie and talked about random 'adult' things. I still didn't see myself as a proper adult; I felt like I was missing something, but it was probably the lifestyle. Immortality aside, being in a band that catered to the unruly youths keeps the rebellion in you.

Talking to my sister put me at ease; she was always a straightforward woman who cared deeply yet was unafraid to say things with brutal honestly. That night helped me to forget everything from the night before, until I checked the news before bed and found out how in the early hours of that morning, there had been another death—right where I'd been patrolling before I got the call from Mars.

I should have been there to stop it.

Ben
November 2018

"I'm worried."

"What?" Casper asked, looking at me funny. It had been a week since his birthday and the Arlo incident. After saying goodbye to Kathy and the kids, we'd driven to Alnwick for the day to clear our heads. I was much better at taking charge now and making decisions for us. We needed a break. I knew Casper blamed himself for the death of the third victim, even though it wasn't his fault. I confronted him—another thing I was better at now—and he confessed his feelings. We kept it from the others, but eventually, I think I got through to him. We were a nightmare sometimes.

"Arlo. He's troubled and has a lot on his mind; I could sense it the other night," I admitted. I barely knew the kid, but ever since our first meeting, I couldn't fight the feeling that I was somehow responsible for him. I couldn't explain it. The day after Casper's birthday, after leaving him with his family, I managed to speak with Arlo. He was out for a walk near the cathedral after dark and I called him over. It was weird... talking to him felt like talking in a mirror, and I believed we bonded, but I was unconvinced *he* believed we had true intentions to help him. I saw too much of myself in him.

"It's early days. I mean, we definitely had a few teething problems, if you'll excuse the pun." Casper laughed, but not at the situation. He understood what I meant. "Marianne has told us to keep an eye on him, and Mars is keeping a close watch. If something is wrong, I know Mars will sort it."

"You know how you felt with Lawrence? Well, I've got this gut feeling with Arlo," I spoke my thoughts.

"Lawrence was in serious danger."

"And Arlo isn't? We're all on edge right now, we have to admit that. Three deaths in less than two months? This Lucy person, that was the name Arlo gave, right? The person who tried to kill him? How many more deaths are going to happen because of her? Home isn't safe anymore."

Casper rubbed my leg. "I know, I know."

I leaned against the window. "He's lonely."

Casper frowned again; I could sense it. "How do you know that?"

I turned the engine back on as the traffic started moving. "Have you seen him with anyone other than that pretty girl?"

"You mean his girlfriend? The kid is allowed to have a partner, you know." Casper rolled his eyes.

"She's not his girlfriend."

"And how do you know that? How closely have you been following the poor kid?"

"He told me! I told you we spoke. He doesn't have a partner. He spends a lot of time on his own—*a lot*."

"Right, but he's only just moved here; he's probably not settled in yet."

"Casper, trust me. I know this. He reminds me of myself when I was in secondary school. I only ever really had Jake, and..." I paused. That was the first time I'd brought up Jake in years. I froze at how freely it slipped from my mouth, as if I'd finally moved on. Wow.

Casper gave me a sympathetic look. "Okay, so you think he needs what? More friends? People to talk to? We offered to help him, and he refused."

"What?"

Casper tapped his lips. "Okay, maybe that was a bit harsh. We don't know him; he's clearly quite distressed. I do believe he will be alright, though. His friend—girlfriend or whatever—she's there for him. Sometimes, having a smaller group of friends means more. The ties run deeper."

I nodded slowly, eyes on the road. He had a point, so why couldn't I shake the intense feeling that I needed to do something? To stop something from happening? I didn't know what, but... I had a headache all of a sudden.

"You okay?"

"Yeah. Sorry. We're nearly there."

ARLO WENT AWAY to spend Diwali with his friend Rani, and while Mars and Marianne seemed a little stressed at the idea, Arlo seemed to be following their advice and looking after himself. We needed him to believe we trusted him, so Arlo left with a human and spent days in human company without us. Yet when he came back, despite no damage having been done, he looked different— paler, thinner. It made no sense.

It was my idea to follow him into the supermarket. There was no denying I was borderline stalking him at that point, but I couldn't ignore the signs. "Did you see his face?"

"Ben, you're taking this a little too seriously now. He's been away, you might have just forgotten—"

Casper was trying to be the voice of reason, thinking about me above anyone else, but I still needed to do my job.

"He's not sleeping, maybe. He looks like he's been punched in the eyes..."

"He's a very pale boy. You look like death half the time, too." Casper pointed out with a slight laugh. "Look, I think we need to let the kid be. It's taking over your mind; you need to let yourself breathe. I know you think you have this moral obligation to protect him, but we're all doing the same thing. The poor kid has half the city on his shoulder at the moment."

"I know. I'm sorry. Let's go home."

Casper

"CARMEN DID WHAT?"

The band sat in our usual studio room. Lawrence was dangling on the windowsill with his cigarette while Fran threw out solos on her guitar when Ben stormed into the room, announcing that Carmen had told Rani who Arlo was. We now had another human in on our secret. One step closer to being caught. Ben looked exasperated.

"She just told her?" Fran tuned up one of her strings. Then: "Wait, fill me in on who Carmen is again, she's the human, yeah?"

We all nodded. Fran really did try to keep herself away from the vampire part of our identities. She said it was the best way for her to convince herself nothing was going on.

"She said she'd been following Rani for a few days and thought the only way for us to go on as normal would be to tell her the truth." Ben sounded out of breath.

"Well, maybe she's right." Fran shrugged. "I mean, how long did it take for you lot to tell me? Would you ever have told me if *Draculita* over here hadn't tried to take out a chunk of my neck?" She gestured to a hazy Lawrence, who blew a plume of smoke directly into the room. I wafted it out of my face, wrinkling my nose in disgust.

"Hey, I said sorry!" Lawrence rolled his eyes, and Fran threw him the middle finger. At least they'd both moved on finally.

"So, that means she's fully aware of us then?" I asked, steering the conversation back to Ben.

"I don't know. I mean, I presume so. Carmen said she asked Marianne because she trusts Rani. After all, she is Arlo's only friend."

"He has us." Lawrence winked sarcastically.

I made sure he saw my eyes roll. "Hardly. He probably thinks we're stalking him, just like the rest of The Thorns. The only people who've successfully managed to get close to him are Ben and Mars."

At the mention of our manager, Lawrence tutted.

"I think she did the right thing." Fran pointed out. "Sometimes you lot need human friends to keep your ties. As long as you can keep it in your gums, you need us close."

We all paused to consider.

"Maybe you're right," I sighed. We could all trust Carmen; she was the closest to Marianne besides Mars and knew what she was doing. Arlo would hardly confess to his friend, and it was most likely eating him apart. As long as we kept Rani in the loop, maybe this would work.

"I suppose at least this way, Rani can look after him without us having to get involved." Ben piped up.

"He's fine, you know," Lawrence said directly to Ben, as though he knew everything. That didn't sink in well.

"He's not," Ben insisted.

I looked into my partner's eyes and sighed. No one else spoke a word on the matter.

Ben

"Casper, wake up! Wake up now. There's been an accident."

Casper startled awake, nearly knocking over the glass of water on his bedside table. I didn't mean to shock him, but after Mars' text, I needed to leave immediately, but I couldn't without letting Casper know where I was going.

"What, what? What's wrong?" he asked, panicked.

"Arlo. He had an accident. He went all feral and ran out onto the streets. They caught him, but he's in a really bad way. Marianne had to sedate him." That was all I knew at the time.

"What the hell? Did he hurt anyone?"

"I don't think so." Though, I wasn't sure. I hoped to goodness he wasn't a Turned. That he hadn't fooled us all.

"Come on then, let's go."

"Okay, okay; thank you." I slipped off the bed and ran to the wardrobe.

WE MADE it down in less than half an hour. Mars and the others paced the hall.

"What the heck happened?" Casper asked before I could even form the words.

"He lied, that's what," Mars said bluntly.

My stomach sank. "What do you mean? Did he hurt someone? Rani?"

Mars shook their head vigorously.

"He lied about taking the bags," said Marianne, speaking for them.

"What do you mean? He wasn't feeding?" All I could see were Arlo's purplish eyes and the bones on his wrists.

"Arlo, the idiot he is, thought he didn't need our help and could do this all on his own. He lied about using the bags I gave him and instead fed off his own blood for three weeks straight."

I sensed the anger in Mars' voice, annoyed they hadn't figured it out sooner. Maybe I should have spoken up more, but no one listened to me. Maybe it was inevitable.

"So, where is he now? What are we going to do?" Casper tucked his hands casually in his pockets; he always stayed calm in situations that used to send my blood pressure rising through the roof.

"He's back in the room. Carmen and Rani are with him," Marianne said.

"He's in a room alone with humans? After being starved?" I shouted. I was moments from turning on my heels before she grabbed my arm.

"He's unconscious! They're keeping their distance; two guards are in the corner, *and* I'm checking him every hour. I gave him blood; he's sated."

"Oh."

"Rani refused to leave his side." She looked up to Casper. "Reminds me of someone."

I THINK this day was when it all started to skew. We put new music on hold and joined The Thorns, alongside Arlo, preparing for the worst. Training our minds like we'd never had to before. Arlo hadn't just *'gone feral'*. He'd let something in. Something else had taken the reigns that night—the night we learned something far more powerful than vampires had entered our world. I knew Arlo stood out for a reason. We were no longer just preparing for Lucy to strike again, we were preparing for the end.

Just like that, we went from living our lives as normal, to being reminded of our differences. We weren't human, and we had to start pretending we'd known that all along.

"I FEEL like everything has changed, and I'm scared." I confided in Casper one night. We'd spent the whole day training our mental guards. I was exhausted; I was never as good as everyone else; my mind was always too distracted. It was harder for vampires to

Manipulate each other than it was to control a human anyway, but I really struggled.

He kissed my forehead and rubbed my temples. "You will get better, you know. We will be okay. We always are."

I buried myself closer in his arms. "We've never had to deal with things like this, though. All our issues have come from amps and miscommunication, and now we're becoming warriors for a battle beyond human comprehension. I just feel so weak all the time..."

He held me tight. "You're the strongest person I know, Benjamín Audley. You are a giant."

A MISSION I gave myself throughout all these changes was to keep Arlo's life normal for him. He didn't know me that well, and we didn't see each other a lot, but I remember him telling me he played piano, so one afternoon, I plucked up the courage to ask him to come with me and Fran to our home studio. He seemed startled, his mind always distant, but he smiled and followed us.

I wanted so badly to ask him how he was holding up, if he needed anything from us—analysing his every move, but my goal was to keep him happy. Nothing about his situation was happy; he was constantly on edge.

Marianne told us all to observe any changes. To report if we saw or heard anything out of the ordinary while she researched all she could. "Something is after him," she would repeat every morning. I didn't want to treat him like a test subject, though, so this was my way of doing both.

I didn't tell him I recorded the piece he played. He wouldn't have performed it otherwise. Call me selfish, call me cruel, but I listened to it every night. The whole band wanted to get him back in the studio once this had *blown over.*

"It will blow over. Just another hurdle," Fran said. I knew she was lying though, she tried so hard to distract us, bless her soul.

We did a few small, local gigs, just like when we first started out. The tone was bittersweet, but it was the best we could do to keep ourselves distracted in the moments of freedom from The Thorns. Freedom from this impending reality. The world had no idea what was going on, we had to keep it that way.

THE FINAL CHANGE that hit me was when I realised how much this was affecting not only Arlo, or The Thorns in general, but my own band. We were so intrinsically connected to all of this now, there would be no escaping.

"Ben? Can we talk?" Lawrence pulled me aside after a gig we did mid-December. Arlo and Rani had been in the front row, Carmen our stand in photographer for the night. I remember thinking it would probably be our last gig for a while. Tensions were really rising, and we were Thorns at the end of the day. We had our duties.

"Everything alright?" I asked, noting the shallow tone of his voice, as if it was coming from the shadows. He was sober, which helped me relax a little.

"Not really. But I..." It wasn't like Lawrence to be lost for words. I indicated for him to follow me into the empty break room, flicking on the buzzing light. I sat, patting the sofa beside me for him to join me.

"How are you managing with the, you know, Manipulation stuff?" he eventually asked.

Not that well. "I get by. Why?"

Lawrence squirmed in his seat, looking around the room as he got comfortable.

"I just... Has a vampire ever made you say or do something you didn't mean?"

What?

This concerned me. I asked him to elaborate, questioning if he was referring to the training Marianne had made us do over the past month or so.

He ignored my direct questions, but unintentionally answered them with his next question. He wouldn't stop fidgeting. Like he was about to admit something that would take away his pride. "Has a vampire ever successfully Manipulated you? Made you use your own Manipulation? I dunno. I feel like we're similar, I know you've said you struggle..."

"Lawrence, who is Manipulating you? Is this going on outside the training? Is it something Marianne should know?"

At the mention of The Thorns leader, he hummed in distress.

"Nope. No. It's nothing like that. I just... Oh never mind, it will be the drugs. It always is." He stood up and headed straight for the exit.

"Hey, wait, Lawrence. I'm here to listen if you need to talk, I'm glad you came to me. I can try and help?" I didn't want him to leave the conversation this *open.*

Lawrence smiled with his eyes. "No, honestly. It's okay. Just forget I ever said anything. It's my problem, I understand that. I know what I need to do."

He never spoke about this to me again.

December 25th 2018

Casper probably never expected me to do it, which is exactly why I did. Everything that happened since October really forced me to stop putting things off and to just go with my gut.

Mars helped me pick the ring. They laughed and said they would be useless aid, but I believed they knew us the best and would give me an honest and non-biased opinion. I didn't want anything too flashy or dramatic. Just something plain and classy, subtly displaying our love.

Three years on from publicly coming out, I still felt a shiver down my spine at the thought of everyone knowing I was gay. It's silly, but I'd accepted at that point that I would always have a slight sense of unease being so publicly *other*. I was just thankful no one who knew me from school had ever advertised my sexuality on social media before I was ready. Or if they had, no one acknowledged it enough to spread the word.

But fears aside, this was something I needed to do—*wanted* to do.

We spent the day with my mum and gran. We cooked for them for the first time and played our annual game of charades. We even attempted a board game. The stakes weren't high, seeing as it was only the four of us, but it was fun nonetheless. I loved my family.

I'd told my mum my plan a few weeks earlier but insisted there was no rush for them to leave. I would wait until they'd gone to bed, but she was adamant. She drank carbonated grape juice then drove my gran back home at teatime. She wanted us to have this time to ourselves.

I waited until we'd washed up before I started dropping hints.

"I'm going to pour us a nice glass of something, and maybe you could pick a movie?" I said, grinning.

"Who are you, and what have you done with Ben?" Casper joked, wide-eyed. "When was the last time we watched a movie together?" He raised his brow and pursed his lips.

"I just thought it would be a nice wind down for us. Completely your choice; I won't complain." I continued grinning as I headed for the kitchen.

Casper hesitantly reached the bottom of the stairs, slowly turning towards the living room. "Okay, well, if you insist. And it's my choice..."

I knew he would choose something I'd despise, but I didn't care. I couldn't stop smiling.

If my heart still worked, I would have been able to feel it in my head then. My hands grew clammy as I waited for Casper to be out of sight, ensuring I could position the ring to face him. I poured us each a double of our favourite rum and dropped an ice cube into each. I took a moment to breathe in deeply, staring out at the backyard, lit with the half-broken fairy lights we'd put up last year. They twinkled, a silent assurance that we would be fine, and the best moment of my life so far was soon to come.

I nodded to myself, deciding I was ready, before making my way with the glasses to join Casper in the front room.

When I reached the doorway, Casper was sitting on the couch, pointing a remote at the DVD player, trying to get it to eject the previous disc. He cursed slightly to himself. Once he noticed my presence, he looked up at me and began laughing.

"I was going to really mess with you, but I don't even think we have the disc for it. I think the player is jammed. I'm hoping it's jammed with the disc I need but I'm losing hope."

I playfully shook my head and moved to join him, popping our drinks down onto the coffee table before us. I stared at him.

"What? Is there something on my face?" Casper rubbed around his lips, embarrassed.

"You look beautiful," I said.

"Oh, hell no. I know that look. You're up to something, Audley."

"Murphey," I said, still smiling.

"Huh?"

That was my cue. *Here goes.*

I stood and walked around the coffee table, blocking the TV. I was the only thing Casper could focus on. His face dropped, but I think he was piecing it together.

With a deep breath, I pulled the ring box out of my pocket and lowered to one knee, holding it out. Casper's eyes widened.

"Casper Murphey, will you marry me?" I said with every fibre of my being, every grain of my soul, every corner of my dead heart.

The second felt like an eternity as Casper stood, covering his mouth with both hands. I followed him with my eyes in a panic, my grip on the box weakening.

"Yes. Yes. Yes!" he cried. "Of course. Of course, Ben. Oh, Ben. My Ben. Be mine." He dropped to his knees before pulling me in for a hug, nodding as tears brimmed his gaze.

"For Eternity," I said through crushed cheeks.

"My Eternal." Casper gripped me tightly.

He finally let me pull back so I could show him the ring properly.

"Oh, it's beautiful, Ben. It's perfect."

He offered up his finger then we embraced once more. We shared many, many tears. It had been a long time coming—too long.

I had one more surprise.

"I've also been looking at the process of potentially adopting. It doesn't have to be yet—there's no rush, but I know you want kids, and I know I said I didn't before, but recently I've been thinking that yeah... I can see a kid being a part of our lives." I was shaking.

And Casper cried again.

"Ben, you don't have to, you know. I was never that bothered, honestly. Don't feel like you have to—"

"I want to." And I did. I'd been thinking more about it lately, and vampiric complications aside, it was something I wanted to happen in our lives. Casper would be a great dad, and our kids would have such an amazing family.

"Oh, Ben." Casper shook his head, tears spilling from his eyes.

"I love you too much," I said. "I love you so much, it hurts, and I know it will never change."

We hugged one final time until our tears settled. Slowly, Casper lifted me to the couch and laid me down against the leather, pressing his mouth and body against mine. We sunk into the chair as his kisses intensified, trailing down my neck. He lingered over the artery and nipped at the skin, a smirk forming.

I held onto his back as his jumper hitched up, pressing my hand against the thin vest beneath. It wasn't enough; I needed to feel him. I pulled at the material until it escaped from his trousers. I pressed my palm flat against his spine, his muscles twitching and tensing beneath it.

"Eternity," he breathed as our kisses broke. "We can be together for eternity, and yet it still doesn't feel like enough." Casper pulled back to take me in, his gaze hungry. I bared my neck for him, and his kisses continued.

I raised my arms to help him remove my thick, knitted Christmas jumper and let him remove each layer until I bared my body before him. His lips lingered over my collarbone, and I instinctively arched my back, needing him closer.

The fire spat beside us while the embers burned strong, heating the room as our bodies became one, sliding together with our well-practised rhythm.

"Casper," I begged, canines clamping onto his lower lip.

At my submission, Casper wrapped his strong arms beneath my body and pulled me up so my knees were bent and straddling his thighs. He let his hands wander up my back and over my shoulder blades. A drop of blood dripped from his lip; I caught it with my tongue.

He breathed a sigh of surrender, then reached a hand down to the belt of my jeans, slowly freeing me and hoisting my legs over his shoulders.

"Ben."

AN HOUR LATER, I ran upstairs for a quick shower and told Casper I was popping outside for a tab. He lay sated on the couch, his chest gently rising and falling as the fire dwindled. I smiled before stepping outside into the cold.

I'd thrown Casper's jacket around my shoulders, laughing at how it drowned me out. I wrapped myself deeper in it.

I stepped around the corner from the house and into the alleyway—a habit I'd formed over the years of fans capturing me at my worst. No fan was crazy enough yet to follow me back to the house, though.

I lit up and watched the clouds of smoke rise into the air. It was so peaceful here. The neighbour opposite had their window latched open, the distant sounds of Home Alone playing into the wind.

Ben Murphey. I thought as I took another drag. We didn't have to take each other's surnames, but I knew I wanted to become a Murphey. I couldn't stop grinning at the thought of it.

"Something amusing you?"

I dropped my cigarette, startled by the voice behind me. I turned towards the figure, assuming it was an innocent fan, until I saw the green hair. My heart sank so low I felt dizzy. There was only one person who I'd ever heard of having hair this colour. Arlo's murderer. The woman most likely to be in charge of *all* these recent murders. *Lucy.*

"You."

She was much smaller than I'd pictured. Based on what I'd heard, I think I expected some seven-foot winged creature from space.

She groaned, emitting a slow, proud laugh. "I see my reputation precedes me." Her voice was cool and confident as she prowled towards me. I edged backward.

I had a million things I wanted to say, but it was no use. The worst thing is, I sensed the strength of her Manipulation before it happened. My brain tingled, and my fists clenched. I was never as strong as the others.

She drew closer. Although she only reached my shoulder, she had me fully in her grasp. I knew then I was her next victim.

"Pleased to meet you, Ben Audley. I've been following you for a while, but don't think that makes you special—it doesn't. You were just my lucky dip." She raised a gloved hand to my forehead and brushed away my curls. I couldn't move. "I'm sorry for picking such an inconvenient time. I'm just getting really, really bored, and I need to start moving forward with everything before I just *scream*." She laughed in my face.

A tiny trickle of worry festered in my body, but I gave in when the arm of the soul behind me came around my neck and covered my mouth. A needle stung my skin. Everything was too strong— her mind, his arm, my weakness.

I struggled once until his other arm wrapped around my wrists and pulled them tightly behind my back, pinning me in place. My eyes never left hers as she pounced, pressing a hand to my chest and bringing her mouth to my ear.

"Sleep, Ben. Sleep, and it will all be over soon."

God, I was tired.

Casper

FIFTEEN MINUTES WAS an awful long time for one cigarette, but sometimes, when Ben felt extra anxious, he'd smoke up to three at a time, coming back stinking of the stuff. But I was confused. What was there to be anxious about tonight?

I waited another two minutes before grabbing my discarded jumper and heading for the door. I reached for the jacket normally hanging on the peg, but it was missing. He must have taken it. So, I left without a coat. I thought I'd only be a few minutes. I'd playfully scold him for stinking the house out, and then we'd laugh it off and go to bed. Never would I have predicted what happened that night.

The night my life fell apart.

Ben wasn't in his usual spot, but I wasn't concerned quite yet. I checked further down the lane and then around the corner to the street opposite the park. Still nothing. I didn't panic, though. Maybe I'd just missed him, and he'd gone back inside.

I remember shaking my head and thinking about how silly we were, but when I reached the front steps to our home, I felt like something was wrong.

I went back inside and called for him. No answer.

"Ben!" I shouted, stomping down the hallway and letting my voice carry upstairs.

He wouldn't pop out of the living room and scare me; he was never one for jump scares—he hated them. We knew each other inside out.

Maybe it was nothing, though. I tried to calm myself down as I went back into the sitting room, sat down, and pulled out my phone to call him.

The phone rang so many times, and with each ring, I lost more and more hope.

And then I realised his phone was on the table.

On silent. No vibration. Face down.

"Ben?" I said out loud again. I was no longer shouting.

I sat for a further ten minutes, waiting for Ben to return, before I rang his phone again and stared at the device beside me. I couldn't think.

A minute later, I left the house. He wasn't coming home. I wrapped his coat around me and walked and walked and walked. It was well past midnight, but my mind wouldn't stop thinking the worst. He couldn't have gone far; why would he wander off? Did he get cold feet and second-guess the proposal? Why did he—

I didn't get home until nearly four. I finally called the police, who said that my call wasn't urgent enough and that I needed to ring back in the morning. It was Christmas Day. He was a grown adult and would likely return home soon. They didn't believe it was serious.

But when I got home, he still wasn't there.

When I fell asleep and woke up, he wasn't beside me.

And then, I lost it.

Ben was gone.

THE LAST WEEK of that year was the hardest thing I've ever had to experience. Every single day, I searched everywhere. He'd completely vanished. At first, I thought maybe he panicked and needed time to rethink the things he promised me, but those thoughts lasted mere seconds. He hadn't run away. Someone had taken him.

The others helped. Oh, they tried so hard. But it was no use.

When the parcel arrived and Marianne refused to let me see it, that was when it sunk in. I was never going to see him again. I was going to kill Lucy; I was going to destroy her.

I'm not a cruel person, but the insurmountable rage I felt that day made me believe I could have done anything and wouldn't have cared. I did not fear the law or what people thought. If Ben was gone, then so was my humanity.

The thought frightened me. All my undead life, I made it a priority to remain as human as possible, constantly reminding myself of my morals and beliefs and what I stood for. Ben felt things too deeply, while I worried I didn't feel enough. But I did. I always did, deep down. I was human. We were human. Nothing would ever change, no matter how long we lived. I'd seen how evil the world could be. That could never be me.

By killing a murderer, you continue the cycle.

It tried me, though. It really tried.

. . .

Lucy had a plan. She knew we'd all turn up, it must have made her so pleased with herself.

That day in the forest, the world tipped upside down. From the moment I felt her inside my head, I knew nothing would ever be the same again.

Ben

I remember feeling a lot of pain. I remember the church rafters, the crumbling, mossy walls and her voice in my head. I remember crying out as she seized my fingers and picked away at them bit by bit.

I remember her getting me to talk, but I had no energy by then.

By the third night, I craved blood—a cruel hunger I'd never felt. She poked needles into me and laughed as the silver burned my bloodstream.

By the fourth night, or what I guessed was the fourth night, I'd forgotten who I was.

And by the fifth, she had taken my eyes.

I think an angel came for me that night. I really believed it was my time, and though I couldn't see it, I heard it cower at the sight of me and fall to the ground. I blamed myself for everything and waited for hell to burn me.

She knew everything about us. She needed nothing from me; I was just the starter. The appetiser. The toy.

I don't remember much else.

I do remember holding Casper's hands one last time, feeling his warmth, and hearing his voice sooth my mind. He made me feel safe in my final moments.

I don't remember dying, but maybe that's for the best.

Casper

FOR AS LONG AS there is air in my lungs, I will never forget the weight of Ben's body in my arms: the colours staining the ground —things I should have never seen. I told myself I still felt his grip digging into my shoulders, but that sensation was long gone. I'd awoken from a cruel dream, only for it to play out exactly like I'd feared.

The jade in his eyes. The elegance of his smile. The beauty of his soul.

I will always love you, Ben. I will always love you.

You just can't hear me anymore.

<u>Interview of Jake Walters: June 2019</u>

INTERVIEWER: Thank you for sitting down with us. We really appreciate your time, Jake.

Jake: Yeah, thank you for having me. To be honest, I'm still baffled I agreed to this.

Interviewer: Just take your time, the interview ends when you say so.

[*redacted*]

Interviewer: After you left, did you ever think about re-joining or getting back in touch with them?

Jake: I'd be lying if I flat out said 'no.' We all let our minds wander at times, but I was pretty set on my decision. I knew it was the best thing for me. I had a lot of shit to unpack by myself, and I don't think I would have ever managed it if I stayed. And that's nothing against them; I loved them like family—we *were* a family. But sometimes, we change. It hurts, of course it hurts, but it hurts everybody. At the end of the day, we had to do what we thought was right in the moment, and I made my decision. Do I regret *when* I left? One million percent. I did it at the most selfish moment because, to me, I was on a train careering off a cliff, and if I hadn't jumped then, I would have taken the ride all the way to the end. I thought the end was nigh, as they say. [*laughs*] But I knew my best friend was suffering; I made it clear to the others as well—they knew what was going on, but I couldn't hold on anymore; it was a ticking time bomb. At the time, I thought the best thing was to cut the wire as quickly as I could. Should I have helped my friend first? Without a shadow of a doubt. But our minds are funny sometimes. Sometimes, it all gets a little cloudy.

I knew he was in good hands. I knew they would find him the help he needed, while I found the help *I* needed, too. I got better; I healed. And I'd like to think he did, too. In fact, I know he did.

Interviewer: Just to be clear, you are talking about Ben here, right?

Jake: [*smiles and takes a deep breath*] I mean, you would have figured that out regardless of my answer, but yeah. He's the only reason I'm doing this interview.

Interviewer: We're all deeply sorry for your...

Jake: Let's not do that. I appreciate the sentiment, but I, you know, don't really...

Interviewer: I'm sorry, we'll move on. So, you mentioned you met up then?

Jake: [*nods*] Yeah. Last summer, he came home. I bumped into him, and I thought, fuck it, I'm not just gonna stand and exchange pleasantries over a shopping trolley. We'd definitely left it a little too long. He looked exactly how I remembered him, as if he hadn't aged a day. And his smile... his beautiful smile. I missed him. I think he missed me, too—at least, I hope he did. But it was all my fault; I'd never blame him for anything now, and that's not just because, you know, he's not here, but I came to terms with my actions many years ago, and if I'm being honest, I chickened out trying to rectify things. But we went for a coffee; we caught up with each other's lives—what was it, six years or something? Seven? God, I can't believe I dropped out of uni because of this. Wow. Things worked out, though.

But yeah, we met, we talked, we hugged. I apologised, then he did tenfold, even after I told him not to. But that was Ben; he never changed.

Interviewer: So, in those whole seven years, you hadn't been in contact?

Jake: It was seven years, then? You did your research. God. Well. Erm, I mean there was passive contact—like following each other on social media and stuff. I kept up to date with the band and had a few conversations with his grandmother. But I don't think we ever texted, other than to wish each other a happy new year or something. I left Durham, you see, and came back home. It just wasn't for me. I didn't want that life anymore; I needed to escape fully, so yeah, we kind of went no contact for those first few years. Again, they all knew I was okay; I didn't just drop off the face of the earth, but I got out of there as soon as I could.

[*redacted*]

Interviewer: Do you regret leaving, now looking at the band's success? You know, when Lawrence joined, and when the band really blew up. After their albums, tours, and fanbase?

Jake: I know you're dying for me to say yes, but honestly, not really. I thought that was all I could ever want for a time; I thought I was on top of the world and would never come down. But eventually, something shifted in me, and I knew deep down that I couldn't really handle that life: the journalists, the media outlets, [*pauses then laughs*] the interviews.

Interviewer: [*laughs*]

Jake: I mean, look at how long it took for them to tell the world about their relationship. Those boys were together for five years before they went public. *Five years.* Of hiding, of lying, of teasing. You remember when everyone thought Ben and Fran were dating? You know how long they—*we* let that lie sit? Because it was mundane news. Hell, things are a lot better now, but at the time, they weren't even legally allowed to get married in either of their birthplaces. But the internet gobbled that lie up. We fed it to them and laughed from the side-lines, but it was all just really sad. Do you think I wanted a life like that? To have my every move observed and scrutinised? I don't know how they coped with everything, but they did, and that band—my friends—are the strongest people I know.

I hope Ben knew that.

Interviewer: He did. From what I researched, he only ever spoke highly of you and your friendship.

Jake: [*pauses and looks away from the camera*] I just miss him, man.

Interviewer: That's understandable.

Jake: [*inaudible*] Can we leave it there, sorry? I need to go outside.

Part Six
'Forever Red'

2019

Casper

It's March now. Two months since it happened. Two whole months without him.

People say grief gets easier with time. I suppose I can't vouch for that yet, but I'd like to hope it does. I can't let myself go on like this forever. For eternity.

After the first two days, I flew home, Jesse waiting for me at the airport. I needed my brother.

"I'm here, little brother. I'm always going to be here," he'd said, wrapping me into the biggest hug. But how could he know? How does anyone know how long they're going to be here?

He'd grown a beard since I'd last seen him, and looked much older. But then again, he was allowed to age normally; he was nearly thirty-six. I, however, was going to look twenty-one forever. A joke I used to make because everyone wishes they could be twenty-one forever, but now I wished I could be close to my thirties, closer to completing my life. I didn't want to die, but I no longer enjoyed the idea of living forever. It was fine when I had Ben because we had each other; we would have never grown lonely. But now, I was doomed to watch everyone I love disappear whilst I constantly reinvented myself and my identity. I couldn't be Casper Murphey forever; the world would catch on.

I suppose I still have time to figure that out, but I'm already getting the 'wow, you look so young for your age' comments, and I'm not sure how much longer I can endure them without screaming.

Kathy is in her forties, Sam and Rhonda close behind. I'm still a child. I grew with Ben, but now I'm stuck. We did everything together; we had our whole future planned, and then it just *stopped.*

WE CAME BACK for the funeral, but flew straight back home after; I didn't tell anyone where I was going except Mars and the band. Band? Can we even call ourselves that anymore? We hadn't made any new music for ages.

I got on the plane with a bag barely packed enough for two nights, but I just wanted to be away from everything—away from our bedroom, our house, his clothes hanging in the closet, his toothbrush, his shampoo, his shoes. His favourite cereal going soft in the cupboard. His eyeliner pens scattered across the coffee table and windowsills. His guitars, his keyboard, his records, his phone. *He didn't even have his phone on him when he...*

I didn't dare move anything.

And the longer I stayed there, the more his scent would fade from the house, and the more things I would accidentally knock out of place. It was eating me up, and I was suffocating.

"YOU WANNA TALK?" Jesse offered once we got into the taxi picking us up from the airport. We'd barely had a full conversation during both flights.

I shook my head but smiled at him, my chest tightening. "I just wanna go home."

He understood.

I'M SAT in my childhood bedroom, peering out of my tiny back window onto the field behind us, staring into the trees where the rope remains from the swing my dad built for us. A thread bare memory of halcyon days. I watch my childhood-self running around, with Sam and Rhonda chasing me until we collapse with adrenaline. My mom shouts for us to come inside for dinner. I was a happy kid; I had the best family. I was and still am eternally grateful for that.

In 2005, Hurricane Katrina hit, and we had no idea how far it would reach. I feared for Kathy, who lived much closer to the evacuation zone than we did, and I genuinely believed it could be the end of the world, because that's how it seemed. I remember my whole family sat on the couch downstairs, eyes glued to the TV, expecting the power to go out at any minute. I tried to act big and brave, but I was terrified. We all were, but Jesse held my hand tight and promised nothing bad was ever going to happen to us.

He was right. We weren't hit, and no one we knew suffered massively, but he couldn't have predicted the future. It turns out, bad things always happen, and that's just life.

Life. Something I still need to remind myself I have.

I didn't talk much in the first week or so after moving back home. It was just Mom, Dad, and Jesse in the house now. They all gave me my space whilst stating many times that they would be there whenever I was ready to talk.

One afternoon, when the sun was out, I went for a walk into town with Jesse. We talked a little about our memories and laughed as we passed houses and streets with childhood stories attached. We went to my favourite coffee shop. (Well, the place had been rebranded about four times in my lifetime, but it always kept the same layout, and I always sat in the window.)

Jesse told me he'd found a place and hoped to move in soon. I was happy for him. He finally knew what he wanted.

"It's got a spare room, you know. You're welcome to it for as long as you need it," he offered with a sincere smile. I thanked him and even said I might take him up on the offer.

The more I stayed, the more I didn't want to leave, and the less and less I thought about the band. We were relatively unheard of in the US. We had our followers, but we were by no means as grand as we were back home.

I said home, didn't I?

Hmm.

IT'S APRIL NOW, and Lawrence called me twice to say he was flying out. I was mad at first, but then I told Jesse, and he said I shouldn't run from everyone. They were all hurting.

I met with Lawrence, who told me about home (I called it home again, didn't I?) and how everyone was doing. Not very well, inevitably, and I was overcome with a wave of guilt. I abandoned everyone at the worst time. The Thorns were falling apart, and not just because of Ben.

Mars was not letting go of the fact that Arlo had disappeared. Poor Carmen and Rani had had their memories from the day wiped, and the rest of The Thorns wanted nothing to do with Marianne anymore; she endangered them too much.

I wouldn't comment on Arlo, though Lawrence seemed pretty opinionated on him.

Arlo tried to save Ben.

Arlo killed Lucy.

But Arlo was no longer human, he'd *transformed*, and I would not stand in his way. I wasn't even ready to think about what happened to him. Despite all our training, none of us were even remotely prepared.

I've kept the ring; I will never take it off. We promised each other eternity, so why should I ever break that? Every time I touch it, I see his face, half lit by the fireplace, half from the static of the TV. Ben's look of sheer joy and relief as I nod and let him place the ring on my finger. Less than two hours later, he was taken from me, suffering so much for nothing. It should have been me; I should have gone outside instead. I should have gone with him. I should have, should have, should have, but I didn't. I did none of those things. I let them take him and hurt him and hurt him and hurt him until he lost all hope of ever being saved.

I remember his body in my arms: his frail, cold shell, shattered and slipping through my fingers. He couldn't even see that he was safe, or that I had him. That I held him. He didn't have a chance for anything.

Lawrence buys me lots of coffee during his stay. He sits and listens. He holds my hand, and he lets me cry.

"He's safe now. He had his faith." He tries to reassure me.

I think about the cross warming my chest. I never held a strong faith, but I had Ben. He was my faith. He never spoke about his beliefs, not even to me. He just had his ways, his connections. I haven't taken it off since the funeral. And I never will. It's the last thing I have that keeps him truly alive with me.

It's May now, and I fly back to England with Francesca and Lawrence. We go back to my house—*our* house. Mine and Ben's. I sleep on the couch at first, and then I move back up to our bedroom.

His clothes still smell like him, even after all these months. I pull out his blue and black striped jumper and put it on, falling asleep atop the covers with my legs curled to my chest. I loved him in this. I love him in it still, in my head.

I don't believe in ghosts, but sometimes at night I feel his weight beside me. I'm warmed and relaxed, and although I never turn, I feel his eyes on me. He asks me why I'm still crying.

Francesca calls me one morning and invites me for breakfast. I don't want to go, but I know I must—for him. He wouldn't want me to give up like this.

Over brunch, she tells me she's moving here permanently and thinks it would be good for us to stay here for a while and stop avoiding things. She doesn't say or mean it harshly, but it hurts to hear regardless. I've been avoiding a lot.

Four months after the funeral, the three of us decide to visit him together. Mars comes, too.

Mars has seen him more than I have. They've been tending to his grave and making sure it's always well-stocked with pretty purple flowers: Ben's favourite colour.

Fran has been leaving photographs, happy ones, developed from her 'retro' cameras.

I reach down to the headstone and hold on tight—closing my eyes so I can talk to him in my head. We talk for a while. When I'm done, I smile and step away.

Everyone stands close and pats me on the back.

Even Ben. His touch is faint and barely there, but I feel it.

I smile again.

It's June now.

Happy birthday, Ben.

⚜

<u>Home video filmed by Ben: November 2018</u>

Ben: [*adjusting viewfinder then sitting down*] Okay, I think this is recording. I'm crap with technology, even with something this old. [*gets comfortable*] Right. So, hello future me. I didn't get a chance to make this before because the battery died and we got distracted, but things are getting a bit weird lately and I can't tell whether I'm coming or going. I don't know what is going to happen, I don't know how it's going to affect me, or Casper, or just life in general, but I wanted to make this video now, just in case, I dunno, anything.

As of today, {29/11/18}, I'm twenty-seven, I live with my long-time partner Casper, and life is… well life is still good. I have my best friends Fran, Mars and Lawrence and we're in a really cool band. I never thought we'd get to the stage we're at now, and we've had some serious ups and downs, but everything brought us to this point, and I wouldn't change it for the world.

So, hello future self. How are you? Is the world any kinder? Are you still touring and performing in front of a crowd that doesn't terrify you? Never forget the first time you saw a pride flag in the audience, and it made you stop and realise you weren't afraid anymore. You *were* proud. Do you still feel that deep down in your gut? And did you have the guts to propose? God, I hope Fran doesn't show Casper this yet. [*clears throat*] Did you propose? Or did he beat you to it? I bet he beat you to it. What was the wedding like? Where did you go for your honeymoon? Hopefully not somewhere too expensive and hot, you know you don't do well in heat.

Did you tell him you've been looking at adoption agencies? Do you have any kids? Are you as good of a dad as Casper? Kids, are you watching? Who's your favourite dad? [*laughs to himself*] God, no. Stop that. Urgh. Right. Haha.

Is Lawrence still functioning? Is Mars a famous designer? Does your dad show his face at all? Ahh, Ben, for goodness' sake, why are you so negative? Okay, scratch that, I don't care. I just want my friends to be happy. Do you become real friends with Arlo? Is he still in your life? Did he go on to become a famous poet?

Oh! And Fran, do you have any more room for tattoos? Have you beaten your dad's guitar collection? Are you living in France with your cats?

Did you make all of this into a documentary?

A NOTE FROM HARVEY

I've been putting off publishing this story, and I'm still scared to share it even now. It's not that I didn't want to write it, of course I did. I've wanted to have the opportunity to tell Ben and Casper's story for years now. I've been carrying them around with me since the very early stages of Fallen Thorns and I could never just *neglect* them, their story was always hanging in the back of my mind, waiting to be told.

But why didn't I want to publish this? After everything? Well because in all honesty, I have zero recollection of actually writing it.

I sent Fallen Thorns off to my editor in May 2023 and then I just vomited up this whole story so incredibly fast, and in the blink of an eye, it's March 2024 and I'm sending Forever Red off to my editor and... I don't remember writing it. I remember the plan and everything I wanted to convey, but I just wasn't present for the process. Life's a funny thing, and I'll spare you the details, but here I now have a project that is easily the most personal and thera-peutic project I've ever done, but it also just took so much out of me.

Ben's journey throughout Forever Red and Fallen Thorns means the world to me, I can't even put it into words. I poured my soul into his character, and his personal arc of growing and coming to terms with the life he has paved for himself has been such a relieving story to write, but then I hear you asking — why did you 'kill him off'? Why did you give him such a promising arc, only for him to die? Authors may seem cruel with your favourite characters, but I promise you we always do things for a reason.

I'll admit I was extremely scared that people would completely miss the point and think I just wanted to force unhappy things upon one character in particular, but I assure you, that was not my intention at all. Ben's whole story was him realising how much he really wanted to live, and so he did. And when he died, it was out of his control, but that didn't change anything about him. Ben was at a point in the middle of the story where he thought if he wasn't going to be around anymore, it would be because of himself. He would end things. But he was given a second chance and he learned to live and love again. I had to write this story for myself, as all authors should be doing first and foremost, but I also wanted to write *his* story to show how complex life can be, even in a fictional sense, but despite everything, you are loved and wanted in this world and I want everyone to hold that close to their hearts.

I hope, moving forward, when people read the sequel to Fallen Thorns and see every one of my characters get their arcs completed, that you understand how much of my own heart I sewed into this whole story.

Ben's story is still not over. It will all make sense soon.

I didn't *have* to give this disclaimer, but I wanted to. Otherwise I would have shoved this manuscript under my desk and moved on, never going back. I do want to thank my beta readers though, because you all single handedly revived my love for this manuscript and helped me make it the best it could be. Something to really be proud of.

Thank you for reading,

Harvey x

Forever Red Playlist

'7th Time' by Clan of Xymox
'Love Like Blood' by Killing Joke
'Kick The Tragedy' by Drop Nineteens
'My Heart' by The Danse Society
'Soul In Isolation' by The Chameleons
'Drowning' by Sixth June
'Kasvetli Kutlama' by She Past Away
'Suffocation' by Crystal Castles
'Eyes Without a Face' by Billy Idol
'Lullaby' by The Cure
'Imitation of Christ' by The Psychedelic Furs
'Faith in Me' by ELZ AND THE CULT
'Lithium' by Labyrinth Ear
'The Eternal' by Joy Division
'When Doves Cry' by Prince
'Criticize' by Alexander O'Neal
'Summertime' by A House In The Trees
'True Faith' by New Order
'Lorelei' by Cocteau Twins
'Remains' by Zola Jesus
'Why' by Carly Simon
'When the Lights Go out' by Naked Eyes
'Stripped' by Depeche Mode

Acknowledgments

I'm not really sure how to do acknowledgements the second time around. It's not even been that long since Fallen Thorns came out. BUT.

Thank you to everyone who has either followed me from the start, or joined my journey after Fallen Thorns was released! I never in a million years expected it to be half as successful as it has been so far, so I cannot thank you all enough! It's been a wild few months!

Thank you to Dorian Valentine for being the first person to read this book. Long live queer vampires!

A huge, huge thank you to my wonderful beta readers who are the reason the version you have in your hands now, is one I'm *insanely* proud of. So thank you Dorian, Syd, Lozzie, Matthias, Belle, Simon and Achilles.

Another enormous thanks to my wonderful editor Eden Northover, thank you for continuing to work your magic and sharing your advice.

I also want to shout out my local indie bookshop, Bookwyrm in Durham. You guys are amazing and I will be forever grateful for the support you've given me! It means the world!

Thank you to my friends and family again for continuing to be supportive and encouraging me through the start of my hopefully very long career! I never want to stop creating my weird little stories.

And thank you to dark wave/goth music for keeping me going through all my ups and downs. RIP Ben, you would have loved Harsh Symmetry. <3

ABOUT THE AUTHOR

Harvey Oliver Baxter is an author and illustrator from the North of England.

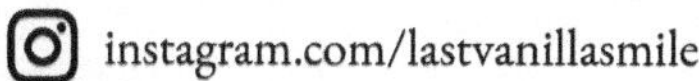 instagram.com/lastvanillasmile

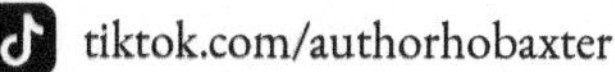 tiktok.com/authorhobaxter

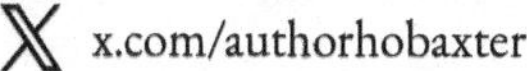 x.com/authorhobaxter

www.ingramcontent.com/pod-product-compliance
Lightning Source LLC
Chambersburg PA
CBHW051136190726
48290CB00006B/1873